GW01454298

Command

COMMAND

ANTONY MELVILLE-ROSS

LUME BOOKS

LUME BOOKS

This edition published in 2021 by Lume Books
30 Great Guildford Street,
Borough, SE1 0HS

Copyright © Antony Melville-Ross 1985

The right of Antony Melville-Ross to be identified as the author
of this work has been asserted by them in accordance with the
Copyright, Design and Patents Act, 1988.

All rights reserved. No part of this publication may be
reproduced, stored in a retrieval system, or transmitted in
photocopying, recording or otherwise, without the prior
permission of the copyright owner.

ISBN 978-1-83901-332-4

Typeset using Atomik ePublisher from Easypress Technologies

www.lumebooks.co.uk

For all those Richards centred on
Long Close Road, Stamford, Connecticut

Chapter One

Night as black as hate and a world where there was nothing but water. Water all-powerful, merciless. Water without end. Water exploding at the stem and smashing over the conning tower. Water trickling, running on his skin inside his foul-weather gear and saturating the air he breathed. Water the enemy. Not the Germans. They didn't matter any more. Just the storm-driven ocean. That and the tiredness. And the cold.

A secondary sea, wind-propelled, running diagonally across the path of the gigantic swells, churning their tops and flanks into flying avalanches of spindrift, avalanches powerful enough to force the surfaced submarine off course; the course it was vital she maintain in order to live. For to present the beam to such a swell was to capsize and die. It was worse, much worse than anything Harding had ever before experienced, worse than anything his imagination could have stretched to encompass, and it had been going on for three days and five hours.

Against the jet Arctic sky a lighter shade of black, warning him of the arrival of the next in line of the towering mountain ranges, a range advancing with a speed which was awesome, looming to a height beyond belief. He watched it through slitted, red-rimmed eyes, hearing the shout of the look-out at his left shoulder, 'Big'un coming, sir!' the words reduced by the wind to the wail of a lost soul, only nodding in reply to spare his cracked lips the effort of acknowledging the report.

The bow rising steeply until Harding's weight was supported as much by his spine pressing against the forward periscope standard as by his feet, then the whole hull soaring upwards as though over a thousand tons of steel were no more to the ocean than a child's kite to the wind. The crest still far above, but closing rapidly with what appeared to be the submarine's hurtling progress. That such progress was an illusion Harding knew well, and knew also that reality was a slow backward drift towards the Norwegian coast twenty miles astern. But there was no time to think of that now. Now was the time to brace himself as he felt he had been doing for a year rather than three days. The forepart of the ship clearing the crest, protruding beyond it for almost half its length. Harding, mouth open because his nostrils were blocked with salty mucus, caught by the full force of the wind, feeling his cheeks vibrate like a badly set sail, braced himself.

Momentary disorientation while the bow scythed down to rejoin its proper element and a feeling of weightlessness. A stunning shock vibrating through his body, the hull whipping along its length, the careering charge down the far side of the mammoth roller ending in sudden deceleration jerking tight the heaving-line securing him to the periscope standard. Then the water was everywhere, beating down on him, dragging his legs with it as it swept thigh-deep across the conning tower deck.

With tired resignation Harding disentangled his limbs from those of either the port or starboard look-out, which it was he didn't know, and dragged himself upright wiping his oil-skinned forearm across his face, more to clear his thoughts than his eyes. He had hit his head on something and it was aching dully. Vision showed him little more than the glint of foam obscuring all traces of his command forward of the conning tower except for the long barrel of the 4-inch gun, but above the racket of the storm his ears detected the high-pitched whistle of air down the twin voice-pipes on its way to feed the hungry diesels. That meant that the lower conning tower hatch had been slammed shut to prevent the flooding of the control room. Eardrums, he guessed, would be hurting down below in the partial vacuum and they would continue to hurt until it was possible to open the hatch and the air could resume its normal unrestricted course to the engine room.

There was the taste of blood in his mouth now and his probing tongue told him that a front tooth had snapped in half when he had been thrown to the deck. 'Oh, damn it all to hell,' he whispered to himself, then returned his attention to the storm. Another watery mountain range was approaching and still the forward casing was submerged, unable to lift itself clear of the ocean's clutch.

'Come on, old girl. Come on up,' Harding whispered again, but this time the whisper carried urgency.

His Majesty's Submarine *Trigger* was *not* old. She was straight out of the builder's yard of Vickers-Armstrongs at Barrow-in-Furness, fresh from her acceptance and sea trials and now on her first war patrol. It was also the first war patrol in command for her captain, Lieutenant Peter Harding, an event he had looked forward to with keen anticipation and guardedly hopeful expectations; expectations far from realized, with *Trigger*'s baptism of fire indefinitely postponed by this appalling battering.

The hissing whistle from the voice-pipes ceased just as the bow heaved itself sluggishly free of the tons of water which had been holding it down, shedding it from both sides of the casing like weirs on a river in spate. Then the next maniacal upward rush began.

There had been nothing complicated about Harding's orders. He had been instructed to proceed to the vicinity of Alten Fjord in northern Norway where, intelligence sources stated, the big German battleship *Tirpitz* lay at anchor. If the *Tirpitz* sailed she was to be attacked and so was any other vessel which did the same. It had all been perfectly simple until the simultaneous arrival of *Trigger* and the great storm in the patrol area had made attack impossible and survival itself problematical.

By some obscure process of thought Harding had persuaded himself that he was at fault for his inability to carry out the tasks entrusted to him and had repeatedly taxed his tired brain for solutions which didn't exist. Only a flash of insight revealing to him that exhaustion and aberration frequently walked hand in hand had enabled him to put the enemy out of his mind and concentrate on riding out the storm. That was when he had reduced the number of look-outs on the bridge from four to two and, against precedent, included himself in the roster of his watch-keeping officers to make life a little easier for them. Having done that he began to wonder if he had done anybody a favour because, the biting cold apart, conditions inside the hull were probably as bad as those on the bridge.

Lieutenant Peter Harding was insufficiently experienced in command to recognize a correct decision of his for what it was. It wasn't altogether surprising. Lieutenant Peter Harding was just a trifle over twenty-four years old.

When he thought of himself which, because he was an introvert, was often, Harding pictured an average man of average intelligence, average ability and a shy disposition. His mirror showed him to be of average build, with washed-out pale blue eyes in a nondescript, pleasant face crowned by indeterminate mousy brown hair. A very average man indeed, discounting the stubborn set to the mouth which he failed to detect, and not, in his view, one possessed of the necessary attributes required for command of an enormously powerful warship. Had he overheard himself accurately described as highly professional, intelligent, dedicated, likeable and attractive to women, he would have taken it as sarcasm or a description of someone else with the same name. But now he was neither dissecting his own character nor overhearing anything other than the banshee howling of the wind. He was bracing himself again for the next precipitous toboggan ride into another dark canyon of the sea.

By the time his first lieutenant clawed his way onto the bridge to take over the watch from him day was approaching, a day during which the sun would barely top the southern horizon before sinking down once more in surrender to the long Arctic night.

'Anything new down below, Number One?'

'Afraid we've got our third broken-bone case, sir,' Lieutenant Maddox shouted back at him. 'Leading Seaman Willard. Got thrown through the water-tight doorway into the torpedo stowage compartment and bust his left leg. Gascoigne and the Cox'n are working on him now.'

That made an arm, a wrist and a leg fractured on top of the assorted cuts and bruises marking every member of the ship's company.

'Oh,' Harding said. 'Anything else?'

'Signal for us, sir. Westerly storm in this area increasing to hurricane force. Can it really get any worse than this, sir?'

'I don't think so,' Harding bellowed. 'This is a hurricane already. They're a bit late with their met report, that's all.'

With Maddox secured in place, Harding released himself from his own

10

length of heaving-line, chose his moment carefully, then swung round the forward periscope standard and into the conning tower. Making his way down the vertical brass ladder took him almost a minute. There was little strength in his frozen fingers and the motion of the ship flung him repeatedly from side to side bringing his shoulders into painful contact with unyielding steel. In the control room he stood blinking in surprise at the canvas hammock slung between the after periscope hoist wheel and the corner of the passageway leading to the galley.

"Ope you don't mind, sir. We don't 'ave much use for a control room at the moment, except for the 'elmsman that is, and Willard'll be more comfortable 'ere than at either end of the ship.'

Harding looked at the coxswain and smiled. He was very fond of Chief Petty Officer Ryland who had been coxswain of the S-class submarine *Shadow* of which he himself had been second-in-command a year earlier.

'Certainly I don't mind, Cox'n. It's a very good idea. How is he?'

"E's okay, sir. A bit pissed off, but mostly because I 'ad Ordinary Seaman Norris clock 'im under the ear'ole so we could set 'is leg while 'e was out and 'is muscles was relaxed. I've doped 'im up now and 'e's asleep.'

Ordinary Seaman Norris was the ship's strong man. Harding smiled again, nodded and lurched forward to his tiny cabin, grasping for handholds at every step. Once forward of the strong current of air sucked from the conning tower to the engine room by the pounding diesels, the stench of vomit enfolded him in a disgusting cloud. Grimacing with distaste he slid the door of his cabin open then turned at the sound of the coxswain's voice.

'Like a word with you about Petty Officer Strachan when you've changed, sir. I'm much more worried about 'im than Willard. 'E ain't eaten for three days and now 'e's bringin' up blood.'

'Oh Christ!' Harding said. 'Let's look at him now.'

'You get dry first, sir,' the coxswain told him. 'You're shakin' like a baby's rattle. Can't 'ave *you* ill.'

There were dry clothes lying on Harding's bunk. Underwear, socks, a pair of bell-bottomed trousers, a shirt, a heavy white woollen sweater and a blue coverall. From the insignia on its sleeve he saw that he had been demoted to leading stoker. Everybody not required to keep watch on the bridge had been at pains to keep those that were, well supplied with clothing to replace that soaked within seconds of the wearer reaching the open air. Given a reasonable fit nobody cared about badges of rank. Duffel coats had proved very difficult things to dry and the engine room had taken on the appearance of a Chinese laundry in the attempt to keep them available. Fleece-lined sea-boots had been found impossible to dry at all, and the users had taken to inserting electric light bulbs on wandering leads into them for a few moments so they could at least put their feet back into warm moisture. The smell of charring fleece made a welcome change to the stink of vomit. The most fortunate were those with plain leather boots, and wives or girl friends who had supplied them with laddered silk stockings which were readily dried and provided remarkable insulation.

Undressing, towelling himself dry and dressing again took Harding almost fifteen minutes because the only safe way to do it was sitting on the deck, but the effort involved stopped him shivering. When he had finished, sometimes climbing the deck, sometimes sliding down it, he went in search of the coxswain and Petty Officer Strachan wondering what made people sea-sick. He never was himself, but took no pride in that fact. Nelson, he had read, had often been. It seemed that one either was or was not, and there wasn't a great deal anybody could do about it.

Strachan was a big, ruddy-complexioned Scot, but the only colour in his face when Harding found him strapped into a bunk was smears of blood on the pale stubble around his lips. He was unconscious.

'Send somebody to the galley for soup, Cox'n,' Harding said. 'I want it warm, not hot, and have the cook told to shove everything into it. Meat, vegetables, bread, everything. It doesn't matter a damn what it tastes like. Oh, and he's to crush up some of those vitamin tablets we're supposed to take, and put them in too.'

''E won't drink it, sir. I've tried.'

Harding glanced at Ryland. 'Just organize the soup, please. He'll drink it even if I have to kill him to make him do it.'

'Aye aye, sir,' Ryland said.

Minutes later Harding pinched Strachan's nostrils together between the forefinger and thumb of one hand and forced the petty officer's mouth open by pressing down on his chin with the other.

'Pour it in, Cox'n. Not too much.'

With the ship shuddering, rolling, pitching, most of the soup missed the gaping mouth, but some of it went in and Harding snapped the jaws together, covering the mouth with his palm.

'Stroke his throat hard, Cox'n, as though you were trying to make a cat swallow a pill.'

Strachan swallowed. Harding maintained his grip on the mouth and nose for a moment before removing his hands. Immediately Strachan's back arched, then his head jerked forward and he ejected a stream of liquid, spraying Harding with a mixture of soup and blood.

'All right,' Harding said. 'Let's do that again.'

They did it again and again and again until, forty minutes later, there was no blood in the fluid which fouled Harding's face and clothes.

'All right,' he said for the second time. 'That's stopped him tearing his stomach lining to shreds and his system should have absorbed at least a fraction of that stuff. I want him fed like that every two hours day and night and I want to be informed at once of the slightest change in his condition either way. Understood?'

'Understood, sir. What 'appened to your tooth, sir?'

Suddenly more tired than he felt he could stand, 'How the hell should I know?' Harding snarled. 'I probably dropped it somewhere!'

He staggered away to change out of his reeking leading stoker's coverall.

His face grave, the coxswain watched him go. Very quietly, 'You're okay you are, Skipper,' he said.

Chapter Two

In Norway the most powerful battleship in the world lay almost motion-less, almost as motionless as the rocky sides of the fjord, heedless of the raving of the elements which made her smaller consorts jerk fretfully at their moorings even in the sheltered anchorage. But for the men on the upper deck of the *Tirpitz* the gale was not something to be ignored and the young *oberleutnant* found it necessary to clutch his cap with one hand and use the other to drag himself forward against the whooping wind as he clawed his way towards the captain's quarters. When he reached his destination he took his cap from his head and stuffed it inside his jacket because he needed both hands to open the heavy armoured door of the lobby leading to the big cabin, then force it shut again against the pressure of the air. Inside at last he stood for a moment enjoying the silence, the stillness, before smoothing his hair and striding across the lobby to knock on another steel door painted to resemble wood.

'Come!'

He went in.

'Ah, it's you, Ernst. What have you got for me?'

The *oberleutnant* took a sheet of paper from his pocket and put it on the desk in front of the officer with the four gold stripes on his sleeve.

'Enemy report, sir,' he said. 'Our U-boats state that a large convoy west-bound out of Liverpool has turned north, presumably for Murmansk. Bad weather precluded any attack and they've lost contact with it now. Details in that signal, sir.'

The other looked down at the paper, began to read, then whistled softly.

'In excess of eighty ships, eh? Two rescue tugs. Escort of eight or more destroyers. Yes, it's a large one, as you say. See that the Admiral's Chief of Staff is shown a copy of this as soon as he returns aboard, get me the latest weather report and, er, the Admiral's due back from Berlin at noon tomorrow, isn't he?'

'Yes, sir. Flying conditions permitting.'

'Very well, we'll anticipate his wishes and bring the Fleet to forty-eight hours notice for steam. See to it, please.'

The *oberleutnant* clicked his heels and left.

*

In Scapa Flow another battleship, older, slower, but with nine enormous 16-inch guns in three triple-turrets, heaved her anchor clear of the mud in which it had been resting and swung ponderously towards the harbour entrance preceded by a line of four destroyers. The storm hit them as soon as they emerged into the Pentland Firth, throwing the destroyers about like toy boats, making even the battleship twist and plunge like a whale in torment.

Clear of the island of South Ronaldsay the force of warships turned east and then north. Not one person aboard any of them was looking forward to the task of providing protection against enemy heavy units for a convoy carrying arms and supplies to the Russians. A hurricane was raging across their course no more than five hundred miles ahead of their bows and that, for the destroyers at least, could prove insupportable.

*

In Berlin the admiral commanding the Arctic Squadron adjusted the Iron Cross at his collar and let himself into the commander-in-chiefs office. Grand Admiral Erich Raeder glanced up, smiled and gestured him to a chair.

'It was good of you to come and see me, Manfred,' he said.

'Good of me, sir? It's an honour and always has been.'

The older man shrugged before saying, 'Well, it's an honour you're unlikely to be experiencing again. I've handed in my resignation and no doubt Doenitz will be appointed in my place within a week or so.'

'Erich! What on earth are you telling me? You've been C-in-C since 1928! You can't leave now! Not at this stage of the war! Anyway Doenitz knows nothing about surface vessels. He's a U-boat man!'

'Try telling that to the Führer,' Raeder told him. 'I've been falling progressively further from grace with him for a long time, first over the losses during the Norwegian campaign, then the sinking of the *Bismarck* and now our failure to stop the Allied convoys to Russia.' He sighed before going on, 'He got a little over-excited the other day and threatened to have the entire surface fleet melted down for scrap. That passed over, but a week later he and I had a tearing row at the Wolfsschanze HQ when he told me that the Navy lacked the will to fight. Beginning with the scuttling of the *Graf Spee* back in 1939 he listed virtually every warship we've lost since. That tirade left me with no choice but to do what I've done.'

'I'm appalled, Erich,' Admiral Manfred Stresemann said.

'Are you? If you had met the *Führer* as often as I, you wouldn't even be surprised.'

Both men stared unseeingly at the desk-top for nearly half a minute before Stresemann asked, 'Are you instructing me to attack this latest big convoy regardless of cost, sir?'

Raeder replied obliquely. 'What the *Führer* fails to understand, Manfred, is that even such a large convoy is a mere trifle within the context of the magnitude of our campaign on the eastern front. What he further fails to appreciate is that the very existence of your *Tirpitz* in northern waters forces the English to keep a minimum of three battleships and their attendant vessels in the area to contain her. With *Tirpitz* sunk they would be free to move those battleships to the Mediterranean theatre where, without doubt, they would demolish what little there is left floating of our Italian ally's fleet. In other words, Manfred, our leader's grasp of strategy is sketchy in the extreme.' He paused there before adding, 'Destroy that convoy if you can, but don't throw *Tirpitz* away doing it.'

Admiral Stresemann stood up. 'I'll abide by your advice sir.'

Grand Admiral Raeder nodded his head slowly then said, 'Bad advice for an old friend who would prefer to go down in a blaze of glory, Manfred, but the best for Germany in my view. Be that as it may, off you go and do what you must. The future's in your hands, not mine.'

Stresemann was old Navy. He didn't click his heels as an *oberleutnant* was doing at that moment in Alten Fjord. He held out his hand instead and the commander-in-chief took it in his own.

Chapter Three

Lying on his bunk, Harding thought, was an extremely tiring and uncomfortable occupation, but he knew that he was far better off than those of his men trying to sleep at either end of the ship. There the prodigious soaring rise and sickening jarring drop, endlessly repeated, made life barely supportable for them. Grimly he subdued the urge to get up, and concentrated mind and body on the exhausting business of resting.

An hour later he was still doing it when the cry 'Man overboard!' reached his ears through the thin partition separating him from the control room voice-pipe. For a moment the shouted words seemed to freeze him where he was, as though the ship's motion had been miraculously suspended, then the orders 'Starboard thirty! Full ahead together!' had him snatching for the quick-release hitch in the line holding him down. Catapulting from his bunk, he fell heavily to the deck, struggled to his feet and jerked the sliding door of his cabin open. Three paces carried him to the helmsman's side.

'Belay those orders,' Harding said. 'Half ahead together. Steady as you go.'

'But, sir...'

'Just do as you're told! Get that starboard wheel off and maintain course 275!'

There was disbelief in the man's voice when he replied, 'Aye aye, sir,' but he wound the steering wheel obediently before the ship could start to swing. Harding leant across to the voice-pipe, hearing it magnify the sounds of the storm.

'Number One?' he called.

'Yes?'

'Captain here. I have countermanded your orders. As I have already instructed you, you are to maintain our present course and speed for anything short of a collision. Is that understood?'

As the helmsman had done, 'But, sir…' Lieutenant Maddox said.

'*Is that understood?*'

'Yes, sir.'

'Very well. Now, who went overboard?'

'Able Seaman Roberts, sir. He just vanished when the last big wave washed over us, sir. He…'

The voice-pipe fell silent except for the noise of the wind, and water poured down the conning tower, soaking the sailor standing by the ladder and swirling across the control room deck. The man reached for the lower hatch, slammed it shut and immediately evil-smelling mist rose from the bilges as the diesels began to consume the air inside the hull. For a long moment Harding's eardrums screamed a protest at him, then some member of the engine room staff slowed the diesels, the pressure equalized and the sailor forced the hatch open again. More water fell on him, but that was only the residue left in the tower. The mist streamed aft to be swallowed by the main engines and Harding's ears cleared themselves.

'Bridge?' he said. 'Bridge, are you all right up there?'

There was a pause before Maddox's voice replied, 'Yes, *we're* all right, sir.' He sounded simultaneously out of breath and coldly formal.

A more than usually violent lurch broke Harding's grip on the valve wheel he was holding on to and threw him across the control room. His shoulder striking the mainvent levers on the diving panel halted his progress painfully. Then, ludicrously, he found himself back where he had started when the deck reversed its tilt. Wincing, he grabbed his valve wheel again.

'Bridge?'

'Sir?'

'I want you to send the other look-out down below, Number One. Officers will stand watch alone until the weather moderates.'

'Aye aye, sir.' The icy formality was still there in the three short words and they signalled the beginning of the end of Maddox's submarine career.

Harding stood, swaying back and forth, trying to keep his face expressionless, feeling the hostility of the five men in the control room like some tangible force, aware of their eyes regarding him as though he were an unwelcome stranger. Then the dripping figure of the remaining look-out appeared through the lower conning tower hatch and staggered away forward with barely a glance at his captain. The adage 'Never complain, never explain' came into Harding's mind. In most circumstances he considered the second half of that maxim an absurdity because without explanation there could be no training, but he had no intention of justifying his actions to men who would never be burdened with the responsibilities of command. Maddox was a different matter. The probably unthinking disobedience of his first lieutenant might charitably be put down as an excusable humanitarian reflex although Harding felt very dubious about that. What could not be excused was his subsequent open disapproval which demonstrated not only disloyalty but an alarming ignorance. A worried frown began to form on Harding's forehead, but he erased it quickly at the sound of a familiar voice behind him.

'Terribly sorry to hear about Roberts, sir.'

He pivoted, still gripping his valve wheel, and looked up at his navigating officer. Lieutenant Gascoigne was tall, dark and handsome which, provided that he was out of earshot, was what the crew called him.

'Hello, Pilot. News travels fast,' he said. 'Yes, it's tragic, isn't it?'

There was nothing but concern written on the good-looking face and Harding felt no surprise at that. He had not expected to read resentment there because Gascoigne, like the coxswain, had served with him in *Shadow*; and unlike the rest of the ship's company, who knew him only slightly, both would know that he'd never leave a drowning man to his fate without a compelling reason. They would also know what that reason was which, incredibly, his second-in-command appeared not to do.

'Will you be holding a service, sir?'

'Yes,' Harding replied, glanced at the swaying hammock containing Leading Seaman Willard and added, 'There isn't much room in here, so we'll have the coxswain find out who his particular mates were and have them along.' He paused, sniffed, then asked, 'Can you smell chlorine gas?'

'Not sure, sir. My nose is pretty well bunged up.'

'So's mine. Oh well, there's nothing we can do about drying off the battery cells with half the Atlantic swilling around in here. Have the First Lieutenant report to me in my cabin when he comes off watch, will you?'

'Aye aye, sir.'

Harding sat on the chair he had had secured to the deck in his cabin, resting his forearms and head on the little desk-top which covered the wash-basin. He jammed one foot against the drawers beneath his bunk and the other against the bulkhead to hold himself there, but the resultant unnaturally splayed position of his legs induced almost instant cramp in his thighs and he abandoned the attempt, wondering bleakly if riding an unbroken horse at a rodeo could cause any more discomfort than the motion of his ship, wondering too for how much longer he would have a ship.

From somewhere came the familiar sound of smashing crockery. There couldn't be much of it left he thought. Not that it mattered. They could eat out of cans. That made him think about Petty Officer Strachan and about the likelihood of others being reduced to his condition. Already some dozen men were useless, although not unconscious, and unless the hurricane blew itself out quickly the number would not stop there. The situation was extremely grave and there was absolutely nothing he could do about it, not even pray.

Coming from him, Harding considered prayer to be an impertinence towards whatever god there might be. He attended religious services solely because the Navy required it of him and certainly not from belief. Anthropomorphism he saw as an astonishing human conceit as he could not accept that God would have made man in his own image when, with the exception of pretty women, many of the rest of the earth's creatures were far more attractive to look at and, for the most part, possessed of much nicer natures. Christ he thought of as a great man, but nothing more. His practical mind baulked at the concept of a Creator who, during his time on earth, had had nothing to say about the fabric of the universe he was reported to have had the moulding of, and did not apparently know either that the world was round or that it orbited the sun.

Aware that he might somehow have missed the entire point, and having heard the aphorism 'To the worm the world must appear all mud', Harding was still not prepared to appeal to a divinity he had denied ever since he had been old enough to think for himself, because that, in his view, would have been impertinent.

Sleep enfolded him, then cast him away with savage petulance, making him grab blindly for anything to support him when the deck dropped like a runaway lift. It happened frequently and he came close to despair, for he, more than most, had to remain an effective unit of the team if they were all to live. It was a relief to concentrate his mind on something else when Maddox knocked on the door, opened it and half-fell into the cabin.

'You wanted to see me, sir?'

'Yes. I want an explanation of why you saw fit to disregard my orders about the course to be steered when there was no risk of collision with another vessel.'

'Well, obviously there was an emergency with a man over the side. I couldn't just do nothing!'

'I see. Did Roberts's safety-line part?'

'No, he had released himself and was making his way to the hatch when a wave came over the bridge.'

Harding looked at Maddox's strained pale face, unimpressed by that because everybody's face was strained and pale, but noting the ugly set of the mouth.

'There's one short but rather important word missing from your statements, Maddox,' he said.

'I beg your pardon, *sir.*'

Deciding to ignore the sarcasm, deciding too not to point out to Maddox that Roberts need not have died had his officer of the watch supervised the change of look-outs, timing it to take place between the towering rollers, 'That's better,' Harding told him. 'What, precisely, did you propose to do for Roberts?'

'Pick him up, sir. What else?'

Dropping his gaze to the deck for a moment, then looking up at Maddox again, 'Do you have any idea for how long a man can live in the sea at this latitude in winter?' Harding asked. The other didn't reply and he went on, 'Two minutes, Maddox. Just one hundred and twenty seconds and then it's all over. That was all the time you had to reverse course, locate him and, because no man can go onto the casing in these conditions, extract him from the water by some means known only to yourself. It was a manifest impossibility from the start and yet you were prepared to risk the almost certain destruction of this ship for that impossibility.'

Trigger corkscrewed wildly and neither man spoke again until they had regained a precarious balance, Harding on his chair, Maddox standing, clinging to the side of the bunk. It was the latter who broke the silence between them.

'This needn't have happened, sir, if we weren't all so tired. If Roberts hadn't been shagged out he could have chosen his moment better. If we could just dive for fifteen hours or so and everybody get some sleep we'd be all right. We'd have more chance of hearing *Tirpitz* by sonar than sighting her anyway.'

Again Harding refrained from saying that the officer of the watch should have been the judge of the correct moment to choose, as he had no desire to saddle anybody with the responsibility for the death of another. For seconds he searched his own conscience, questioned his own training of his officers, then brought his mind back to the present.

'That was something of a *non sequitur*, wasn't it?' he said. 'Still, never mind that now. What's all this about diving? Do you fancy doing that with chlorine gas coming off Number 3 battery?'

Maddox opened his mouth to say something, but Harding forestalled him.

'Don't bother to answer that question, the gassing has only just started but, tell me, what do you know about metacentric height?'

Receiving only a shrug in reply Harding went on, 'The metacentric height is the distance between the centre of buoyancy of a ship and its centre of gravity. Obviously the first has to be above the second or the ship would turn turtle. When a submarine is either diving or surfacing those two centres move very close together, so there's no righting moment, no stability, and a single nudge from waves the size of these would roll her over. That's why we can't dive. That's why I didn't dive three days ago. Do you understand what I'm telling you? Do you understand that diving or surfacing in such conditions as these would almost certainly kill us all?'

Harding watched his first lieutenant swaying, jerking to the movement

23

of the ship, saw his eyes flicking around the cabin as though searching for something, heard him say, 'The crew don't like this Roberts business at all. Not one little bit. I can't say I blame them.'

Quietly, sadly, 'Go to the wardroom, Maddox,' Harding told him. 'You are relieved of all duties. Gascoigne will take over from you.'

He waited for remonstrance, but none came. For countable seconds Maddox remained where he was, then turned abruptly and lurched out of the cabin.

Alone again, Harding rode his bucking chair wondering if it had been his intention to dismiss Maddox from his position ever since his suicidal attempt to rescue Roberts; recalling that, possibly unconsciously, not once had he addressed him by the first lieutenant's unofficial title of 'Number One', but always by his name. He thought that it probably had, for not only had Maddox's action been utterly foolish, but also a direct contravention of orders. Then had come the further demonstration of professional inadequacy, of ignorance of what a submarine could and could not do. If all that had not put the question beyond doubt, the man had finally damned himself beyond any hope of redemption by the irrelevance and disloyalty of his final statement. It was very unfortunate and not only for Maddox but for everyone. The loss of his services would place a greater strain on...

'Cap'n, sir?'

He turned and looked at the face of the sailor peering at him round the partly open cabin door.

'What is it, Norris?'

'Bridge says to tell you the wind's dropped down to storm force, or maybe only gale, sir. It's veered north, sir.'

'Thank you, Norris.'

There was no lessening yet in *Trigger*'s gyrations, nor would there be for some time to come, but the strangest feeling grew in Harding that his earlier musing on religion had been monitored by some power outside himself and approved because he had not been impertinent.

'Oh, come on!' he said to himself. Then, muscles and head aching, eyes gritty from lack of sleep, he struggled into protective clothing to go and look at the weather.

Chapter Four

Trigger, diesels burbling idly, ghosted over the long smooth swells, all that remained of the hurricane's passing, a white phantom on a black sea. It was bitterly, frighteningly cold.

Harding looked down at the 4-inch gun, which might have been canvas-covered for all its coating of ice had left of its real shape, then up at the jumping wire and aerials, their sheaths of frozen water thick as a man's thigh. He wondered how much more weight they could stand without parting, how much more *Trigger* could without capsizing; then he stopped wondering, as for him to conjecture about the unknown was both pointless and harrowing to the nerves. With the submarine's slow roll, a roll from which she was increasingly reluctant to lift herself upright against the drag of the immensely swollen superstructure, the nerves needed no additional strain applied to them.

Instead he listed in his mind those facts he could be thankful for. That Petty Officer Strachan was conscious and would live without further help from anybody else. That the bone fracture cases were comfortable and on the mend. That the ship no longer stank of vomit and had suffered only minor structural damage. That the crew members were rested and had stopped looking at him as though he were something nasty they had stepped in.

Grateful as he was for that last fact, it embarrassed Harding a little that he had Maddox to thank for it. Virtually if not actually under arrest, the ex-first lieutenant had, without being asked, made it known to those members of the ship's company unable to see it for themselves that his decision to attempt the rescue of Able Seaman Roberts had been a dangerous error of judgement which held out no hope of success. A large part of Harding's embarrassment stemmed from the knowledge that Maddox's public confession would be of small help to his future prospects and for that he was sorry, but could do nothing. Something in Maddox had snapped under tension and it would take a great deal more than a subsequent generous admission to repair the damage, if it could be repaired at all.

'Bridge?'

Harding bent to the voice-pipe.

'Yes?'

'Permission to rig the jury aerial, sir?'

'Yes,' he said again.

He had done what he could about the ice with men chipping and hammering it off the periscope standards, off the deck and sides of the bridge, off anything they could reach and safely belabour. But what could be done from the safety of the bridge was pathetically little, the ice reformed rapidly on the cleared areas and continued to thicken over the rest of the near-hundred yard length of the submarine. Diving would have removed it rapidly enough, but to dive was impossible with no way of calculating *Trigger*'s volume and displacement.

Heading south to warmer latitudes would have removed it too, although much more slowly, but that would have left *Tirpitz* free to sail not only unmolested but undetected as well. More than his orders, it was the mental picture of the great ship rending the packed, almost defenceless vessels of convoy after convoy like a fox in a chicken-run which decided Harding to remain on station. That picture took little conjuring up. The awesome thunder of 15-inch gun broadsides. The almost instantaneous impact of eight giant high-explosive shells from every salvo, their weight alone, without even the necessity to erupt into the appalling detonation each was capable of, enough to drive a merchant ship under. The long winter night banished by the light from blazing hulks. The carnage, the deaths of thousands by fire, water, or merciful disintegration.

There was also the matter of the loss to the Russian armies of urgently needed weapons and ammunition; but Harding, too young, too inexperienced yet to view the war as a global conflict, could find little of concern in himself for the fate of hard-pressed Russians. It didn't matter. His sense of duty towards his own kind was more than enough to hold *Trigger* where she was.

Two men, like himself and the look-outs, so heavily clothed and hooded that only their eyes could be seen, struggled through the upper conning tower hatch and drew the spare aerial up after them. Harding watched them attach it to the periscope standards, then draw it far forward and aft with heaving-lines passing through loops which Gascoigne and a team of men had attached to the jumping wire near bow and stern. Two other sailors, one at the front of the bridge and one at the back, kept those lines in constant motion when the aerial was not in place, to prevent them becoming rigid with cold and acquiring their own icy sheath. Securing the loops to the jumping wire had been a difficult and dangerous operation on the treacherous casing, but Harding had to have that aerial as a replacement for the normal one now rendered useless by its thick shrouding of compacted frozen snow. It was essential that the telegraphists could listen every hour to the big transmitters at home so far away to the south, and be able to transmit when their captain had anything to report to his superiors.

Twelve minutes after the aerial had been positioned, 'Wireless room says nothing for us on the hourly routine, sir,' the voice-pipe announced.

'All right,' Harding said, then ordered the aerial unrigged. The heaving-lines had already assumed a bar-like rigidity which, together with their icy adhesion to the loops invisible in the darkness, had to be broken by a combination of persuasion and brute force.

Temporarily distracted by the activity around him, Harding had forgotten the small nagging pain centred on his broken front tooth, but it reminded him of its presence now and he pressed the back of his hand against his mouth. The act revealed the absence of feeling in his nose and, cursing softly, he began to massage it. It was difficult with the double layer of glove on his hand, so he stripped both layers off and tried again. The mucus in his nostrils was frozen solid, but that was nothing new and he ignored it, rubbing and kneading until sensation returned to the flesh of his face. *Trigger* started one of her slow rolls then and, automatically, Harding grasped for support, his hand closing on the torpedo night-sight secured to the side of the bridge. It stuck there as though clamped in position by some powerful magnetic force. He swore again, loudly this time, and there was more than a hint of agitation in his voice.

'You okay, sir?' The words were muffled by the scarf covering the speaker's mouth. Harding turned his head to the lookout.

'Is that you, Chivers?'

'Yessir.'

'Come and hold me up in case I keel over when I pull my hand off this night-sight. It's frozen to it.'

'Fucking hell!' Able Seaman Chivers said, grasped his captain under the arms, heard the sharp hiss of breath when Harding tore his hand clear of the metal, felt him sag, then straighten again. Both of them peered at the hand in the darkness, saw blood well blackly against the pale flesh, congeal, freeze.

'You'd better get a relief up here a bit sharpish and go below and get that seen to, sir.'

'No, I'll be all right, Chivers.'

The able seaman brushed past him to the voice-pipe and said, 'Control room! Get one of the officers up here quick to relieve the Skipper! He's hurt his hand bad!' Then he faced Harding. 'No arguments, sir.'

Harding smiled through the pain. 'No arguments, Chivers. I expect you're right.'

'I'm bloody sure I am, sir.'

It was shock rather than cold, Harding supposed, which kept him trembling jerkily for twenty minutes after he had come down out of the sub-zero temperature on the bridge. It was the excruciating agony of disinfectant applied to the flayed flesh of three fingers and the palm of his hand by Gascoigne and the coxswain which made him faint.

The next day fever took hold of him.

*

At the head of Kaa Fjord, close to the little town of Alten, *Tirpitz* still lay moored by two anchors at the bow and with huge wires connecting her stern to the shore, but she was alive now. Smoke and steam were drifting from the great cowled funnel; men worked by flashlight on the forecastle around the cable winches and aft on the mooring wires; the 15-inch gun turrets traversed from right to left and left to right in almost constant motion to prevent the roller bearings on which they moved from freezing, the smaller weapons of the secondary armament following suit; sailors moved purposefully, enthusiastically about their tasks, the discomfort and racking boredom of the Arctic winter forgotten because they were putting to sea to destroy a vast English convoy. It did not occur to them that a considerable proportion of the assembled ships they hoped to attack would be manned by the other races of the British Isles as well as Americans, Norwegians, Poles, Danes, Dutch, Belgians and French, in addition to many from the Commonwealth and Empire. Even if it had occurred to them, it would not have interested them. England was the old enemy so, regardless of its composition, to them the convoy was English.

Admiral Manfred Stresemann was by no means so simple in his outlook. He knew only too well the extent of the world's rage directed at his country, a rage which transcended the act of war itself, knew some of the reasons for it and, in part, accepted it as a natural reaction to the behaviour of the maniac who was his nation's leader. For a long time he had allowed himself, disloyally he had thought, to wonder if the *Führer* was mad and after his last meeting with Raeder in Berlin had become convinced that he was.

Standing, a lonely figure, on the admiral's bridge deck, he recalled with complete accuracy his brief exchange with the grand admiral. With less accuracy he called to mind the sneering voice of von Ribbentrop before the war recounting a warning given to him by Churchill, then only a member of the British parliament with no official position in the government. 'Mr Ambassador,' Ribbentrop had said, mimicking the now well-known growling tones, 'you should advise *Herr* Hitler not to underestimate the British. They are very clever and if you force them into war they will bring the whole world in arms against you.' Stresemann wasn't certain after a gap of five years that he had Churchill's words exactly right, but he *was* certain that Ribbentrop should not have ended his mimicry with laughter.

There was little to laugh about now either, even with the great opportunity facing him of the annihilation of a major enemy convoy, for intelligence reports had confirmed that a 16-inch gun British battleship had sailed from Scapa Flow and was believed to be steaming north to provide heavy cover for the merchantmen. That meant either *Nelson* or *Rodney* as they were the only two ships with guns of that calibre in the Royal Navy. Which it was, made no difference. They were identical. They were also more heavily gunned than *Tirpitz*, but she had a distinct speed advantage and Stresemann, with his staff, had worked out a number of tactical moves which could lead to the destruction of much of the convoy without the necessity for a direct confrontation with the British battleship. It saddened him that such hit and run methods should be forced on him and it saddened him the more that it had been the calculated policy of his masters to divert financial resources away from the surface ships of the once proud High Seas Fleet in which he had served as a young man to other branches of the armed forces; forces which had inflicted and suffered casualties amounting to millions while achieving nothing of permanence.

Stresemann thought of the *Luftwaffe* so mauled over England in 1940 that it had never fully recovered, of the *Wehrmacht*, once invincible, routed at Alamein and Stalingrad, of the seemingly endless Russian reserves of manpower and the rapidly growing capability of the Americans to produce armaments of every kind. He thought too of the massive Anglo-American bombing assault on German cities and of the startling increase in U-boat losses. He would have been desolated, rather than saddened, had he known that, within less than three months of this February day in 1943, Admiral Doenitz, the new commander-in-chief of the *Kriegsmarine*, would be obliged to withdraw his U-boats altogether from the North Atlantic because of those losses. That knowledge was not available to him, but the writing on the wall was so growing in clarity as to be almost legible.

As though seeking encouragement from any source he let his mind wander. It settled on Peenemünde and the research taking place there on the V-1 pilotless jet-propelled aircraft and the V-2 long-range rocket. Reprisal weapons the *Führer* called them, the *Vergeltungswaffen* from which their initial letter came and which, he claimed, would blow the English and their American fellow-bandits off the British Isles. Stresemann didn't believe it and although, out of the wind and with a steam radiator at his back and another at his right side it was not cold on his private bridge deck, he shivered.

'I am instructed to inform you that we are ready to proceed, sir.'

He glanced at the *leutnant* who appeared to have materialized beside him, then at the assembled ships seen dimly through the gloom of the Arctic day. The last of his five destroyers was moving slowly away from the big *Altmark*-class tanker from which she had taken her fuel, the other four lay stationary along the length of Kaa Fjord and directly ahead, beyond *Tirpitz's* flaring bows, a gap had opened in the triple line of anti-submarine nets by which the battleship had been enclosed.

'Thank you,' he said. 'My compliments to the Captain, and the squadron will put to sea.'

Her crew buoyant, excited, her officers thoughtful, her admiral in sombre mood, the vast steel edifice, like some huge blacked-out city block, began to move towards open water, the only sound coming from her the subdued roar of the forced-draught fans feeding air to her boilers. Then darkness swallowed her and there was only the wake of her passing lapping at the banks of the fjord to show that she had ever been.

*

'No, sir, I won't dry up and get on with the job,' Gascoigne said. 'A few days ago I was just the navigating officer of this ship. Then you ordered me to take over as first lieutenant and now I'm sort of acting captain. If anything happens to you I'll *be* the captain. I've got to know what the situation is so that I can at least try to make the right decisions.'

Harding smiled up at him from his bunk. 'So it's a dead man's shoes now, is it Number One? I've had you and the coxswain labelled as a couple of raving sadists since this business started, but I didn't think you'd carry things that far.'

The tall young man sighed gustily. 'Please be serious, sir. I know you're better and your hand's mending, but if it gets infected again and you nod off into another sort of semi-coma, we'll all be in it right up to here.'

31

'Oh, I shan't be that stupid a second time. After dinner I'll get up and have a practice canter through the ship.'

'No you won't,' Gascoigne told him. 'Apart from going to the heads, you're staying right where you are, sir. You'd never even have got that far this morning without Norris and me to help you.'

'Christ, you're a bossy lot,' Harding said. 'First Able Seaman Chivers has me thrown off my own bridge, then you and the coxswain take turns at ordering me about. Still, I must admit that I feel rather like a bit of chewed string. Sit down and tell me what you want to know.'

Gascoigne folded his long length into the only chair in the little cabin before saying, 'It's like this, sir. I'm assuming that it's pretty important that we stay here. Otherwise, with injured men on board, you out of action and the ship getting steadily more unstable, you'd have signalled that you were withdrawing from station and then headed south if only to get rid of all this ice. Add to that the facts that we can't dive and that the five external torpedo tubes are frozen solid, all we can do if *Tirpitz* does sail is send off an enemy report and carry out a suicidal surface attack with the six internal tubes. Well, I don't imagine that you're contemplating the latter, so I take it that the enemy report is the essential thing.'

'Right on all counts, Number One. They *must* be told at home if *Tirpitz* is on the loose. That convoy is depending on us. Every other convoy too for that matter. Think what could happen with a ship of that power running wild in the Atlantic.'

'Yes, sir, I have thought about it and that's what's puzzling me. Are we the only people able to check on *Tirpitz's* whereabouts? What about the cloak and dagger boys and the bloody RAF? If they're both on the job I'm going to head for home, if you get sick again, before we collect more ice up top and capsize. There are still blizzards about.'

Frowning, Harding opened his mouth to say that he had no intention of getting sick again, realized that that was a stupid remark to make, and closed it. Then, after a moment's thought, he began to speak.

'You've got a point, Number One, and I really can't see that there can be any possible objection to my telling you what the form is in the circumstances. Give me a glass of water, will you?' He nodded his thanks when

Gascoigne filled a glass at the wash-basin and handed it to him, then went on, 'The Germans caught up with our agent before we sailed for patrol. Well, I suppose it would make more sense to say that they found the transmitter, as probably every Norwegian is our agent. Anyway, they've gone off the air. As to the RAF, they're pretty badly placed because of the distances involved and the darkness at this time of year. Also, I don't suppose that hurricane we all enjoyed so much helped them a lot.'

Feeling renewed tiredness pressing on his eyelids Harding sipped from his glass of water and said, 'In summer they can keep the northern Norwegian coast fairly well covered by operating Photographic Reconnaissance Unit Spitfires out of Vaenga airfield if the Russians happen to be feeling cooperative which, I was told, isn't often. Then there's another scheme using Mosquitos fitted with long-range tanks flying from Scotland to Murmansk and, in both cases, a shuttle service of Catalina flying-boats going way out over the sea to avoid German fighters to bring back the photographs taken by the Spits or Mozzies, but the Russians succeeded in lousing that up too. Did you know that the Catalinas have carrier pigeons aboard in case they have to land on the sea out of wireless range?'

'No, sir.'

'Well, they do, and the Russians objected to the flights because, believe it or not, it's illegal to import livestock into the Soviet Union.'

'Good grief!'

'As you say. Then the whole damned thing gets even more complicated in winter with the difficulty of dropping flares in high winds from forty thousand feet, or whatever the Mozzies fly at, and getting decent night photographs. Are you beginning to get the picture?'

'I've already got it, sir. We have to stay here.'

'That's right,' Harding said. 'We have to stay here, and you forget all the RAF stuff I've told you. Now, how's the watch-keeping situation? You and the Pilot aren't getting too worn out, are you?'

'No, with the Chief standing a watch, sir, we're okay with two hours on and four hours off. He claims that, with an engineer officer at last in control on the bridge, the executive branch has finally come to the end of whatever usefulness it ever had and…'

Gascoigne saw his captain's eyes close and the glass in his hand tilt slowly sideways. Taking it gently from him he put it in the holder above the wash-basin, left the cabin and slid the door shut behind him. He was simultaneously relieved and alarmed to know the weight of the burden he had temporarily to carry.

Chapter Five

The white wraith that was *Trigger* slid across the flat black sea, ten miles to the north, ten miles to the south, then ten miles to the north again. She wasn't rolling now, more maintaining a list of some fifteen degrees one way for long periods before, for no apparent reason, heaving upright and assuming the opposite angle like a sleeper turning in his bed. Snow drifted lazily, not going anywhere in particular.

Lieutenant Walker, who had taken over navigational duties when Gascoigne was made first lieutenant, said, 'All right, I'll take over the watch, Number One. I can see now.'

'What can you see?'

'Same as you. Snow, and the nearer bits of the ship. And you of course. You look like the Abominable Snowman. Must be something to do with the size of your feet.'

'Well, if they offend you look somewhere else,' Gascoigne said. 'How's the Skipper?'

'Says he had a good sleep and feels better now. Apparently he began to get disorientated lying in his cabin, so he's had a chair put in the control room and he's sitting on that, drinking soup. Probably prefers it to looking at Maddox's gloomy face in the wardroom.'

Gascoigne grunted, but made no comment.

In the control room Harding finished his soup and put the empty cup down on the chart table beside him. After his bout of fever he was still not strong enough to stand for long unaided, but his mind was clear and he used it to remind himself of the function of every one of the massed columns of dials, valve wheels and levers on the diving panel. Those levers, their film of metallic blue anti-corrosion compound tinged mauve by the ship's red night-lighting would, with little more than finger pressure on them, send *Trigger* sliding beneath the surface of the sea. 'Or they would,' Harding said, 'if we didn't have all that bloody ice to hold us up.' He had not meant to speak aloud and was not aware that he had done so until a voice asked, 'What, sir?'

He looked at the chief yeoman of signals and said, 'I was just muttering to myself about our covering of icing, Yarrow. Makes me feel like the captain of a wedding cake.'

'An iceberg more like, sir. There's no marzipan under this lot,' Yarrow replied, smiled and went on his way.

Harding returned his attention to the control room fittings, to the twin hydroplane controls with the depth gauges above them, their pointers indicating zero feet as they had done for so long with the ship unable to dive for one reason or another; to the brass columns of the two periscopes, one binocular, one monocular; to the radar mast, inoperative like almost everything else which protruded outside the hull above the water-line; to the steering wheel which was something that still worked and was in constant use. When he had looked at all that, he raised his eyes and examined the maze of electric cables and pipes running from forward to aft above his head, identifying each one and its purpose. He did it rapidly, accurately and automatically, because the knowledge was deeply engrained in him. The bewildering array held total logic for him and that made it simple and almost aesthetically pleasing. It was a pity, he thought, that a few degrees drop in temperature should be able to reduce so much advanced technology to virtual uselessness.

That made him think about the hurricane which had had exactly the same effect. Remembering that he had felt momentary gratitude to someone or something when that had eased to a mere storm, he wondered if they were better or worse off now. Unable to decide one way or the other he came to the conclusion that God, if he existed, really was a terrible tease.

'Hydrophone effect bearing Green 125, sir,' Petty Officer McIntyre said. 'Very faint, but I think it's turbine.'

The suddenness with which Harding swung to face the chief sonar operator made his head swim and for a moment he was afraid that he would fall off his chair. Then the control room steadied about him and quite unnecessarily loudly he barked, 'Stay on it! Never mind the all-round sweep for now!'

'Aye aye, sir.'

Petty Officer McIntyre sat, hunched forward over his sonar set, eyes screwed tightly shut in concentration, moving the knurled knob controlling the ship's electronic ear fractionally this way and that. Harding watched him doing it, biting his lip in anxiety, realizing that, but increasing the pressure of his teeth to prevent the escape of a demand for more information, information not yet available. McIntyre would tell him when it was. Seconds dragged themselves into minutes. McIntyre didn't speak. Air whistled past some obstruction in the conning tower. Gascoigne appeared through the lower hatch and stood, beating himself about the body, stamping his feet, white eyebrows and lashes turning quickly black in the higher temperature. His captain beckoned to him and whispered something as though the Germans might overhear. The first lieutenant nodded and both officers turned their gaze on the chief sonar operator. Oblivious to everything else McIntyre listened to the sounds of the sea, to the sounds *in* the sea.

At last, 'Confirmed turbine, sir,' he said. 'Several sets of 'em bearing Green 130 to 135.'

Gascoigne glanced at the gyro repeater tape in front of the helmsman, made a simple mental calculation and looked at Harding.

'Söröy Island, sir?'

'Yes.'

Söröy Island masked the approaches to Alten Fjord, to Kaa Fjord where *Tirpitz* lurked like some gigantic Moray eel in its cave.

McIntyre removed his headset and turned to face the captain.

'Can't swear to it, sir, but it sounds like a big ship and several littler ones.'

'I see,' Harding said. 'Number One, have the jury aerial rigged and tell the Chief to start ciphering a signal. It begins "Sonar indicates *Tirpitz* and escorts at sea off Söröy Island". Prefix it "Most immediate". I'll add to it if we learn anything more in the next few minutes.'

'Aye aye, sir.'

Aware of the sudden activity around him, ignoring it, Harding picked up the second pair of earphones and tried to fumble them onto his head. It was difficult with one hand swathed in bandages.

''Ere, let me, sir.' A voice behind him, the headset taken from him and placed in position over his ears.

'Thank you,' Harding said.

The sea whispered at him. The sea always had something to say but, unlike McIntyre, he was unskilled in its language, incapable of interpreting its hisses, clicks and occasional birdlike chirpings. In his brief professional life there had been so many things to attain at least a working mastery over, that there had been no time to make himself competent in all of them. That was bad and he decided that he would have to devote more of his attention to detail, to high-speed Morse, to diesel engineering, to reading the message of a radar screen, instead of to his newly acquired command responsibilities which called for the curious blending of fact and hypothesis in such a way that... 'What the hell do you think they've given you petty officers for? Either leave it to McIntyre, or shut up and listen,' Harding told himself and concentrated his mind on listening.

It took him a little while even to detect the susurration of distant propellers and even when he had done so he could neither tell their number, nor whether they were driven by turbines, reciprocating engines or anything else, but he avoided falling again into the trap of envying Petty Officer McIntyre his educated ears. Then he saw the sonar operator's lips move, and pushed the earphones out of the way.

'What did you say?'

'The change of bearing is very irregular, sir.'

'Meaning what? That they're slowing and then speeding up again?'

There was a slightly pained look on McIntyre's face when he said, 'Oh no, sir. The revs are constant. I think they're doing an almost constant zig-zag like they're heading away from us part of the time, towards part of the time and at right angles the rest. The rise and fall of sound intensity fits the idea, sir.'

'Good for you. That makes sense to me. They're a long way off, aren't they?'

'Yessir, but I can't say how far.'

'Can you guess at their speed?'

'Going like hell, sir. Very fast revs. More than twenty-five knots I shouldn't wonder. They're warships all right. Bearing about Green 160 and I'm beginning to lose them in the noise from our own screws.'

'Stop both engines,' Harding said. 'Where's the First Lieutenant?'

'I'm here, sir.'

'Oh, so you are. Is that aerial rigged yet?'

'Very nearly, sir.'

'Very well. Add to that signal "Course westerly zig-zagging at 25 knots plus". Get it transmitted as soon as you can. Chivers, tell the bridge we've stopped to listen to a sonar source. Somebody tell the crew over the Tannoy as well.'

Trigger lay dead on the surface of the sea, her 70-man crew silent, or so it seemed to Harding with only the subdued humming of the ventilation system audible. It was, he thought, as though everybody on board was trying to detect the sounds that only the sonar operator could hear. Eerie, very eerie to be sitting on a chair in the hushed control room of a submarine in contact with the enemy many miles inside the Arctic Circle when normality would have called for the crew at diving stations and the thunder of the diesels urging the ship at her best speed along an interception course. It would be eerier still on the quiet bridge, he imagined, with only the loom of the periscope standards, the icy battlements of the conning tower and the gently drifting snow for visual distraction. He had even stopped them chipping at the ice up there lest the sound should frustrate McIntyre's efforts.

'Hydrophone effect directly astern now, sir.'

'Thank you.'

Worry nagged at Harding, the worry that what he had so faintly heard was not the *Tirpitz* at all or, if it was, that she had put to sea only for exercises and that she posed no threat to the Murmansk convoy or any other. 'Sounds like a big ship and several littler ones,' McIntyre had said. 'I think they're doing an almost constant zig-zag,' McIntyre had said. 'Going like hell, sir. More than twenty-five knots I shouldn't wonder. They're warships all right,' McIntyre had said. No, it had to be the *Tirpitz* and the absence of sonar transmissions was significant too, transmissions which would have been audible over a much greater range than the noise of propellers. They were maintaining sonar silence, trusting in the zero visibility to protect them from submarine attack, in an attempt to slip away unnoticed into the vastness of the ocean. Presumably they were maintaining radar silence as well, for although his detector aerial was ice-shrouded and so could not tell him, he could assume it on the grounds that none of the ships had come to investigate his presence. Well, they'd know of that presence very shortly now when his powerful wireless transmission blasted out of their search receivers. That would tell them, as surely as if they could read the ciphered message, that their furtive departure from harbour had been observed. It would also tell them, if they were alert and brought their radio direction finders into operation quickly enough, his bearing from them. He must alter that bearing by using high speed as soon as they had established it.

Harding grunted irritably at the realization that that would be of no help as, knowing themselves discovered, there would be no point in the Germans not using radar. That would pin-point him fast enough. What would they do? Detach one of the escorts to hunt him down or press on in the knowledge that they could swiftly out-distance him? In what knowledge? There was no way in which they could be certain that the sudden spate of fast Morse had come from a submarine and not from a destroyer or some other vessel with the speed to trail them and report their every movement. So they would come hunting.

Fleetingly he considered the possibility that the enemy's radar would be as solidly frozen and as useless as his own, but he pushed the wishful thought away from him. They had steam hoses and, with those, ice could be cleared from almost anywhere.

'Any change in the situation, McIntyre?'

'Beginning to fade on Red 170, sir.'

Something the chief yeoman had said, something about an iceberg and no marzipan, pushed its way to the forefront of Harding's mind and gave birth to an idea there.

'Has that signal gone yet, Number One?'

'It's being transmitted now, sir.'

'Full ahead together,' Harding said. 'Steer 360 and ask the Engineer Officer to work up to maximum revolutions as soon as he can.'

Trigger came alive, vibration building throughout her length as she began to race north towards the dangerous haven of the polar ice-cap. To those on the bridge her momentum gave the drifting snow a spurious appearance of purpose.

*

Admiral Stresemann's sombre mood deepened, but he allowed no sign of his disappointment to show in his face when he said, 'That is unfortunate, but it was always a possibility. We must now endeavour to ensure that we are not shadowed. Kindly detach one of the escorts to establish the source of the transmission and to destroy it if possible. If it turns out to be an enemy heavy unit, *Tirpitz* herself will engage it.'

'The communications office doesn't think the signal was strong enough to have come from a heavy ship, sir.'

The admiral looked up from his desk at his chief staff officer. 'Is that so?'

'Yes, sir.'

Stresemann permitted himself a slight frown before saying, 'I am not particularly interested in opinions at this moment. Don't just stand there. Do as I say and find out for certain.'

He picked up his pen and began writing to indicate that the exchange was over.

*

'What the blazes do you mean by an evaluation, George?' Flag Officer Submarines asked. 'If young Harding of *Trigger* says that his sonar indicates that *Tirpitz* and her escorts are at sea, he means that his sonar indicates that *Tirpitz* and her escorts are at sea. What do you want me to evaluate? The efficiency of his sonar, his ability to communicate, or the threat posed by *Tirpitz* loose on the high seas?'

He listened to the telephone receiver for almost half a minute before going on, 'Well, that's your decision, old boy, but if you've got *Duke of York* pottering about that far to the east of Iceland you seem to have an excellent chance of trapping *Tirpitz* between her and *Nelson* and earning yourself another knighthood. You know, "*What?* Twice a knight at your age?" as Somerville said to Cunningham, or was it the other way round? Good luck anyway and if your original point was intended to establish if Harding has his head screwed on the right way, the answer's in the affirmative… What?… Oh, good for you. Give her what the *Bismarck* got. Are you lunching at the club?… Right, see you in an hour. 'Bye.'

Flag Officer Submarines replaced the receiver on its rest, turned to the officer who was Deputy Director of Naval Intelligence, waited for him to put down the extension phone, then asked, 'Was that all right?'

'First rate, sir,' the DDNI said. 'I'm much obliged to you and Admiral Shanklin. A verbatim report of that conversation will be in Berlin by tonight. This has really been a most fortunate set of circumstances.'

The admiral watched the door close behind the departing Intelligence officer, then stood up, walked round his desk and sat down in the visitor's chair as though preparing to be interviewed by himself. He was thinking about the fortunate set of circumstances, about the breaking of the latest U-boat code, about the intercepted signal from U-261 reporting the sighting of a *King George* V-class battleship to the east of Iceland, about *Trigger's* enemy report. That battleship, the *Duke of York*, had started her race to the support of *Nelson* and the Murmansk convoy hours before the fabricated telephone conversation in which he had been coached and had concluded moments earlier, but that fact would have been of only peripheral interest to the officer who had just left him. His object had been to convince the German Secret Service of the continued reliability of one of their agents now working under the control of M15, by forcing the man to provide them with accurate information of which they were already aware from the U-boat's message.

It had, the submarine admiral thought, been a very strange experience to talk about secret matters, however flippantly, on a telephone line tapped by an erstwhile enemy agent. That the tapping had been made possible by an officer of the section of M15 responsible for the control of double agents and that the spy's subsequent wireless transmission would be closely supervised did nothing to lessen the strangeness. He had asked why the charade was necessary at all, why the man should not simply be given a transcript of a conversation and made to transmit it and had been told by the DDNI that participation, however fraudulent, helped 'turned' spies to retain a grasp on reality. In addition when, as was often necessary, they were sent to report to their German superiors in a neutral country, it was easier for them to survive in their new role if they had actually done what they claimed to have done and been where they said they had been.

Flag Officer Submarines sat for a moment longer wondering what disinformation would now be pushed through the chink in the enemy's armour which *Trigger's* report had been used to open, then brought his mind back to the more immediate present. He was aware of Manfred Stresemann's appointment in command of the German Arctic Squadron and had known him personally before the war. He knew him to be a disciple of Grand Admiral Raeder and a strategic rather than tactical thinker who would prefer to preserve *Tirpitz* as a force in being, as a Damoclean sword hanging above the heads of the Allies, rather than risk her very existence for a questionable gain. The *Nelson* alone he might well have engaged in battle, but the fortuitous coincidence of *Trigger's* warning and the convenient presence in the area of the *Duke of York* having enabled the Admiralty to confront him with virtually overwhelming fire-power, and M15's double agent ensuring that he would know that he would be facing just that by turning a possibility based on a U-boat sighting into a certainty, would drive him back to the safety of Alten Fjord.

And that, Flag Officer Submarines thought, would be excellent for the Murmansk convoy which would escape involvement in a battle between giants and excellent, too, for *Trigger* who could place herself in the optimum position to attack *Tirpitz* on her return to harbour.

He went back to his own chair and telephoned a staff officer about a signal to be sent to *Trigger*, not knowing that the submarine was racing towards the edge of the pack ice with a German destroyer at her heels.

Chapter Six

To Gascoigne *Trigger* seemed to be careering through the perpetual night, to be achieving a hurtling progress far beyond the velocity at which her engines had been designed to propel her. It was, he knew, an illusion created by the snowflakes living briefly within his field of vision before vanishing astern, by the extreme vibration transmitted through the ship's structure from the diesels to his cold feet, by the now constant slow roll coming more from the torque of the twin screws than any motion of the sea. But knowing those things and accepting them was not the same with the mental image of the jagged wall of ice somewhere beyond the invisible bows clear in his mind, ice twenty miles ahead, ten miles, one mile, perhaps only five hundred yards.

How far away the ice was Gascoigne had no idea and the fact that his captain didn't know either only served to increase his alarm and, in his imagination, *Trigger's* speed. From moment to moment he lived in anguished anticipation of the fatal crunching impact when more than a thousand tons of fast-moving steel struck an immovable floe, hearing the scream of tearing metal and injured men, feeling the deck canting further and further until the Arctic Sea flooded over them, ending all sensation with the shock of its frigid embrace. So strong was the impression of riding a runaway sledge blindfold towards a precipice that he had constantly to remind himself that the sonar's probing electronic finger should enable them to avoid disaster. Should? How thick did ice have to be for sonar to detect it? How thick did ice have to be to wreck a submarine?

Despite the cold Gascoigne was sweating.

*

Frigaten-Kapitän Franz Heyde said, 'Give me the distance to the ice and the range of the object.' Heyde was a precise man, precise in his use of words and, therefore, not yet prepared to refer to the object radar had detected as a target because he was not certain what it was.

Beside him a *leutnant* spoke into a telephone, waited, listened and clipped the instrument back into place on the side of the destroyer's bridge.

'Nine thousand and five thousand metres respectively, sir. The object is approximately thirty degrees on our port bow.'

'Approximately!' Heyde said. 'When will they provide us with accurate equipment? I don't like those nice round figures in metres either. I suppose they're approximate too.'

'Yes, sir.'

'Then they're useless for gunnery control. Slow down so that the "sound" room can hear. Perhaps they can do better.'

'*Sofort, Herr Kapitän!*' the *leutnant* replied and began giving orders.

*

Sitting in *Trigger's* control room beside the chief sonar operator Harding searched his mind for something to be positively pleased about other than that his ship hadn't been sunk yet, but found only the knowledge that the temperature was rising. Not much, not enough to melt the carapace of ice *Trigger* was carrying on her back, but enough to let the snow fall. Or was it warmer because the snow was falling? For a moment he wondered about that, then moved his shoulders irritably. What did that matter? The thermometer reading was higher than it had been and if that trend continued he might again find himself in command of a submarine which could submerge. That, he thought tiredly, would make a nice change from his present utterly unseamanlike sightless charge across water which might not only be bearing enemy vessels in the immediate vicinity, but would certainly turn from the liquid to the solid state very soon.

He turned and watched Petty Officer McIntyre periodically depressing the sonar transmission key, searching for an echo off the barrier of ice lying across their bows, caught his eye and saw the negative shake of his head.

'All right,' Harding said, 'we'll do some more listening. Chivers, tell the bridge I'm stopping again for an all-round sonar sweep. Stop both engines.'

Vibration ceased and silence descended on *Trigger*. Seconds grew into a minute. Two minutes.

'Nothing, sir. Not a whisper.'

'Very well. Tell the engine room to...'

'Wait, sir! I'm getting sonar transmissions on Green 125 now, sir.'

'In contact?'

'No, sir. Sweeping, but – hang on! Sweeping in our general direction, sir. They seem to know roughly where we are, but no contact.'

'Diving stations,' Harding said and in saying it thought it was the most incongruous order he had ever given, as the ship could not dive. Not that anybody else would find it odd. Surfaced or submerged, 'diving stations' was the synonym used by the Submarine Service for the surface fleet's 'action stations'.

Feet pounding. Muttered imprecations. Men milling in orderly confusion. 'Get out of me way, Shorty!' The scene settling as appointed stations were reached. A late arrival bumping into Harding's chair. 'Sorry, sir.' Silence and a taut expectancy.

'Any change in the situation, McIntyre?'

'No, sir. Still sweeping.'

Harding stood up, swayed and felt his arm grasped.

'Thanks, Selby. Just steer me over to the ladder, will you?'

Supporting himself with one hand on a rung of the brass conning tower ladder, Harding took down the microphone of the Tannoy public address system with the other and spoke into it, wincing a little from the pain the small pressure brought to his flayed palm.

'This is the Captain speaking. Sonar has detected an enemy vessel off our starboard quarter. It doesn't seem to be quite sure where we are, so with the visibility less than half a ship's length I'm going to lie doggo for a bit. You never know, they might get bored and go away. You needn't maintain strict silent routine at this stage, but don't clatter things about. That's all.'

The microphone back on its hook, he turned and made his way to the voice-pipe beside the helmsman to tell Gascoigne what was happening. Petty Officer Selby, arms half extended, followed him like a mother behind a toddler, not touching him, but ready to grab.

*

'Well?'

'The "sound" room isn't sure, *Herr Kapitän*.'

'The "sound" room isn't... Oh give me that telephone,' *Frigaten-Kapitän* Heyde said irritably, snatched the instrument from the *leutnant* and shouted, 'What aren't you sure about?'

'What's there, sir,' a tinny voice told him. 'If there's anything there. When we first slowed down I thought for a moment I could hear propeller beats, but I can't now.'

'Can you classify those beats? Think hard.'

'I'd only be guessing, sir.'

'Then guess, damn you!'

'Diesel, sir,' the ear-piece said.

Without acknowledging the statement the captain returned the phone to its bracket, then stood chewing his lip for a moment before saying, 'Check with radar again.'

Seconds later, 'Four thousand five hundred metres, bearing thirty-five degrees to port, sir.'

'Plot that.'

The head and shoulders of the *leutnant* disappeared under the canvas cover screening the chart table with its tiny light at the side of the bridge. Heyde watched him because there was nothing else to look at, saw him re-emerge.

'So?'

'We're overtaking at about the same rate, sir.'

'Ah!'

'Sir?'

As though thinking aloud, 'The same rate, eh?' Heyde said. 'And we've slowed right down which means that he must have stopped altogether. That's why the "sound" room can't hear him. There's a submarine lying stationary on the surface over there, Otto. It must be that. Zeitzler thought he heard diesel engines. For some reason it can't submerge, otherwise it wouldn't have been making for the shelter of the pack ice.' He paused before adding, 'Perhaps it suffered damage during the hurricane.'

'Then we've got him, sir!' Excitement in the *leutnant's* voice.

'Yes, we've got him,' Heyde replied in the same thoughtful tone. 'We've got him just as surely as if we'd got a cobra in a darkened room. The problem is doing something about it without getting bitten.'

*

Back on his chair Harding looked inward at the outlines of the picture McIntyre had begun to paint for him, exercising his command function of juggling fact and hypothesis in an attempt to block in the rest. Mentally he began to list the items of knowledge available to him.

There was a hostile destroyer somewhere not very far away on his starboard quarter. McIntyre had said so, so that was a fact. Wrong! He hadn't said anything of the sort. He had simply identified a sonar source in that direction, a source now moving slowly forward towards the beam. Nothing about a destroyer at all. Oh, stop nit-picking. What else would it be? Assume destroyer.

The destroyer had located him by radar because there was no other way in which it could have done it, so accept as fact. But then why weren't shells falling around *Trigger*? On *Trigger*? Why was the enemy probing, unsuccessfully as yet, with sonar impulses? Because the *Kriegsmarine's* radar was less precise in definition than the Royal Navy's? It was certainly reported to be so, but he was not prepared to bank on it. Because they thought *Trigger* might be a U-boat? Nonsense! They *must* know the disposition of their own forces. Perhaps they had taken her for a breakaway chunk of ice. Well, that had been his intention in hurrying north, but he wasn't prepared to bank on that either.

'Bearing Green 120, sir. Still sweeping.'

'Thank you, McIntyre.'

Still no contact. That was good. Where had he got to? Oh, yes. A breakaway chunk of… Green 120? Bloody hell! Don't just sit there like a pregnant duck offering almost the whole length of the ship as a sonar target! Turn end on! Which end? Quickest to port, presenting the stern. That would carry him further away too. Stupid! They'd still have his approximate bearing on radar and all of the stern torpedo tubes were above the water-line and frozen solid. Six of the bow tubes were submerged and ice-free. At least point your teeth in the right direction!

'Group down, slow ahead together, starboard 20,' Harding said and glanced at the illuminated gyro repeater tape in front of the helmsman. Even with no steerage way the ship's head had swung only three degrees away from due north on the calm water. He thought east would be about right and added, 'Steer 090.'

The orders were repeated back to him, the telegraphs tinkled their message and *Trigger*, propelled by her electric motors, began to move ahead again, turning slowly, silently, towards the east and the enemy. When the turn had been completed he ordered the motors stopped.

It was as though adopting a posture of offence had at last fully awakened Harding from the lethargic legacy of his fever. It was an unpleasant awakening, bringing with it the realization of how slowly his mind had been working. Bringing with it fear too, fear whose sharp spur ripped away some opaque substance which seemed to have been clouding his intellect and prodded his brain into frantic activity.

He found himself on his feet, moving towards the voice-pipe, his tendency to stagger gone but with an unsettling inward tremor replacing it.

'Bridge?'

'Yes?' Gascoigne's voice.

'What's the visibility like, Number One?'

A pause, then, 'Well, now you mention it, sir, I think it's a bit better. I hadn't noticed before, but I can almost see the for'ard hydroplanes. The snow seems to be easing up a bit.'

That did it for Harding. With the anaemic light of the Arctic dawn less than two hours away, time was running out.

'Now, listen carefully,' Harding said. 'We're going in to ram, and this is what I want you to do.'

49

*

Admiral Stresemann took a pair of pince-nez from a velvet-lined case and clipped them to the bridge of his nose, then looked down at the two signals the *oberleutnant* had placed on the desk in front of him.

'For admiral commanding Arctic Squadron,' he read. 'U-boat sighting and subsequent confirmation from intelligence source indicate that heavy cover for target convoy will be supplemented by addition battleship *Duke of York* repeat *Duke of York* before noon tomorrow. Present heavy cover consists of battleship *Nelson* repeat *Nelson*. Act as circumstances dictate'. The message was signed *Oberkommando der Kriegsmarine*.

'Tautology,' Stresemann said.

'What, sir?'

'Supplemented by addition is taut… Oh, never mind.'

The second signal read, 'Germany expects a famous victory! Engage the enemy more closely! Adolf Hitler'.

'I suppose seeing the name "Nelson" inspired that bit of lunacy,' Stresemann said softly.

'I beg your pardon, sir?'

'Nothing.'

The admiral took off his pince-nez, polished them with a square of chamois leather and returned them to their case. He was not conscious of any of those actions, his mind occupied by images of the two great ships, *Nelson* with her nine 16-inch guns in three triple turrets, *Duke of York* with ten 14-inch guns in one twin and two quadruple turrets. Nineteen enormous pieces of naval artillery against which he could pit only eight 15-inch guns. Quite deliberately he allowed himself to picture the last moments of *Tirpitz's* elder sister *Bismarck*, hammered and blasted into a capsized hulk by just such guns before torpedoes sent her to the bottom. That he did to gauge the extent of his personal trepidation and found none. All his life he had trained for such a confrontation and would have been dismayed had he detected in himself reluctance to face his own chosen destiny. But a chosen destiny and the requirements of his high calling were two very different things and he had no intention of allowing the *Führer's* ill-considered bombast to cloud that fact.

'He got a little over-excited,' Grand Admiral Raeder had said about Hitler, meaning that he had become hysterical. Then, indirectly and kindly, Raeder had told Stresemann where his duty lay, knowing well that he did not need to be told, but doing it nevertheless so that a proportion of the inevitable blame should rest on his shoulders.

Stresemann glanced at the *Führer*'s message again, but without his glasses the words were a blur. It didn't matter. The silly paraphrasing constituted a death warrant which was all that he needed to know about it and the best he could do for Germany was to limit its scope.

Looking up at the *oberleutnant*, 'My compliments to the Captain, and the Squadron will return to Alten Fjord,' he said.

*

His chair moved close to the helmsman now so that he had immediate access to the voice-pipe, Harding watched its brass funnel quivering in sympathy with his ship's vibration, telling himself that his own trembling came from the same source and not believing it. What he was doing was insane and he knew it, but he also knew that if he did nothing he would be guilty of a greater insanity, because then they must either surrender or die. This way they all stood a chance of having to do neither of those things and might, just might, sink an enemy destroyer. It would be by no means a one-sided contest. The destroyer, larger, a lot more manoeuvrable and a great deal faster appeared to have all the advantages; and in anything approaching reasonable visibility would have done so, would indeed have sunk *Trigger* with her 5.9-inch guns at long range and at leisure. But the visibility was not reasonable, although Gascoigne had reported that he could at last distinguish the bows, and that evened the score.

Two images formed almost simultaneously in Harding's mind. The first showed him *Trigger*'s sharp reinforced stem slicing through the thin plating of the enemy's side, deep into its interior. The second, the destroyer riding over *Trigger*, driving her under, but crumpling her own bows in the process, quite likely crushing them as far back as the forward gun when they came into contact with the far thicker steel of the submarine's pressure

51

hull. Any destroyer captain anywhere would hesitate before inflicting such damage on his own ship. In the Arctic with its extremes of weather he would hesitate for even longer and that hesitation, Harding thought, might tip the scales in his favour. He had tried to load the scales further by turning out the forward hydroplanes into their horizontal operating position but, as he had feared, they remained frozen and immovable. That was a pity because one British submarine, blown to the surface and in danger of being rammed, had met its adversary head on and its hydroplane had ripped the side of the enemy vessel as though opening a can of fruit. Well, he would send them some torpedoes to think about first. With so little information available to him the chances of a hit were negligible, but the enemy might find the sound of their approach unnerving. Anything was worth trying.

'Situation please, McIntyre,' Harding said.

'Confused, sir. They've heard us of course, like I said they would. Even if they didn't hear our engines, they could hardly miss the sonar with me transmitting straight at them.'

'Yes, I know all that, McIntyre, but what are they doing?'

'Bit hard to say with all the racket we're making, sir, but they've narrowed their angle of sweep, so they know our bearing but haven't made contact yet. Nor have I. Their bearing's still straight ahead, or maybe a fraction to port now.'

Harding scratched at the stubble on his face and his mind side-stepped to produce the thought that it would be nice to be able to shave again when he could use his hand properly. Angrily he dragged his attention back out of the hole it had sought refuge in and asked, 'Are they transmitting all the time?'

'No, sir. They're alternating transmissions with passive listening watch.'

'So they'll hear our torpedoes coming.'

'Loud and clear, sir.'

'Good, that's what I want them to do,' Harding said. 'Stand by Numbers 1, 2, 3, 4, 5 and 6 tubes. Set the fish to run at four feet. Cox'n, come five degrees to port.'

'Five degrees to port, sir. Aye aye.'

The ship juddering as though it were running on cobbles, snow-flakes tinged pink by the red night-lighting, sucked down the conning tower by the stream of air feeding the racing diesels, dancing and dying, the gaze of half a dozen pairs of eyes on him an almost physical sensation. Harding moved his shoulders uneasily.

'Course 085, sir.'

'Thank you, Cox'n.'

'Sonar contact, sir! Give you a range in a second!'

'Well done, McIntyre,' Harding told him.

*

'Report!' *Frigaten-Kapitän* Heyde snapped.

'Enemy bearing approximately ninety degrees left, sir! Closing rapidly! Range approximately three thousand metres!'

'Approximately, approximately,' Heyde muttered before saying much more loudly, 'Well, we'd better see if we can approximately hit the damned thing, or at least scare it away. Full ahead both engines. Main armament train ninety left, range two thousand seven hundred. Open fire! Salvoes!'

Long barrels swinging in unison, the darkness speared by tongues of flame, the still night splintered by thunder, Heyde feeling his head driven down between his shoulders by the concussion of the broadside, the ship lurching to starboard at the recoil of the guns, the urgent metallic voice of the sonar operator blaring from the bridge speaker, '*Torpedo! Torpedo! Torpedo!*' A second broadside drowning speech, then Heyde shouting, 'Cease firing! Hard a' port! Depth-charge crews stand by! Close all water-tight doors! Prepare to ram!'

*

McIntyre's words, 'Torpedo running, sir,' and an excited cry from the bridge reached Harding's ears simultaneously. He looked quickly at the man at the steering wheel.

'What did the First Lieutenant say, Cox'n?'

'Gun flashes dead ahead, sir.'

'Ah,' Harding said, then into the voice-pipe, 'Any sign of their shells, Number One?'

'None, sir! Didn't even hear them. Ooops! More flashes!' Seconds passed before Gascoigne added, 'No sign of them either, sir.'

'That's nice,' Harding said. 'Now listen. We've just fired a fish at them. They'll either alter course towards or away when they hear it coming. We'll let you know which as soon as we get some Doppler effect, but things are likely to happen rather fast now if they turn towards, so don't nod off.'

There was no reply and Harding asked. 'Did you hear me?'

'I'm sorry, sir,' the voice-pipe told him. 'I was just stifling a yawn. Yes, I heard you.'

Harding grinned because it was the sort of remark one was supposed to grin at. He had never felt less like grinning – with some external source of low-voltage electric current seemingly playing along every one of his nerve fibres, oscillating current from the way his whole skin area was quivering. Hoping very much that the effect was not visible he turned and looked enquiringly at McIntyre.

'Can't distinguish nothing, sir. Our torpedo's making a noise like a dive-bomber.'

Unaware that the rictus-like grin was still on his face Harding nodded, trying to picture what the sonar could not describe to him, not liking the picture his imagination painted of two ships charging head on at each other like blind rhinos. Imagination? No, fact if the enemy had altered course towards. A droplet of sweat detached itself from his hair-line, ran across his forehead, then wandered more slowly down the side of his nose to lodge in the stubble on his upper lip. He licked it away. There would be a crash like the end of the world in a minute, part of his mind told him, only to be silenced by another part shouting, 'Work it out, you stupid bastard! "In a minute" means nothing!'

Lieutenant Walker standing at the chart table could not help him because he had insufficient data to plot anything worthwhile, but Ordinary Seaman Norris was squatting on a tool-box nearby, patiently jotting down the times of events on a pad. Harding snatched it from him, checked the time of the firing of the torpedo, looked at the control room clock and began to estimate the build-up of the destroyer's speed after its sonar operator first heard the scream of the torpedo's 300-horse-power engine coming from his earphones. The enemy's turning-circle had to be taken into account too, as well as *Trigger's* own velocity.

His mental arithmetic had not yet arrived at the possible distance apart of the two vessels when it was driven from his head by McIntyre saying, 'Got it! Bearing Red 7! Range six hundred yards! Doppler up! Closing fast!'

'Come seven degrees to port, Cox'n! Quickly now.'

'Sir!'

Harding watched the illuminated figures of the gyro repeater tape flick rapidly from 085 to steady on 078, stabbed the firing button of Number 2 tube with his thumb and another twenty-two-foot length of gleaming torpedo leapt from *Trigger's* bows in pursuit of the first.

*

'Never mind the telephone. Use the bridge speaker as you did before until further orders,' Heyde told the operator in the 'sound' room. 'I must know immediately and precisely what is going on!'

The metal trumpet on the bulkhead behind him hummed experimentally, then said, '*Jawohl!* Torpedo has missed to port, *Herr Kapitän*, but I can't make out much of the enemy. We're moving too quickly and I'm losing the echo. I'll try listening watch.' A sound like a sharp inhalation and the shouted words, '*They've fired another one!*'

Quietly, 'Hard a starboard,' Heyde said and felt the deck tilt beneath his feet as the rudder bit into water streaming past at sixty-five kilometres an hour, feeling, too, the after part of the ship skidding sideways with the violence of the turn, praying that he had not left it too late.

It was then that he saw the English U-boat, a phantom only vaguely perceived, neither dark nor light, seeming to swing across an arc from his right to his left towards the stern with a mobility not of this world. For a long moment he stood as though hypnotized before the realization came that it was his own ship's sharply curving course creating the illusion and that he might, just might, have acted in time to avoid being rammed aft, but there was going to be only a metre or two in it.

Raised voices of men calling out their own sightings of the long low hostile shape so perilously close; the *leutnant* ordering search lights trained astern and the guns to stand by; Heyde himself, thrusting a sailor out of his way, leaping to the side of the bridge and slamming his gloved hand against the three knobs on the depth-charge control panel there, hearing the throwing mortars cough in response, picturing the charges arcing away through the darkness to either side, others dropping over the stern.

A searchlight beam stabbed out then, blunting itself, flattening against the curtain of softly falling snow. It traversed to the left and the miracle happened, men standing transfixed as a billion crystals of ice reflected its violet glare as though a star had burst. But the brilliance faded quickly as the ships separated, before flicking out of existence, leaving only the beam of the searchlight probing ineffectually at the blanket of drifting whiteness.

'My God! What was that?' the *leutnant* asked.

'Ice,' *Frigaten-Kapitän* Heyde told him. 'The enemy U-boat is coated in it. That's why it can't dive! "Sound" room and radar! Get me a range and bearing as soon as you can!'

*

It was worse than the rush towards the ice, Gascoigne thought. Much worse. Better to hit a stationary floe than a destroyer moving at thirty-five knots in the opposite direction! He began to sweat again and tried to persuade himself that that was because it was warmer. It *was* warmer. Not that it felt any less cold on the exposed skin around his eyes, but several pieces of compacted frozen snow had fallen from the periscope standards and thudded onto the bridge deck. A large chunk had struck Able Seaman Jameson on top of the head, knocking him sideways, but all Jameson had said was, 'Fuck those seagulls!' which had made Gascoigne laugh nervously. Now, with the suspense growing by the second, he had no inclination to laugh nervously or any other way at...

'Ramming!' Gascoigne shouted into the voice-pipe when, in a single instant, the blurred nothingness he had stared at for so long had become the side of a destroyer sweeping from starboard to port only yards beyond *Trigger*'s bows. It looked appallingly solid and he grasped at the front of the bridge, bracing himself for an impact which never came, although at what particular moment the enemy ship drew clear he could not tell with the blinding violet glare of a searchlight in his eyes. Distant shouts reached his ears and a double thump as though somebody had fired something which was not an ordinary gun. With spray everywhere, as *Trigger* plunged into the destroyer's wake and water surged over the fore casing, nobody noticed the splash sent up by a depth-charge hitting the surface of the sea almost directly alongside the conning tower.

The heavy metal canister was fifty feet beneath the surface and several yards astern of the fast-moving submarine when it exploded, its shock-wave creating a whiplash effect along *Trigger*'s entire length, making her heel to starboard and knocking Gascoigne off his feet.

'You all right, sir?'

Jameson crouching beside him, supporting his head. Chivers pushing great shards of ice off his body and legs.

'Yes, I think so. Give me a hand up, will you?'

The voice-pipe saying, 'Bridge? Bridge?' and Able Seaman Chivers answering, 'First Lieutenant's just coming, sir. He fell over.'

Upright again, Gascoigne lowered his head to the voice-pipe and said, 'Cap'n sir?'

'Yes?'

'We missed their stern by a whisker, sir, and they turned a searchlight on us. Then I think they must have dropped a depth-charge.'

'They dropped ten, Number One, but only one near us.'

'Oh, I see, sir. Sir, it's gone!'

'What's gone?'

'The ice, sir.'

'All of it?'

'Yes, sir. The casing's clear fore and aft. So's the gun, the periscope standards, the Oerlikon platform, the jumping wire, the – yes, it's all gone, except for the stuff trapped on the gun deck and we're knee-deep in it up here, of course.'

'I thought you might be. Quite an avalanche came down the hatch.' There was a short pause before Harding added, 'All right, Number One. Dive the ship.'

'Aye aye, sir,' Gascoigne said and stood for a moment admiring what he felt to be a remarkably novel command after so many days on the surface before ordering the look-outs below, forcing shut the two voice-pipe cocks and crunching over splintered ice to the conning tower hatch. When he had lowered himself into the tower he pressed the klaxon button twice, heard its double snarl come from the control room and swung the heavy metal lid down above his head. It closed to within an inch of its sealing ring and stopped.

For some seconds he struggled with it, banging it up and down against its counter-balance weight, unaware of the broken end of the wireless aerial, which had finally succumbed to the combined drag of ice and the shock of the explosion, jammed in the hatch's hinge. As he pictured the sea rising up the sides of the conning tower, fear rose with it until a shouted query from below brought him back to himself.

'Coming!' he said and dropped rapidly down the vertical brass ladder, slamming and clipping the lower hatch as soon as his feet reached the bottom.

'What happened, Number One?'

'Upper lid's jammed, sir.'

'You'd better start pumping ballast water out of "0" tank,' Harding told him. 'We'll be pretty heavy when the tower floods.'

Gascoigne had given the orders for that to be done and for 'Q', the emergency quick-diving tank, to be blown clear of water when the uproar began, an insane cacophony of sound beating at the eardrums, tugging at the nerves and rendering coherent thought almost impossible. Disorientated, he jerked his head in the direction of movement caught by peripheral vision and saw Petty Officer Selby pull two fuses from a panel. Immediately silence returned and, nearly as quickly, Gascoigne understood.

'Thank you, Selby,' he said, took down the Tannoy microphone and spoke into it. 'It's all right, everybody. We've flooded the conning tower and that shorted the circuits of the alarm and the diving klaxon. No panic.' He replaced the microphone, turned to the captain and asked, 'What depth, sir?'

'Stay at ninety feet until you're sure of the trim, Number One. It's ages since we last dived.'

'Hydrophone effect bearing Red 110, sir. Very fast turbine.' McIntyre's voice.

'And shut off for depth-charging,' Harding said.

Chapter Seven

There was no depth-charging. There was no sound at all except for the quiet breathing of men, the whisper of the ventilation system and Petty Officer McIntyre's periodic reports on the progress of the enemy destroyer apparently withdrawing at high speed to the west of south. Harding found it almost impossible to believe that it was doing that, that it wouldn't return to hunt him down.

Seventeen minutes after *Trigger* had dived, 'Quiet all round, sir,' McIntyre said.

Still unable to accept the evidence presented by the chief sonar operator because it made no immediate sense to him, 'Do you think they may have stopped?' Harding asked.

'Can't swear that they haven't, sir, but they done it in a funny place if they have, right at the limit of audibility. What would they want to do that for, sir?'

There seemed to be no answer to that and Harding's tired mind having ruled out coincidence he nodded his head. The small physical action, with its tacit acceptance that there would be no long-drawn-out hours of waiting interspersed with thundering under-water bombardments, knocked the prop which had been tension from under him. He could feel the deck rocking beneath the legs of his chair and see the fluctuating brightness of the lighting. There was no rocking and the bulbs glowed without a flicker. Somehow he knew that to be so, but it was difficult to convince his body of the facts with exhaustion settling around him like a cloud of anaesthetic gas. When after a long moment he succeeded, the ship and the lights steadied.

'You may go to patrol routine now, Number One, and I expect the Cox'n could be prevailed upon to issue the rum ration to the crew.'

Harding had spoken casually to demonstrate vocal as well as physical steadiness, but the words carried with them a tone of bored indifference which made him wince at his own theatricality. 'Don't ham it up!' he told himself, then watched almost furtively as the men dispersed, laughing, chattering, but theirs was the laughter of relief, not derision, and he relaxed slowly.

For several minutes he continued to sit where he was, wondering about what seemed to be an almost miraculous escape from an extremely hazardous situation. The enemy's withdrawal didn't make any sort of sense and the thought occurred to him that God, assuming that He existed and disregarding a degree of prevarication on His part during the hurricane and subsequent bitterly cold spell, had come down finally on the side of *Trigger*, first by enveloping her in a cloak of impenetrable darkness and then causing her to materialize, a scintillating apparition of brilliant light, before the eyes of an astonished foe.

The realization of the track his thinking had followed made him grin, but the reaction transformed itself into the embarrassed yawn of a dog that knows it is being laughed at. That made him wonder too.

*

In the petty officers' mess Chief Yeoman of Signals Yarrow rolled the dice and made his move on the Ludo board before saying, 'I wonder why that Jerry buggered off sharpish like that.'

'Christ! You'd have buggered off sharpish if you'd seen the look on the Skipper's face,' McIntyre told him. 'Grinning like a wolf he was when we was going in to ram.'

'Is that so? And I suppose you pinged off a message to the destroyer in Morse on that contraption of yours. "Dear Jerry, our Skipper's grinning. You'd better piss off or else".'

'Oh, knock it off, Lofty,' McIntyre said to the chief yeoman.

After that there was silence broken only by the clatter of the dice. It lasted for nearly three minutes until, as though there had been no gap in the conversation, 'Right fed up he was when I told him they'd scarpered,' McIntyre announced. 'Real disappointed. You could tell it from the way he ordered patrol routine. Is he all right in the head? I mean charging around after a…'

'That'll do, Ian!' Chief Petty Officer Ryland had spoken sharply and with the full authority of the ship's senior non-commissioned officer.

'Sorry, 'Swain. No offence intended.'

The coxswain nodded. 'All right then, but no more talk about Lieutenant 'Ardin' bein' off 'is 'ead. 'E's a very fine officer. We was together for two years before this lot, so I should know. That was in Shadow. Good ship *Shadow* was.' He pronounced it 'Shadder' both times.

'I practically seen 'im grow up from a kid,' Ryland went on, 'so I know 'im, and I can tell you that what you 'ave just seen was a battle of wills between 'im and them Krauts. Now you tell me, which one stayed ice-cool and which one run for it with 'is tail between 'is legs? Just you tell me that!'

Out of a facial expression which had been nothing more than a nervous acknowledgement of a mildly humorous remark of Gascoigne's, and an over-played attempt to keep his voice steady, the legend of Harding grew and spread.

*

At the tiny desk covering the wash-basin in his cabin Harding sat chewing at the end of a pencil. His whole being was crying out for sleep, but wasn't going to be allowed it until after *Trigger* had been taken to the surface, the conning tower drained and the obstruction jamming the upper hatch located and removed. But that task he was not prepared to deal with before he felt reasonably certain that the enemy destroyer had travelled far enough to place it beyond the range at which its radar could detect a surfaced submarine. Meanwhile he was filling in the time by trying to bring his patrol report notes up to date.

His vision blurred repeatedly as he read what he had already written, but he rubbed his eyes and persisted until he had finished, then took the pencil from his mouth.

'The only conclusion I can draw from the foregoing,' Harding wrote, 'is that the enemy broke off the action after he had obtained visual confirmation that he was in contact with a submarine, that is to say a vessel with insufficient speed to overtake a squadron of warships which I believe to have included the *Tirpitz*. Knowing that we constituted no immediate threat to that squadron he may have decided, or been ordered, to rejoin it.'

Not entirely satisfied with his own argument Harding shook his head irritably, slid the door of his cabin open and called, 'Who's the officer of the watch?'

'Me, sir. Walker, sir.'

'Switch over to red lighting. We'll be surfacing in thirty minutes,' Harding said.

*

On the bridge of the speeding destroyer *Frigaten-Kapitän* Heyde stood belabouring himself with his arms, enjoying the explosive sound the palms of his gloved hands made when they struck the back of his shoulders. The activity didn't make him feel much warmer, but it did serve as an outlet for the elation he felt at the destruction of the English U-boat, elation it would not have been seemly to give vent to verbally. Being a precise man Heyde acknowledged to himself that relief was also present in his pleasure, relief that the insane game of blindman's-buff carried out at maniacal speed had ended in his favour.

That it had done so somewhat fortuitously he also conceded, while giving himself credit for his foresight in having the depth-charge crews standing at the ready, as well as for his fast reactions which had sent the charges on their way during the infinitesimal time-span in which they could achieve anything.

For all that, their having achieved so much had been fortunate in the extreme but, fortunate or not, they had done it. When, shortly after the explosions, a U-boat incapable of diving had quite rapidly disappeared from the radar screen there was only one conclusion to be arrived at. At first Heyde had suspected his already suspect radar, then absolved it of blame when it continued to paint a clear picture of the polar ice. The English U-boat had sunk and he had ordered a ciphered signal to that effect to be broadcast with a request for information which would enable him to rejoin the squadron.

The reply, when it came, congratulated him on his success and instructed him to return to Alten Fjord. The second part of that message puzzled him because it was highly improbable that the attack on the Murmansk-bound convoy could have been concluded so soon.

*

On top of the conning tower which he had reached by way of the gun tower, Gascoigne located the broken aerial lead which had jammed the hatch and sent for a telegraphist to repair it. At the next hourly routine a cipher prefixed by *Trigger*'s call-sign was received. Its time of origin was several hours in the past and it instructed Harding to patrol a certain line off Söröy Island with a view to intercepting the *Tirpitz* on her return to harbour. *Trigger*, her conning tower cleared of water and her diesels pounding again, was already proceeding in that general direction and only a minor alteration in course was necessary to comply with the order.

A second signal followed an hour later. It cancelled the first – the *Tirpitz*, it said, being already back in Kaa Fjord; told Harding to return to Scotland as *Trigger*'s sister ship *Tusker* was closing the area ready to replace her; and ordered him to report his position by radio.

Glad as he was to be relieved of an arduous and unpleasant duty the message both depressed and puzzled Harding. His depression stemmed from his belief that throughout the long weeks of the patrol he had achieved absolutely nothing. *Tirpitz*, as he had feared might be the case, had sailed simply on exercise as every warship must if it is to remain an effective fighting unit. He found some consolation in the assumption that either the clandestine wireless link between Alten and the United Kingdom had been restored, or that the RAF had solved the problem of their over flights, because his superiors now knew where the *Tirpitz* was and that knowledge would be of assistance to *Tusker*.

The reason for his puzzlement lay in his being told to report his position. For a submarine to be instructed to break radio silence for such a purpose was a rarity and implied the fear that it had been lost. He wondered what had given anybody that idea and continued to wonder without any success at all. Harding was not one of the handful of people who in the entire world knew of the existence of a group of buildings near the Buckinghamshire town of Bletchley which housed an organization code-named 'Ultra' whose strange electronic machines enabled the German armed forces' 'Enigma' ciphers to be rapidly translated into plain language. It followed that he was unaware that *Frigaten-Kapitän* Heyde's signalled claim to have sunk a British submarine had been intercepted and deciphered at Bletchley Park.

With his ship racing towards its home base Harding was free to go to his bunk at last, but there depression took a stronger hold on him and fended off the sleep he so badly needed. For almost an hour he lay worrying about the as yet unwritten report on Lieutenant Maddox and the letter of condolence he would have to send to the parents of Able Seaman Roberts. Had he known how at that moment the sailor's death was being paid for in kind it would have given him no pleasure.

*

In the little town of Alten, Admiral Manfred Stresemann knelt on the stone floor of the police station's only cell with his wrists manacled in front of him. In ordering his execution the *Führer* had described him as spineless and the man from the *Gestapo* shot him eight times in the back in order to make it so.

Chapter Eight

'Finished with main engines,' Harding said, then stood for a moment looking around him at the snow-clad slopes of Holy Loch, at the squabbling gulls, at the three other submarines lying motionless on the scummy water at the points to which they had withdrawn to give him the berth directly alongside the depot ship. Last, he looked up at the grey mass of the depot ship itself and the rows of faces staring down at *Trigger*. It was all so familiar, but at the same time unreal after so many days of storm, darkness and ice.

Someone shouting, 'Where's your "Jolly Roger", then? Didn't you sink nothing?' One of his own crew replying, 'Just a few tots of rum. The Skipper said we was all to take it easy as this was our first patrol.' Beside him Gascoigne calling, 'All right Norris, that's enough. Keep your reminiscences until you get inboard.' Norris saying, 'Yes, sir. Sorry, sir.'

The steadiness of the deck beneath his feet felt unreal too and so did the absence of vibration from the diesel engines, but his bandaged hand and the small nagging pain from his broken tooth were there to remind him of what had been. That and the tiredness.

Harding glanced at Gascoigne and asked, 'All secure?'

'Yes, sir.'

'Okay. Let's go and report to Captain Submarines.'

'Who, me as well, sir?'

'Certainly you as well. You were doing my job for half the time. He'll want an eye-witness account of that business with the destroyer. Not hearsay from me.' Harding turned away, then back again and added, 'By the way, in case you're worrying about it I'm recommending that you stay on as permanent First Lieutenant. You handled everything very well.'

Gascoigne frowned a quick worried frown, gone almost as soon as it had formed.

'I thought you might say that, sir, and I'm grateful, but...'

'But what?'

The last sailor from the bridge party was just lowering himself into the conning tower and Gascoigne waited until the man's head had disappeared from sight before saying, 'I'm not sure if I'm reliable enough, sir. When we were running towards the ice-pack and after that when we charged the destroyer, well sir, I was a bit windy.'

'You were a bit *what?*'

'Windy, sir.'

'Dear God,' Harding said. 'I didn't know we had a man of iron aboard. Personally, *I* was absolutely petrified! Now, have you got any more silly confessions to make, or can we get on with running this ship together?'

Gascoigne grinned, shrugged his shoulders, murmured the word 'sir' and followed his captain.

Harding stopped in the great gaping portal through which the gangway entered the depot ship's side and looked back at his command, remembering the shouted query about the 'Jolly Roger'. He didn't really like the submarine custom of flying the black flag with its grinning death's head and symbols recording the destruction of hostile targets. It seemed to him in poor taste to flaunt a record of the death and destruction spread by oneself but, for all that, he regretted its absence now because the lack of it pointed directly at his failure to open his account with the enemy. Disappointed that so much mental, nervous and physical effort should have gone for nothing, he walked on with Gascoigne at his heels.

*

Captain Submarines was short, stocky and clearly fighting to control his temper until Gascoigne should finish his report on the attempted ramming of the German destroyer. He succeeded, dismissed the tall lieutenant, waited until the door closed behind him, then seemed to bounce out of his chair.

'Kindly explain yourself, Harding!'

'There's nothing to explain, sir,' Harding said levelly. 'I had no choice but to go over to the offensive before it got light enough for them to see me. I couldn't dive and…'

'I'm not talking about that, dammit!' the flotilla captain broke in. 'I'm referring to your appalling stupidity in failing to inform me of your physical condition. Look at you now! You still look bloody awful to me and what sort of use you could have been to anybody for the days after you hurt your hand, goodness knows. It's the worst case of rank irresponsibility I've ever encountered in a commanding officer. Why didn't you signal? Why didn't you report that you were no longer in command of your ship?'

'Because I was unconscious, sir,' Harding said.

'Don't be impertinent, Harding. You know perfectly well what I mean. After that you were confined to a chair in your control room almost until you got back here. What sort of command do you call that? Why, you had even fired your first lieutenant which means that that – that *kid* Gascoigne was effectively in charge! What possible justification had you for permitting a situation like that to continue?'

'The detection of the *Tirpitz*, sir. Achieving that was justification enough. Or it would have been if she'd intended to do anything more than carry out routine sea trials.'

The older man closed his hands into fists, propped himself on the desk with them and glared angrily at Harding before speaking through clenched teeth.

'I'm not in the least interested in the clarity of your hindsight, Harding,' he said. 'You made the decision to remain on patrol and conceal your inability to reach your own bridge *after* you had recovered consciousness and some considerable time *before* your sonar identified the sound of the *Tirpitz*. It's all written down here, so don't try arguing about that!' He raised one of his clenched fists and banged it down on the sheaf of typewritten pages which was Harding's patrol report before going on, 'What I am interested in and distressed by is your lack of forethought, of officer-like qualities, of plain common or garden sense! Can you give me one good reason why I shouldn't ask the Admiral to order a court-martial assembled to try you on a charge of hazarding your ship?'

For a moment Harding sat, staring at the report he had put ashore in the Shetland Islands when he had called in at Lerwick to refuel on the way home from the Arctic. Flown south by the RAF it would, he knew, have been in the hands of his superiors for a number of days. His conclusions and recommendations were missing from it, still in pencil form aboard *Trigger*, because he had needed more time, needed the residue of the fever out of his head, to enable him to present a theory in its clearest form.

He looked up at the flotilla captain and said, 'Only that for some time past, sir, I've had this idea that the right place for the captain during a surface action in poor visibility is in the control room, not on the bridge.'

'Ah!' Captain Submarines said. 'Go on,' and sat down as abruptly as he had risen. Harding thought he could see an expression of relief on his face.

'I've written an addendum to my patrol report, sir,' he began, 'but it hasn't been typed yet. It's in my safe aboard *Trigger*. Shall I get it?'

'No, I'll read it later. Just give me the gist of it.'

'Aye aye, sir.'

Harding had answered automatically, almost absently, his thoughts centred more on the threatened court-martial than on what he was going to say. They must, he supposed, have stayed there for longer than he had imagined as he was only brought back to himself by the sharply spoken word 'Well?'

'I'm sorry, sir,' he said. 'It's all so much against tradition that I'm finding it a little difficult to express, but… Well, it's like this, sir. During our working-up period before we went on patrol, I carried out a couple of practice night surface attacks on friendly ships using radar and sonar. The visibility was very good on both occasions, sir, and I did them from the control room with the First Lieutenant on the bridge. That was Maddox at the time, of course, not Gascoigne. His job was to take over and get us out of trouble if I made a mistake, or the electronic equipment was faulty. It worked like a dream both times and he didn't have to do anything. In fact it worked better than if I had been on the bridge because I could see everything on the radar screen for myself and listen directly to what the sonar operator was saying. That cut out all the delay in passing the information up the voice-pipe and also meant that I didn't have to rely on somebody else's description of what was happening. Am I making sense to you, sir?'

'Keep going. I'll tell you when you're not.'

Nodding, Harding ran his fingers nervously through his mousy hair and went on, 'It feels as though I'm talking heresy, or blasphemy, or something, suggesting that the captain can be anywhere other than on the bridge during a surface action, still…'

He paused there until the flotilla captain said, 'Blaspheme away,' then resumed his discourse.

'The weather played a part in my thinking too, sir. It really was rather bad. In fact the bridge was almost untenable at times during the hurricane, which was why I reduced the standard number of four look-outs to two and finally to none at all. I only wish I'd done that sooner, then Able Seaman Roberts wouldn't…'

Harding snapped his teeth together so sharply that they made an audible click, scowled and began to speak again. 'The point is, sir, that nobody could have done anything about anything whatever we sighted, and I blame myself for not abandoning standard procedure much earlier. All I needed was an officer of the watch to –' He stopped abruptly. 'Do you know something, sir? I'm not honestly sure what I needed him for either except to look for a change in the direction the sea was running. If we'd run into the entire German navy all we could have done was wave at each other.'

Again Harding paused before saying, 'Actually, sir, that isn't the point – as I stated just now. The point is about when the hurricane blew itself out and the real cold came and we iced up. After I had injured my hand I was faced with two choices. Either I had to signal that I was withdrawing and leaving the *Tirpitz* uncovered, or I could stay where I was. Having thought seriously about it, I decided that my inability to make it as far as the bridge was irrelevant because, except during a couple of hours of what is laughingly known as daylight up there, visibility was about the end of your nose and there was little sense in trying to squint at that. Admittedly the radar was on the blink, but the sonar wasn't, and that could hear a damned sight further than anybody could see. That's self-evident. It detected the German squadron for us, enabled me to fire two fish at the destroyer and guided us to within a coat of paint of ramming it. None of those things could have been done visually from the bridge.'

All trace of his earlier anger had gone from the flotilla captain's face when he said, 'That's excellent, Peter. Both we and the Americans have been taking a classified look at the possibility of submarine captains carrying out attacks in precisely the manner you have described. Well, very nearly precisely. The sole difference being that, for our part, we believe that the officer on the bridge should also be qualified in command, which rather rules it out for us as we don't have any to spare for that purpose. Still, that's by the way and does not invalidate the conclusions which you arrived at independently.'

Tired, still feverish, the sudden reprieve took Harding the wrong way. Stiffly he asked, 'In that case, sir, may one be permitted to enquire what all that court-martial stuff was about?'

He got no direct reply and watched, chewing his lip, while his superior removed two letters from a folder, placed one on his desk and tore the other across and across until the fragments of paper were little larger than postage stamps, then listened to him say, 'That, young man, was a communication which you would have received from the Admiral via me had you, as I very much feared would be the case, been unable to give a logical explanation of your actions. As you see, the letter no longer exists. This one does, and is now your property.'

Harding took the sheet of paper held out to him and read,

'I am required by Flag Officer Submarines to inform you that he has read with considerable satisfaction of your steadfastness under trying circumstances during your recent patrol. He wishes you to know that your dedication to duty had a direct bearing on the frustration of an enemy foray against an important Allied target and adds that your conduct was plainly all that he could ask'.

'Gosh!' Harding said and the flotilla captain smiled for the first time.

'Quite. Now, you'd better take that hand of yours along to the sick-bay. Oh, and do arrange to have your tooth capped. I don't much care what my commanding officers look like, but I do hate them lisping at me.'

Smiling in his turn, Harding stood up, then asked, 'Could you tell me why you told me to report my position, sir? I somehow inferred from that, that you thought I was in trouble.'

'I did,' the other told him. 'A Russian submarine reported hearing heavy depth-charging in your area. Their definition of "heavy" seems to be somewhat at variance with ours and I didn't know that only ten charges were dropped, or that you were on the surface at the time, until I read your report.'

'Yes, I see, sir,' Harding said.

He didn't see, nor did the flotilla captain. Neither was in a position to know that the Russian submarine existed only in the imagination of those at Bletchley Park responsible for concealing with cover stories the existence of 'Ultra' and its ability to read the German 'Enigma' ciphers.

Harding walked slowly towards the sick-bay, simultaneously pleased with the message from the admiral he had been given and worried about the contents of the one he had not. Then he patted his pocket, heard the faint reassuring crackle of the letter inside it, shrugged and quickened his pace.

Chapter Nine

Ordered to be ready to sail for the Mediterranean theatre of war in eighteen days time, Harding told Gascoigne that he could send the crew on leave in two batches for six days each. Amongst the first to go was Ordinary Seaman Norris. By some four and a half days he was also the first to return, something he achieved with the assistance of an escort provided by the Naval Police. Within twenty minutes of his arrival aboard *Trigger* he was standing, badly bruised about the face, in front of his captain at the defaulters' table in the control room.

Harding listened while Chief Petty Officer Ryland read the charge, then looked at Norris.

'Well?'

'I didn't do nothing, sir,' Norris said.

'Nothing? Are you telling me that these US Marines assaulted you without cause?'

'I only sang their song, sir, and a whole bunch of them jumped me, but there's at least two of 'em that'll remember they was in a fight, sir.' The sailor drew back his shoulders and bunched his fingers into fists in happy reminiscence.

'You sang their song, Norris?'

'Yessir.'

'Remind me. How does it go? Don't sing it, just tell me the words.'

'Yessir. It goes "From the halls of Montezuma, to the shores of Tripoli, sir.'

'So it does. What follows after that? It's your version I want.' Harding guessed what was coming, but wondered if Norris had thought of a new variation on the taunt.

Norris had not. Addressing the deckhead above him he recited, '"We're bloody fine hands in harbour, but oh my Christ at sea!". Sir!'

'Look at me, Norris,' Harding said, saw Norris's gaze flick down from the deckhead to meet his own and asked, 'Do you know a lot of jokes about the American Services, Norris?'

'Yes, sir. Dozens, sir.'

'I see. You didn't happen to be born in Berlin, did you?'

'Eh? Oh, no, sir. In Stepney, sir. London, sir.'

'Then perhaps you're a member of the British Union of Fascists.'

'Who are they then, sir?'

'They,' Harding told him, 'are a bunch of traitors locked up on the Isle of Man for the duration of the war and from the way you're going you might well be joining them.'

For the first time it seemed to occur to Norris that something serious was being discussed. 'Eh?' he said for the second time.

If there were two things in life Harding disliked more than any others, the first was dealing with defaulters and the second going to the dentist. He was due to have his tooth capped, which involved drilling out the nerve, in a quarter of an hour's time and concluded that this was not his day. He steeled himself to dispose of the first of his hates, at the same time chiding himself for having employed sarcasm which the average sailor rarely understood.

'Norris.'

'Sir?'

'Listen to me, and listen very carefully, Norris. Those dozens of jokes you know about Americans, and the dozens of jokes they know about us, almost certainly originated in Germany for idiots like you to tell to other idiots. It's a nice cheap way of creating dislike and distrust between us and our chief ally. Our chief friendly ally anyway. The only people to get any real enjoyment out of what you imagine to be humour are the Germans. I want you to remember that and, to help you to do so, your shore leave and pay are stopped and you'll do two hours extra work every day until we sail. We have enough enemies to fight without you taking on the United States Marines. Now, get out of my sight and stay out of it.'

The coxswain translated Harding's sentence into naval 'scale' terms, then added, 'And get out of the Captain's sight and stay out of it! On cap! About turn! Quick march!'

Harding made his way towards the dental surgery aboard the depot ship thinking that his final instruction, repeated by the coxswain, had been a particularly stupid one when there was no way in which Norris could comply with it in the cramped circumstances they all lived in. He put it down to his intense dislike of punishing his crew members, particularly when he himself was guilty of having sung the same words to the same tune, albeit not within American hearing.

*

Lieutenant Gascoigne made his own contribution to Anglo-American disharmony by dancing four numbers in succession with the tall wife of a US Assistant Military Attaché. The attaché didn't mind, he was on a visit to the almost completed Pentagon building near Washington, but the American Navy captain who had brought her to Quaglino's restaurant for dinner certainly did.

Her arms draped over Gascoigne's shoulders, the band playing something calling for minimal movement, 'The old bastard's been trying to get me into bed ever since hubby went to the States,' she said.

Gascoigne made tutting noises and added, 'And you a married woman!'

'Yes, it really is disgraceful,' she told him.

The US Navy captain minded even more when Gascoigne and the girl left together but, after that, there was no more disharmony. They continued to dance to music provided by Carroll Gibbons and his Savoy Hotel 'Orpheans' over the radio in the living room of her flat. Both of them were naked except for her high-heeled shoes which, tall as she was, she needed to wear to accommodate him.

Not once during his five days in London did Gascoigne leave the flat and, when he returned to his ship, Harding looked at him with concern on his face.

'Are you all right, Number One?'

'I will be after a good night's sleep, sir,' Gascoigne said. 'I've been staying up with a sick friend.' He didn't much like lying to his captain but, being unable to embark on a description of what he had been doing, he consoled himself with the thought that there was a grain of truth in the statement as it had been his first encounter with nymphomania.

Harding regarded him strangely for a moment, but asked nothing more.

*

Harding took no leave but he too had an American connection, a gently charming one in the form of a golden girl he had briefly lived with. She had seen the distraught officer wandering aimlessly away from a burning street in London during a bombing raid. His parents and one of his crew had died in that street moments before; so, distressed for him, she had taken him first in her arms, then into her bed. From that, during the ensuing days, liking had grown between them, a liking which became love.

Now separated from her by many thousands of miles while she fulfilled her role of war correspondent somewhere in the Pacific, Harding was more than content to find two letters from her on the wardroom mail rack after the dental surgeon had finished with him. With his new tooth cemented in place and the letters in his hand he decided that it was his day after all.

*

Chief Petty Officer Ryland and Chief Yeoman Yarrow crossed the Clyde together daily, venturing no further than Greenock on the far shore. There they drank in solemn communion throughout the entire time span of official licensing hours, returning to the depot ship each night loaded to capacity, but determinedly, ponderously sober as befitted their station and seniority. At the end of their six days they agreed that it had been an excellent leave of absence.

Petty Officer McIntyre was more adventurous, travelling all the way to Callander in Perthshire where he rewired the whole ground floor of his mother's small house. He too felt that his time had been well spent. The work had not been particularly necessary in anybody's view other than his mother's, but he was fond of her and he liked anything to do with electrics.

Lieutenant Maddox, ordered to hold himself in readiness to appear before a Board of Enquiry, broke ship and deserted.

*

'Oh Christ, *no*!' Harding said.

'I'm afraid so, Peter.'

Harding realized that he was cracking the knuckles of one hand explosively inside the palm of the other, stopped doing it and flicked both as though ridding himself of the sensation. Then he looked at the flotilla captain and raised his shoulders in a despairing gesture.

Before he could say anything, 'Now don't you start getting upset,' Captain Submarines told him. 'Pretty obviously this stems from the action you took, but that doesn't make it your fault. You acted perfectly correctly and this running away of Maddox's proves it – if proof were necessary, which it isn't.'

'But it's appalling, sir! Couldn't he – couldn't he get himself shot for this?'

'Oh, I don't think so,' the older man said. 'He hasn't actually deserted in the face of the enemy and even if the prosecution was able to make out a case proving that to all intents and purposes he had done so, I expect the doctors would find a way round that for him. Mentally disturbed or something. No, it'll be dismissal with disgrace I imagine, probably after a period in jail, then drafting into some essential civilian occupation.'

'Oh dear.' Harding sighed the words, then added, 'Well, they'll have to catch him first.'

'And that won't take them any time at all. Where can he go? What do you think he's going to do without ration cards, clothing coupons and money, as well as carrying a naval identity card he's no longer entitled to?' The flotilla captain had spoken abruptly.

'Oh dear,' Harding said for the second time.

'Peter!'

'Sorry, sir.'

'So I should think. Stop making a rod for your own back, go away and arrange for me to have a written deposition from you about Maddox's behaviour aboard *Trigger* before you sail for the Med. I'm not holding back one of His Majesty's submarines from the war for anybody's court-martial.'

'Aye aye, sir,' Harding said.

Lieutenant Maddox gave himself up to the police in Bristol four days later, but by then *Trigger* had left the Clyde astern and set course for the Mediterranean. Captain Submarines decided that there was no point in worrying Harding with the news.

Chapter Ten

Harding opened his account with the enemy while *Trigger* was proceeding south across the Bay of Biscay, and he did it without taking any offensive action whatsoever.

The Atlantic swell heavy, the weather sullen with a low, scudding overcast giving momentary glimpses of a pale sun, the horizon rarely visible with the big rollers repeatedly covering the periscope's upper lens, but showing as a hard dark line when it was.

Lieutenant Walker, navigating officer since Gascoigne had become first lieutenant, glanced at his watch, then at the two men at the hydroplane controls struggling to maintain the submarine's depth.

'Can you two hold her here for a couple of minutes?'

'Be easier if you speeded up a bit, sir,' Able Seaman Chivers on the fore planes replied for both of them.

Frowning, annoyed with himself for not having anticipated that need when he had ordered *Trigger* brought from the stillness of deeper water to the turbulence near the surface, 'Of course,' he said. 'Half ahead together.'

The double chime of the motor room telegraphs and a voice saying, 'Both motors at half ahead, sir.'

'Right. You Jameson, go and ask the Captain if he'd mind coming here for a moment. No panic.'

'Aye aye, sir.'

When Harding joined him in the control room, 'The overcast's breaking up a little, sir,' Walker told him. 'I wondered if you might want to surface and let me try for a noon sight. The sun's reappearing fairly frequently now and it would be nice to know a bit more accurately where we are.'

Harding agreed that it would be nice, took his place at the periscope, turned it through a full circle and said, 'We'll surface at once. Get your sextant, Pilot.'

'Diving stations, sir?'

'No, no. These chaps can do it. Just warn the crew over the Tannoy and ask the First Lieutenant to take over from you while we're up top. I don't want anybody else on the bridge.'

Walker spoke into the Tannoy microphone, Gascoigne arrived, glanced at his captain, saw his nod and said, 'Shut main vents. Stand by to surface.'

Less than a quarter of a minute later, high-pressure air was roaring into numbers 2, 4 and 6 main ballast tanks. *Trigger* seemed to hesitate, then reared upwards to lie wallowing in the swell, the sea still surging over her not yet fully buoyant hull. The heavy metal conning tower hatch swung open at Harding's upward push and the downward drag of its counter-balance weights, then with water which had had no time to drain from the bridge deluging his head and shoulders he dragged himself staggeringly into the open air. Walker followed, cradling his sextant in the crook of his left arm like a baby. Both made their way round the forward periscope standard to the front of the bridge where Harding opened the voice-pipe cock and said, 'Control room. Stand by to write down the time at my call.'

The helmsman's reply, 'First Lieutenant standing by to mark the time, sir,' and Walker's, 'Can you hear anything, sir?' reached his ears simultaneously.

He looked quickly at the navigating officer, eyes slitted as though as an aid to listening, then all around at the heaving grey ocean.

'No, Pilot. What sort of – Wait a minute!'

For long seconds the two officers stood, swaying with the motion of the ship, listening to the wind, to the surge of the sea and to something else.

'It's an aircraft,' Harding said. 'Where did you hear it first, Pilot?'

'Starboard bow I think, sir. It seems to be to port now, down wind from us.' Then, his voice rising urgently, 'Here it comes! Throw yourself flat!' Walker shouted.

Later Harding remembered himself thinking 'I can't do that. I have to know what's going on.' The thought held him upright for long enough to enable him to see, just below the overcast, bright points of light sparkling along the length of a horizontal dark bar with a nearly circular blob at its centre before he followed Walker's injunction and example.

The cannon shells struck then, first around the 4-inch gun Harding guessed, before hammering out a thunderous madman's tattoo against the side of the conning tower. Two of them struck the inside of the bridge and splinters whined briefly like demented hornets. The need for information ingrained in him made Harding roll onto his back, and he did it in time to see the configuration of the plane with the black crosses on its wings live for a second within his field of vision. He pulled himself to his feet, bemused by the suddenness of it all, relieved when Walker lurched upright beside him. Two hundred yards to starboard a column of water rose skywards.

'Rotten shot!' the navigating officer said and grinned in nervous excitement.

'Get down below,' Harding told him, whirled to the voice-pipe and shouted, 'Dive! Dive! Dive!' The double squawking snarl of the diving klaxon came to him as he followed Walker into the conning tower. The hatch clipped shut above his head he dropped rapidly down the vertical ladder to the control room.

As soon as his feet landed on the deck, 'Is that inboard voice-pipe cock shut?' he asked.

'Yes, sir.'

'Good. I forgot to close the ones on the bridge. Better remember that when we surface or the man at the steering wheel will get a soaking. Go straight down to ninety feet, Number One.'

'Aye aye, sir. What on earth happened up there?'

'We surfaced within sight of an Me109. Purest chance. There probably isn't another plane within a hundred miles, but I thought we'd forget about sun sights for today in case he had another fighter with him. He shot us up with his cannons.'

'Dropped a bomb on us, too,' Walker added. 'Missed by miles.'

'No he didn't,' Harding said. 'He went straight into the drink. I've heard that it's very difficult for pilots to judge their height above water when they're making a low-altitude run.'

He was turning away to go to his cabin when Gascoigne snapped, 'Cox'n!

Get the first-aid box quickly! The Captain's been shot through the hand! Here! Let me see that, sir! I've only just noticed, dammit!'

Harding raised his hands. The left one was bleeding profusely from immediately above his knuckles, the fingers obscured by a sticky covering of red, red which formed into drops and fell, spattering the deck by his feet. Something was protruding from what appeared to be the source of the flow. With the forefinger and thumb of his other hand Harding grasped the object, pulled, winced and wiped it on his sleeve.

'I think that's a piece of the Pilot's sextant mirror,' he said.

Walker peered at the small shard of glass held out to him before saying, 'I'm afraid it is, sir. I lost the sextant. Something sort of snatched it away from me. I'm sorry, sir.'

'Don't lose too much sleep over it, Pilot,' Harding told him. 'One sextant in exchange for one Messerschmitt sounds like a splendid deal to me.'

Chief Petty Officer Ryland's voice came from behind him. 'If you'll excuse me, sir, you're still drippin' on the deck and if you don't come along and let me patch you up you won't be able to deal even a busted flush for a week. You and your 'ands is givin' me a 'ard time, sir.'

'Anything to channel your sadistic tendencies, Cox'n,' Harding said and followed the burly man obediently, thinking how very lucky he and Walker had been, how fortunate that he had allowed nobody else on the bridge.

Half an hour later he finished writing the notes for his passage report on the incident with the words 'This must be the first instance on record of an enemy fighter being brought down by a navigational sun shot', then decided that that wasn't all that funny and crossed them out again.

When he had put the papers into a drawer he clambered into his bunk and lay, looking unseeingly at the depth-gauge at its foot, feeling obscurely sorry for the German pilot, wondering what he had been doing seventy miles from the coast of France. After a little he slept.

'Cap'n sir?'

Harding opened his eyes and saw Gascoigne standing in the cabin doorway. 'Yes, Number One?'

'Wills has got something on the sonar. Not sure what it is yet.'

'Right,' Harding said and swung his legs over the side of the bunk.

In the control room, 'Still can't make nothing of it, sir,' Able Seaman Wills told him from his place at the sonar set. 'Except for the bearing. That's about Green 25.'

Nodding, Harding turned to Gascoigne. 'Let's go up and take a look, shall we?'

'Aye aye, sir.'

Trigger began her slow rise back to periscope depth, Gascoigne watching the inclinometer which showed the angle of the ship in relation to the horizontal, and the depth-gauge needles moving slowly round the dial, Harding ignoring them, looking at Wills.

As though forced to speak by the gaze coming from behind him, 'I think it's a diesel, sir,' Wills said.

'Heavy or light?'

Wills looked round and pulled one earphone away from his head.

'What, sir?'

'Can you tell if it's a heavy or light diesel?'

'Oh. Hang on a tick, sir.'

The able seaman replaced his earphone, turned back to the sonar control panel and twisted the knurled knob there fractionally one way and the other before saying, 'Light, I think, sir. Yes, confirmed light diesel, sir.'

And that, Harding knew, ruled out his first guess, a surfaced U-boat. He glanced sideways at the depth-gauges. Sixty feet and rising.

'You'd better send the crew to their stations now, Number One,' he said.

Gascoigne acknowledged the order, broadcast it over the Tannoy and, throughout the length of the ship, bunks and hammocks disgorged their human contents, meals were thrust aside, books discarded, cards abandoned. For twenty seconds all was movement, then stillness reasserted itself and with it came an air of expectancy which Harding could feel as though it were a physical presence.

Forty feet and rising. 'Up periscope,' he said.

The great brass column of the forward periscope rising upwards out of its well, the hydraulic power which lifted it no more than a faint, steady hiss. The double click as Harding jerked the two handles downwards. Gascoigne saying, 'Thirty-four feet, sir.' Nothing to be seen but a shifting arabesque of refracted sunlight on the underside of the sea's surface. Harding saying, 'Come up to thirty-two feet, Number One, and don't hesitate to use speed if you have to.' The upper lens clear of the water showing him the side of a wave moving closer, seeming to engulf him when it rolled over the periscope.

'Come up to thirty feet.'

'Thirty feet. Aye aye, sir.'

A perceptible movement of the deck beneath his feet now with the submarine reacting to the ocean's rise and fall, but a horizon of sorts visible over the swell with a plume of smoke rising from it. Gascoigne saying sharply, 'Group up! Full ahead together!' Harding gesturing for the periscope to be lowered with a downward sweep of his hand and looking at the depth-gauges. Twenty-seven feet. The hull vibrating with the increased thrust of the propellers.

'Sorry, sir. Thought we were going to stick the conning tower out, but we're okay. Group down. Half ahead together.'

'Well done. Up periscope.'

The plume of smoke still there a long way off and, momentarily visible until a wave hid it, a small vessel closer, very much closer and pointing directly at them, spray exploding sideways from its plunging stem.

'Sonar transmissions bearing Green 20, sir,' McIntyre said, then added the word, 'Sweeping.'

Harding glanced quickly at the petty officer who had replaced Able Seaman Wills on sonar watch, looked through the binocular periscope viewer again, then repeated the downward hand gesture he had made earlier. The periscope hissed into the well at his feet.

'Go deep, Number One, and shut off for depth-charging.'

'Flood "Q", sir?'

'No, we still have enough time. Level off at 120 feet.'

Trigger angling downwards by the bow. Five degrees. Ten. Fifteen. Men grasping for handholds. Gascoigne saying, 'Shut off for depth-charging. Shut off for depth-charging,' with the Tannoy microphone to his lips. The depth-gauge pointers beginning to move faster round the dials, passing sixty feet, passing seventy.

'Sonar in contact, sir!' McIntyre's voice. Sharp.

'Group up. Full ahead together. Starboard 30,' Harding said, then turned to Gascoigne. 'She's an anti-submarine trawler, Number One. I expect that Messerschmitt reported our position before it attacked us. There's more shipping up there too. I saw the smoke. The trawler's probably part of the escort.'

'She got into contact damned quickly, sir. Expect they saw our periscope sticking up like a telegraph pole. I'm sorry about that, sir.'

'Not your fault, Number One,' Harding told him. 'I ordered you to come up to thirty feet and you can't expect to maintain depth accurately that shallow in these sea conditions.'

Vibration building up again as the speed increased. The figures on the illuminated tape of the gyro repeater moving more rapidly across the oblong screen in front of the helmsman as the ship turned at the urging of the extreme rudder angle. 198 – 199 – 200 – 201. McIntyre saying, 'Firm contact, sir. Bearing steady. Transmissions shortening. Attacking, sir.' Harding feeling his skin crawl, hearing someone yawn achingly in nervous suspense, watching the compass numbers flicking faster as *Trigger* strove to get away from the track of the oncoming enemy. 214 – 215 – 216.

'Warn the crew to expect depth-charges any moment. Number One.'

'Aye aye, sir.'

Gascoigne taking down the Tannoy microphone, speaking into it. The shallow depth-gauges shut off, their pointers idle. The deep gauge showing 110 feet and falling. The submarine's course reading 223 – 224 – 225 – 226. Little chance of detecting the sound of enemy propellers passing overhead either with the naked ear or sonar above the noise of *Trigger*'s passage and Harding tense, wondering if the charges were about to be dropped, or already had been and were now sinking down through the water to the point at which their hydrostatic valves had been set to detonate them. Wondering, too, what depth that would be, or if the settings would have been varied. Deciding conjecture was pointless. Stopping it.

'Go on down to 200 feet.'

'Aye aye, sir.'

Harding telling himself that he mustn't go deeper than that because there might still be a chance of a torpedo attack on the shipping betrayed by the column of smoke if he could shake off the anti-submarine trawler, that if he did go deeper it would take too long to regain periscope depth. Deep gauge showing 132 feet and falling. Ship heading 239 – 240 – 241 –

Concussion.

The hull whipping from the shock-wave, rolling in the blast of tons of displaced water, the certainty of broken glass and crockery but nobody hearing that because the ears have been stunned, nobody seeing it because there is no light. The emergency bulbs snapping on, dim, sepulchral. Deep gauge showing 80 feet and steady. Harding thinking they were lucky not to have been blown all the way to the surface, hearing Gascoigne telling the Tannoy microphone that all departments were to report damage, anxious about that himself, but thankful for the proof that his ears were recovering from the series of titanic sledge-hammer blows on the steel surrounding them. Ship heading 259.

'Steer 270. Depth 100 feet,' Harding said, saw a flicker of surprise on Gascoigne's face and added, 'They'll expect us to be much deeper than that by now and set their charges accordingly.' Never explain? Why not? Valuable instruction if he was right. A lesson learned if he was wrong. If he didn't kill them all.

The coxswain saying, 'Grab a broom, Jameson, and sweep this glass out of the Captain's way.' Compartments reporting, one after the other, that they had suffered no particular damage, no casualties. Gascoigne asking if he should replace light bulbs. Telling him 'no'. Jameson scooping up broken glass with a brush and pan, cutting himself, muttering, 'Fuck it!' *Trigger* still boring through the water at her best submerged speed.

'McIntyre.'

'Sir?'

'They dropped five charges as far as I could judge. As you heard, they exploded almost simultaneously. Is that enough to keep the water stirred up for a bit, or will they hear us if I don't slow down?'

'Oh, it'll still be churning around out there for another two or three minutes, sir. They won't hear nothing until then.'

'Thank you, McIntyre.'

He had already arrived at the same conclusion, Harding knew, but learning fast just how lonely a condition command was, it comforted him to be able to seek a second opinion on something. The crew didn't mind because they didn't expect their officers to know everything. Indeed they liked being asked and, having provided the answer to some specific point, thereafter regarded the officer as an expert in their entire field. Harding smiled briefly at the thought and inadvertently, as several pairs of eyes were watching him, added to his reputation for complete calm. Feeling very far from calm, with an adversary somewhere above his head who had already demonstrated marked efficiency, he let his ship career west for another minute and a half, then ordered slow silent running. There was battery conservation to consider as well as evasion.

When a quarter of an hour had passed without detection Harding had begun to hope that he had escaped from his pursuer, but then McIntyre resumed his chanted litany of firm contact, steady bearing, shortening transmissions, attacking. The second underwater bombardment was less severe than the first, the charges detonating far below *Trigger* as Harding had hoped they might. It was still bad enough momentarily to blur the vision while the hull hummed like a plucked string in response to the explosions. He ordered speed and an alteration in course, then looked round anxiously for the source of a series of breathy bass exhalations. They appeared to be coming from Chief Petty Officer Ryland.

'Are you all right, Cox'n?'

'Yessir. Just rememberin', sir.'

'Remembering what?'

'When you and the First Lieutenant and me was together in *Shadow*, sir.' He pronounced it 'Shadder' again.

'What about it?'

'The Skipper, sir. Lieutenant-Commander Bulstrode, sir. 'E used to complain about depth-charge patterns because they played 'ell with 'is sinuses, sir. Very funny officer Lieutenant-Commander Bulstrode was, sir.'

The gusty exhalations came again and Harding said, 'I don't remember you laughing at the time, Cox'n.'

Ryland nodded his head in agreement, not taking his eyes from the depth-gauge and hydroplane indicator in front of him. 'No, sir, but Petty

Officer Parr 'ere only just told me what sinuses is. I thought Commander Bulstrode was worried about the navigation.'

'Navigation?'

'Yessir. Sinuses and cosinuses like the Navigatin' Officer uses when 'e's doin' 'is sums.'

Harding bit his lip and held his breath to contain the laughter welling up inside him, then scowled fiercely when Lieutenant Walker began to say, 'They're called sines and co…' Walker fell silent and looked at the deck.

'Yes, Commander Bulstrode was amusing, wasn't he?' Harding said before ordering the speed reduced to dead slow.

The third attack devastating, blowing *Trigger* clear to the surface where for agonizingly long seconds she lay wallowing in plain view of the anti-submarine trawler. The loud hissing of foul-smelling air venting inboard, displaced by the tons of sea flooding into 'Q' tank, the screws thrashing at full power, half in and half out of the water, not gripping sufficiently well to drive the submarine back to the comparative safety of the deep, the black tops and grey sides of his ship remaining stubbornly visible to her captain through the periscope.

The stern of the trawler was visible to Harding too, not even periodically concealed by the swells with the upper lens of the periscope so high in the air. He swung it through a complete circle, but there was nothing else in sight, not even the smoke he had seen earlier, and he returned his attention to his tormentor. Already it had started to turn and he could see the gun mounted on the high bow. Men were running lurchingly towards it.

Forehead still pressed to the rubber shield of the binocular viewer, 'What's the depth, Number One?'

'Still pretty well surfaced, sir. She doesn't seem to want to go down.' Gascoigne's voice, tense.

'Put the after hydroplane to full rise. That should drag the stern down and let the propellers bite properly.' Never explain? Why not? Without the explanation the order sounded stupid and Gascoigne didn't know the trick or he would have done it himself.

'Aye aye, sir.'

A stab of flame, not very bright in the daylight, from the trawler's gun, and a puff of smoke instantly dissipated by the wind. No sign of the shot, but the enemy's turn half completed. Soon they would be on a course to ram. 'Get under! Get under!' Harding said, but said it only to himself.

The gun flashing again, Gascoigne saying, 'We're on our way, sir. Both hydroplanes at full dive. Depth eighteen feet and dropping.' Harding ordering the periscope lowered because there is no sense in continuing to give them a point of aim after the hull and conning tower have submerged. Angle and rate of dive increasing. Thirty feet. Thirty-five. Forty. Get down! For God's sake get *down*! Sensation of sweat forming on forehead. Brushing it away pretending to smooth hair, wondering if they were all as frightened as he, doubting it as only he had any knowledge of his future intentions and only he had witnessed the speed with which the enemy gunners had gone into action, the vessel's rapid swing into position for another attack, its alarming proximity. Fifty feet. Fifty-five. Sixty.

'Blow "Q", sir?'

'No. Keep on down. Blow when we've passed one hundred feet.'

Gascoigne acknowledging his order. Angle of dive very steep now with everybody in sight holding on to something. A series of thuds from the accommodation spaces forward like chairs toppling and the crash of breaking crockery. A slithering sound close to him. Somebody saying, 'Mind your feet, sir!' Stopping an errant tool box sliding across the composition deck-covering towards him with the sole of his shoe. Seventy feet. Eighty. Was that the sound of a propeller passing overhead? Difficult to tell with the racket *Trigger* was making, but the time factor about right, so wait for it, wait for the fast-sinking grey cylinders to reach the depth at which they will release their latent energy in a series of appalling thunder-claps which – *Shut up*!

Harding didn't have to wait for long, little more than three seconds, before the storm broke, its force seeming to cleave his skull and actually rattling his teeth, but this time there was no uncontrollable surge towards the surface.

'Exploded above us I think, Number One.'

'Yes, sir,' Gascoigne said. 'Blow "Q".'

Air roaring into the emergency quick diving tank, expelling the additional ballast. Depth 120 feet. Ship levelling. Compartments reporting minor damage, small leaks of water from outside the hull and high-pressure air from within. Some broken battery cells too because there are reports of loose acid in the sumps.

'Stop blowing. Vent "Q" inboard.' Gascoigne's voice intruding on Harding's thoughts, thoughts that he had better advance his future intentions to the present because he had failed to shake off a highly competent adversary who appeared to have no trouble in following his every move, because the power of his huge battery of 336 giant cells was rapidly becoming depleted through breakage and his repeated demands for bursts of high speed, because depth-charge damage, rarely immediately fatal, was cumulative, remorselessly destroying a submarine's ability to function, because...

'There's a number of earths showing on the board, sir.'

With his electrical insulation failing that did it for Harding. 'All right, Number One,' he said. 'Stand by gun action.'

Chapter Eleven

In the autumn of 1939 Helmut Schobert had accepted the conscription of his trawler and himself into the *Kriegsmarine* with little surprise and less enthusiasm. The rank of *oberleutnant* he accepted with a mixture of irritation and wry amusement for he had no time for authority and its trappings. His crew had always called him 'Helmut' and continued to do so despite the hierarchical wedge driven between him and themselves by the unwanted award to them of more lowly naval classifications. All wore travesties of regulation uniform and continued to refer to their ship as *die Königin* which she had been christened, in preference to Anti-Submarine Vessel J 47 which she had become. Schobert declined to wear the Iron Cross to which he became entitled two years later on the grounds that everybody else had one too and despite repeated warnings that not to do so was an insult to the *Führer*. In fact Anti-Submarine Vessel J 47 started the war as a disgrace and continued to be one after more than three years of it, but no serious action was taken to remedy that state of affairs because Helmut Schobert had turned himself and his men into the finest submarine hunters on the French Atlantic coast. On this day in early March of 1943 they were living up to their reputation.

'Set the next pattern to explode deep, Ernst,' Schobert said. 'Say 80 metres. We'll try to blow them to the surface again.'

Ernst Dieckhoff, unrecognizable in an old oilskin and woollen cap either as a temporary *leutnant* or permanent second-in-command, nodded, turned and shouted down to the depth-charge crew on the trawler's stern. One of them raised a languid hand in acknowledgement of the order.

'Eighty metre depth-setting going on now, Helmut.'

'Thanks.'

J 47 continued to swing in a broad arc back towards the area of sea where the last group of five columns of water had hurled themselves at the overcast before subsiding in a welter of foam. The surface of the swell there was still troubled, still quivering in the aftermath of the explosions.

'Stop the engine,' Schobert said, then looked towards the little hut at the back of the bridge and added, 'Bearing roughly ahead, Hans. The first whisper of an echo you get, give me a shout. Right?'

'I wasn't thinking of sending you a written report,' Hans Bodenschatz replied from his place at the sonar set. Schobert grinned and faced forward again. The swells ahead were smooth to the eye now, but he knew that deep down there would still be a considerable amount of turbulence left by the detonations from his last attack. Hans wouldn't be able to detect anything for a while. He began to wonder in which direction the submarine would be trying to run this time.

*

Lieutenant Randolph, black haired, ruddy, beginning to run to fat, had joined *Trigger* as a numerical replacement for Maddox. Harding had appointed him armaments officer. Now he was standing in the control room listening to his captain, flanked on one side by Leading Seaman Peters, the gunlayer of the 4-inch, and on the other by Able Seaman Chivers. Able Seaman Jameson and Ordinary Seaman Norris stood just behind them, resting the butts of their Vickers gas-operated machine-guns on the deck.

'I don't think it's as big as an 88 millimetre,' Harding was saying, 'but it's a sizeable gun. Could be an old 75. Anyway, I'm not going to risk a long-range bombardment. In this weather it would be pure chance who hit who first, so we'll surface as close as possible and try to finish it quickly. All right?'

Randolph said, 'Yes, sir,' and the others murmured their agreement, not, Harding thought, that they had any choice in the matter.

'Okay,' he went on, 'now you, Peters, take your time. We'll be pitching, or rolling, or both, depending on where the seas are coming from when we surface, not the best conditions for your first gun action. Take it slowly as I said and always remember that it'll be just as difficult for them as for you. Your point of aim is their waterline. That way if one of your shells falls short it'll probably ricochet straight into them. Can do?'

'Can do, sir.'

'Good. Now for you, Chivers. I don't want you to take it slowly at all. I want that Oerlikon cannon of yours in action so fast and so constantly that they won't know what the hell's going on. Your point of aim is the bridge. Smash it to smithereens. Every fourth round of yours is a tracer shell so you shouldn't have any trouble hose-piping onto your target. When you've destroyed their bridge, switch to the gun. That's mounted right for'ard. Okay?'

'Yessir,' Chivers said.

Harding looked past him at the machine-gunners. 'You two. Same as for Chivers. Fast and furious. Your target is their gun. Stop them manning it at all if you can. Knock out any machine-gun fire as well.'

Jameson and Norris murmured 'Aye aye, sir,' in unison.

Trying to think of something less conventionally unhelpful to say than 'Good luck' or 'Good hunting' Harding's thoughts were interrupted by Petty Officer McIntyre calling, 'Enemy sonar in contact, sir.' He looked at each of his gunners in turn then said, 'I'm relying on you chaps to ensure that that's the last time McIntyre needs to tell me that today. Open fire when ready. Carry on.'

Trigger had risen slowly, silently, turning as she did so. Now she lay at a depth of only sixty feet with the anti-submarine trawler approaching rapidly from astern. Having no intention of taking high-speed evasive action Harding knew that there would be no difficulty in hearing it pass overhead and that was important to him because precise timing was essential. He felt himself to be quivering, hoped that the condition was not visible and that it stemmed from suppressed tension rather than fear, but was unsure on both counts. Breathing in and out quietly and deeply to steady himself, listening to a silence broken only by McIntyre's periodic reports on the advance of the enemy, Harding waited for a full thirty seconds then, 'Man the gun tower,' he said.

A thud as the lower gun tower hatch is thrust open. Randolph's legs disappearing upwards. The breech operator following him with the gun's firing mechanism hanging from a strap around his neck. The layer and trainer following in their turn. The ship's cook, head and shoulders showing above the section of deck covering the magazine, the long shape of a 4-inch shell and its combined brass propellant cartridge cradled in the crook of his elbows, ready to pass it up to the next man in line. McIntyre saying, 'Attacking, sir,' in a flat voice. Harding conceding that what he is experiencing is plain fear, trying to subdue the emotion with self-contempt and failing. Trying to convince himself it's just like a drill. Failing again. The flail-like noise of the propeller above their heads loud and clear.

'Gun action. Surface,' Harding said and started up the vertical ladder to the bridge with the automatic weapons party at his heels. The thunder of depth-charges exploding two hundred and fifty feet below obliterated the sound of high-pressure air expelling water from the main ballast tanks.

*

To Ernst Dieckhoff staring astern from the bridge of J 47, it was as though the English U-boat had materialized in the centre of the five thick pillars of sea created by the latest pattern of depth-charges.

'You did it, Helmut!' he shouted. 'Now's your chance to finish the bastard!'

The pillars of water fell back in on themselves in a welter of tumbling spray showing him the figures of men clambering rapidly out of the submarine's hull, some onto the conning tower, others in front of it.

'They're abandoning ship!' he said, spun around and dropped at Schobert's feet with blood pulsing from a gaping hole in his throat. As though it were some party game, the helmsman fell forward over the steering wheel before sliding to the deck to join him.

For two long seconds shock held Helmut Schobert rigid, listening uncomprehendingly to the whip-crack of machine-gun bullets splitting the air, to the bell-like clanging when they struck metal, to the whine of ricochets, then the glass of the foul-weather screen exploding in front of him broke the spell and he threw himself flat on his face. Only at that moment did his ears register the sound of gunfire, the tearing calico of machine-guns, something more powerful joining them with a ranting, hammering bellow of sound, then the single coughing slam of a heavy artillery piece and a column of water leaping into existence close alongside.

'Are you all right, Helmut?'

He turned his head and saw Bodenschatz prone on the deck beside him.

'Yes, Hans! Drag Dieter out of the way! We must get the helm over so the gun can engage them!' Schobert realized that he had shouted the words and that made him frown because he had never been a shouter. 'Quickly now,' he added more quietly, then froze where he was as the ship rolled and a series of small bright explosions stitched across the canted deck, tore at the body of the dead helmsman and shattered the steering wheel.

Almost conversationally, 'Twenty millimetre cannon,' Schobert said, turned and crawled rapidly to the back of the bridge. There he stood upright, cupped his hands round his mouth and called, 'Manfred!'

The four-man depth-charge crew crouching for precarious cover behind their own charges looked fearfully up at him.

'Get down into the tiller flat and put the rudder hard over to starboard,' Schobert told them. 'The wheel's been shot away. You Karl, keep your head out of the hatch to relay my orders.'

The submarine's heavy gun slammed again, its shell falling short but close enough to deluge them with water. Pushing his soaking hair away from his eyes, Schobert watched the men struggling to release the butterfly nuts securing the metal cover to the tiller flat, saw one of them straighten as though he were on parade and topple stiffly over the guard-rail into the sea. More bullets cracked past him, but Schobert didn't move. He had decided that there was no point in doing so because there was no effective cover anywhere and, anyway, he *was* the captain, even if they did all call him 'Helmut'. Then suddenly the metal cover came free and a moment later *die Königin* began to turn.

*

Harding was no longer frightened. He was too busy thinking to be that, but with all the uproar going on around him he was not entirely clear what it was he should be thinking about first. To his left and a little behind him Jameson's .303 Vickers machine-gun snarled in regular ripping bursts at the trawler fine on the port bow and little more than a hundred yards away. To his right Norris was firing too, one leg over the side of the bridge to achieve the angle he needed, like a snooker player addressing an awkwardly placed cue ball. Harding hoped that Norris wouldn't get too excited and shoot away *Trigger's* jumping wire and aerials, but said nothing because he needed the fire-power. Behind him at the back of the bridge with its muzzle pointing as directly ahead as the safety stops would permit, Chivers's 20mm Oerlikon raved out its mind-shattering song. Ahead and a few feet below him Leading Seaman Peters's 4-inch had bellowed twice making him jump both times because there was no way of anticipating when the thunder-claps would come. Peters hadn't achieved a hit yet, but with the submarine soaring and dropping over the heavy rollers that didn't surprise Harding.

What did surprise him was that with the action now into its second minute the enemy had made no attempt to turn and bring his main arma-ment into play. He wondered about that and about the absence of the return machine-gun fire he had been expecting.

At his side Lieutenant Walker, his voice angry, shouted, 'You're in the First Lieutenant's report, Edgecombe! Now get back to watching out for aircraft and stop goggling at the enemy ship!' Harding was thinking how essential and how difficult it was to train look-outs to ignore everything but their own sector, when everything seemed to happen at once.

The trawler swinging fast to starboard bringing its gun into view. Harding ordering a course alteration to port and an increase in speed to stay astern of it. Failing because, much faster as *Trigger* was, she was far less manoeuvrable. Another slamming report from the 4-inch gun, a flash and a puff of smoke low down on the trawler's stern. Chivers swinging his cannon to fire on the starboard bow. A stab of flame from the enemy's forecastle and a shell whimpering overhead to plunge into the sea very close on the port quarter. The Oerlikon raving again, a fourth roar from the 4-inch and an explosion near the waterline beneath the enemy's funnel. Flame glowing darkly red where the first hit had gone home. Men folding, falling like broken toys around the distant gun, scythed down by

95

automatic fire. Two other men clambering from the bridge, leaping the last few feet and running forward to replace the casualties. The trawler still swinging, but more slowly now. A second stab of flame, a coughing reverberating clang from the direction of *Trigger*'s bow, a cloud of smoke quickly dissipated and a jagged hole in the casing where the capstan had been a second before. Somebody on the 4-inch gun platform screaming and Lieutenant Randolph shouting, 'Ammunition party get that man down below!' Leading Seaman Peters's fifth shot and the trawler's gun jerking to point at the sky, one man sitting near it, no other movement. Harding bellowing 'Cease fire!' and reinforcing the order by flinging his arms outwards like a referee at a boxing match.

Silence immediate and total, not the sounds of the sea, not even the throaty rumble of the diesel exhausts audible to shocked ears, the senses recording only the stench of cordite, the burning anti-submarine trawler lying stopped on the heaving surface of the sea, the pressure of the wind.

'Stop both engines. Out engine clutches,' Harding said to the voice-pipe and heard the words boom strangely inside his head.

Her own momentum carried *Trigger* to within twenty yards of the enemy then she too lay dead in the water, her gunners edgily alert for any hostile move. There was none. On the splintered upper deck there were only corpses and the one man sitting, the left side of his face a mask of blood, forearms on knees, looking at them with his single visible eye, seemingly unaware of the flames beginning to climb like some swift-growing creeper up the sides of the bridge behind him.

'Abandon ship!' Harding called to him. 'Get your people up on deck and abandon ship! Hurry! There's nothing more you can do and your depth-charges will detonate inside ten minutes with all that heat aft!'

The eye gazed at him blankly, unblinking, but the man neither spoke nor moved.

Harding bent to the voice-pipe. 'Ask the First Lieutenant to find out if we have any German speakers aboard.' He noted that his ears were recovering when he heard his request repeated and, more faintly, Gascoigne saying twice over the Tannoy, 'Anyone who can speak German, report to the control room at the double.' There was a pause of some seconds before Gascoigne spoke to him directly up the voice-pipe.

'No luck, sir.'

'Sod it!' Harding said. 'I'm trying to persuade some silly bugger to get himself and anybody else alive over the side before they either fry or get blown to pieces, but he…'

'Oh, I can tell him that, sir,' Gascoigne broke in.

'Then why didn't you say so in the first place?' Harding asked him angrily. 'Get up here and do it!'

Gascoigne arrived on the bridge quickly, took in the scene at a glance and raised a megaphone to his lips.

'*Alle Mann das Schiff verlassen!*' he said, then said it again.

Reaction. The eye blinking rapidly, the German stirring aimlessly at first, then staggering upright and making a vague gesture with his arm towards a large canvas-covered object. There were many bullet holes in the canvas.

In a slurred voice, '*Das Boot. Kaput,*' he said and sat sharply down again as though he had been struck across the back of the knees.

'Sod it!' Harding muttered for the second time and looked round him at the endlessly scudding overcast, darker now with the day sliding into evening, at the black line of the empty horizon, at the enemy warship beginning to settle by the stern with steam hissing from the shell-holes in her hull where fire and water struggled for the privilege of delivering the *coup de grâce*. Then suddenly words poured from him.

'Control room. Send up two life-jackets, a torch and a heaving line. Randolph, secure the 4-inch, get your men down below and shut the gun tower hatches. Oerlikon and machine-gunners stay where you are. Number One, as soon as you've got your torch and life-belt, go and examine the pressure hull under that shell hole in the casing. Norris, I want you right for'ard with the heaving line. As soon as I've moved us in close enough chuck it across to that man, get him to secure it under his arms, then pull him over the side if you have to and get him aboard here. The First Lieutenant will give you a hand if he's too heavy. Pilot, take over Norris's machine-gun. Ah, here comes the stuff we need.'

'Gun secured, gun platform cleared, hatches shut, sir,' the voice-pipe said.

'Thank you.'

Trigger nosing closer to the doomed trawler. Gascoigne's legs waving absurdly above the casing, his head and trunk inside the jagged hole. Norris almost dancing with excitement and frustration on the bows shouting. 'No! Tie it round yourself like this, you stupid fucker!' Comprehension dawning on the German's bloodied face and his fingers fumbling the line about his chest, securing it there and struggling over the guard-rail to splash into the sea. Gascoigne shouting, 'Pressure hull's okay, sir! Just scored a bit!' then turning to help Norris. The two of them hauling the dripping survivor aboard and half carrying him towards the bridge at a stumbling run, several pairs of hands helping them up its side. By some instinct the German immediately selecting Harding from amongst the group of men surrounding him saying, '*Danke, Herr Kapitän*. Me, I am Helmut Schobert. *Oberleutnant* Helmut Schobert,' smiling tiredly and adding, 'Your ship is fighting like a very cross cat. Too much spittings for us.'

He fainted then and Norris caught him under the arms.

Chapter Twelve

Everybody thought that Able Seaman Drew's shrapnel wound was very funny, everybody except Able Seaman Drew with a splinter of steel lodged deep in his right buttock. Harding decided to leave it where it was, excused the sailor from all duties until after he had received proper medical attention at Gibraltar and returned to the wardroom where Chief Petty Officer Ryland was shaving the side of the German officer's head.

'Nearly ready, sir.'

'Good.'

'Able Seaman Drew all right then, sir?'

'Yes, as long as he keeps lying face down, Cox'n.'

'Ah. Then take a look at this 'ere, sir.'

Sitting, bent forward with the side of his face resting on the wardroom table, 'My ear is shot?' Helmut Schobert asked.

'No, no,' Harding told him. 'That's just a – just an expression. You've got a gash in the scalp.'

'*Ich verstehe nicht* – I am not understanding these words.'

Harding stood looking down at the German's head, at the shaved area to either side of a five-inch slit which had opened like parted lips to reveal the bone of the skull beneath, bone which gleamed pinkly white when Ryland sponged it, then disappeared under a slow tide of blood. The sight made his stomach heave.

'Wait,' he said, jerked the wardroom curtain aside, walked to the control room and glanced automatically at the depth-gauge. Steady on 120 feet he saw and turned to Gascoigne.

'Number One, get somebody to relieve you on watch and come and interpret for me. We have to explain to…' He stopped talking at the urgent negative shaking of Gascoigne's head, frowned and raised one eyebrow enquiringly.

'You've heard all my German, sir, except "*ja*" and "*nein*". The whole damned lot and I'm not sure if I got that right either. I'll explain when you've got more time.'

'Oh I see,' Harding said. He didn't see at all, but dismissed the matter from his mind, went to the chart table, drew a human head on a piece of signal paper and hurried to the wardroom. A long, distant, rumbling explosion made Chief Petty Officer Ryland's tray of medical instruments tinkle softly as soon as he got there.

'My ship, *ja*?'

'I think so,' Harding told Schobert then, speaking slowly, added, 'She was beginning to sink by the stern when we dived. That will have been the depth-charges detonating when she reached their set depth.'

'Depth-charges?'

'Underwater bombs.'

'Oh, *ja ja*.'

'Sit him up slowly, Cox'n,' Harding said.

With Schobert sitting upright Harding put the signal paper on the table in front of him while Ryland continued to dab at the wound.

'This is your head, right?'

'Very handsome fellow, *nein*?'

'Yes. Well, your scalp is split from here to here.' Harding's pencil traced an arc from two inches above one eye to where the line disappeared over the crown. 'The bone is not broken, but I must stitch the flesh together.' He took a transparent packet from the tray and held it up so that the German could see the ugly curved needle it contained with thread already attached to it and added, 'With one of these. Do you understand?'

'*Ja*. So please to stitch. I do not wish my face to fall off my skull.'

Harding smiled at him, admiring him, and wishing that he himself felt less nervous. Then he looked at Ryland.

'Bring the patient a glass of rum, Cox'n.'

Ryland moved into the passageway, but turned back at the call, '*Herr* Cox'n.'

'Sir?'

'Perhaps you bring another glass for the *Herr Kapitän*. His fingers are not so steady for the needle I think.'

'Good idea,' Harding said. 'Make it two.'

For half an hour Harding and his prisoner sweated through the small operation, then *Trigger* surfaced into the black night and cruised south, recharging her depleted batteries, replenishing her reserves of high-pressure air, putting miles of sea between herself and the scene of the battle. It was not until after she had dived again at dawn and the officers were at breakfast that the subject of Gascoigne's linguistic ability came up. Schobert, having given his word of honour that he would not attempt to inflict any damage on the ship and having been instructed in the mysteries of flushing a lavatory aboard a submerged submarine without inflicting unpleasantness upon himself, returned unguarded from the 'heads' to find one place vacant at the wardroom table. It was next to Gascoigne.

'*Guten Morgen, Herr Leutnant,*' Schobert said to him. '*Ist dieser Platz frei, bitte?*'

Gascoigne gestured to the seat beside him and asked, 'What did you say?'

Schobert nodded his bandaged head slowly, a little sadly, before sitting down and saying, 'I ask only if this place is free for me to sit, but I understand.'

'Understand what?'

'That it is not correct for you to speak the enemy tongue unless there is need.' He paused, shrugged and added, 'But I thank you for telling me what I must do after the fighting. Perhaps I shall be dead now if you had not done so, because I think then I have the shell concussion and am recognizing only German speech.'

'Oh my God!' Gascoigne said. 'You and the Captain seem to have the same idea. That was all the German *I know*!' He turned to Harding seated at the end of the table. 'It was a film I saw in Glasgow, sir.'

'Tell us about it, Number One.'

'Well, it was called "Sailors Three", sir. Claude Hulbert and a couple of other idiots were supposed to be aboard one of our cruisers off South America which calls in at some port or other and the crew is given shore leave and these three get pissed and miss the last liberty boat back and – Sir, it's not really all that funny.'

'Go on, Number One. We'll probably survive the tale.'

Gascoigne sighed and went on, 'They hire a boat, sir, and have themselves rowed out to the ship and climb up the anchor cable to avoid the officer of the watch, but what they don't know is that the cruiser has sailed and that the German battleship *Ludendorff* has anchored in its place. Anyway, they get down to a mess-deck, take off their uniforms and push them through a scuttle into the sea thinking the scuttle's a cupboard. They're still drunk you see, sir.'

'Does this last much longer, Number One?' Lieutenant Walker asked.

'You shut your face, Pilot,' Gascoigne told him. 'If the Captain can take it, so can you. Now, where was I? Oh yes. They wake up in the morning with frightful hangovers and can't find their clothes, so they put on German uniforms and walk about looking busy and nobody bothers them. You know, sir, like that chap at Portsmouth Barracks who carried a clip-board around for a month and was never…'

'Get on with it, Number One.'

'Yes, sir. They find an anti-Nazi – er, they find an Austrian who falls in with their plan to capture the ship and he says what I said over the *Ludendorff's* public address system. The Germans think it's a drill, you see, get into the boats and abandon ship and our chaps steam off with it, sir. Of course, it was a bit more complicated than that.'

The end of the story was greeted by a long stunned silence, a silence broken only when, in a puzzled voice, Schobert said, 'There is not a German battleship of the name *Ludendorff*,' paused and added, 'Please explain again more slower what was happening.'

'I'm sorry,' Gascoigne replied. 'I have to go on watch now.' He was half way to his feet, but sank back again when Harding spoke.

'No you don't. You aren't due on watch for another forty minutes. I think *Oberleutnant* Schobert deserves an explanation of why he owes his life to British film moguls and your spooky ability to recall foreign language extracts from their creations.'

For several seconds Gascoigne sat staring at the table with a small reminiscent smile on his face. He was picturing himself lying in a bath at the flat belonging to the girl he had taken to see the film, hearing again her wild cry of '*Alle Mann das Schiff verlassen!*' seeing the bathroom door burst open and the splash when her body landed in the bath on top of his. The game had gone on until the people in the flat below complained about water coming through their ceiling and by that time the words, correct or not, were firmly implanted in his memory.

When he began talking slowly and clearly to the German he was not surprised to find that they had the wardroom to themselves.

*

Lisbon was abeam to port when Harding saw Chief Yeoman Yarrow at the chart table, stitching a white cloth cut-out of a pair of crossed guns onto the black material of the 'Jolly Roger' to mark the ship's first successful gun action. Beside the flag, not yet attached to it, was the double cruciform representation of an aeroplane.

'Oh come on, Yarrow,' Harding said. 'We can't claim that Messerschmitt.'

'*Not*, sir?' Yarrow sounded extravagantly surprised.

'Of course not. We didn't *do* anything. It just flew into the drink. I can't have you sewing aircraft symbols on there every time a *Luftwaffe* pilot decides to take a bath.'

Yarrow nodded ponderously. 'I get what you mean, sir. That was more a case of "fell in der sea" as one might say.'

'What?' Harding said.

'*Felo de se*, sir. Suicide like. Joke, sir.'

'Oh Jesus,' Harding murmured, then added more loudly, 'This ship is lousy with phoney linguists. I give up.'

Harding had grinned when he had said it and that was enough for Yarrow. He had never intended to sew the aeroplane symbol onto the flag. It had taken most of the forty-eight hours since the sailor who acted as wardroom steward had reported on Gascoigne's confession for the chief yeoman and the coxswain to decide on a suitable bait with which to hook their captain. Now it had served its purpose.

'Fell in der sea,' Yarrow repeated to Harding's retreating back and chuckled throatily to make doubly sure that his and Ryland's laboriously contrived witticism had found its mark.

*

Trigger surfaced in daylight for the first time since the gun action with the trawler when Cape Trafalgar was astern. Ahead lay the southernmost point of Spain, the Straits of Gibraltar and the motor launch sent out to protect her from the unwelcome attentions of friendly aircraft likely to attack any submarine on sight without asking questions. The presence of the small vessel was more than normally necessary this day, Harding thought, because not since the Battle of Britain had he seen so many planes in the air at the same moment. It was an impressive sight, but not one that surprised him. With Rommel's Afrika Korps retreating before Montgomery's rampaging 8th Army to the east and with Anglo-American-French forces advancing towards the Germans' rear through Algeria to the west, Gibraltar had become the natural staging post for the allied air forces.

Harding looked about him at the coast of Spain, at the gently moving swell and at the brilliant pale blue sky, enjoying the warmth of the sun on his back. It was the first day of pleasant weather he had encountered since assuming command of *Trigger*. Then his eyes took in the duffel-coated figures of the look-outs in their Balaclava helmets. He addressed the man nearest to him.

'That's the Mediterranean ahead, Jameson.'

'Is it, sir? Always wanted to see that, sir.'

It never ceased to astonish him how little sailors and, he supposed, submarine sailors in particular knew or cared about their ship's position on the face of the globe.

'Yes,' he said, 'but aren't you a little bit warmly dressed like that?'

'Now you mention it, yessir.'

'Then I suggest that you go below in turn and take off some of that clobber.'

When the down and up traffic had ceased, Harding bent to the voice-pipe.

'Tell the German officer he's welcome to come up onto the bridge if he wants to.'

Schobert joined him moments later, propped himself on the front of the bridge at his side and said, 'It is good to smell new air again. I am not much liking undersea boats.'

Harding nodded an acknowledgement of both statements, but didn't speak and Schobert added, 'Hans Bodenschatz and I do that with the last shot before you break our gun. I am seeing the explosion. It is very good that I am not hitting you harder.'

Following the direction of the German's pointing finger Harding contemplated the large jagged hole in the casing feeling embarrassment stir in him, resenting it.

'Don't talk sentimental nonsense,' he said.

Schobert gave a short barking laugh before saying, 'Is not sentimental. I kill you if I can, but *die Königin* is sinking and if I am also sinking your ship, I am a drowned man. Makes good sense, *nicht wahr?*'

A formation of twelve fighter planes with the insignia of the United States on their fuselages flying close down *Trigger's* port side at an altitude of only some hundred feet blanketed the area with the thunder of their passing and relieved Harding of the necessity to reply. He was glad about that because his embarrassment had increased with the thought that, by voicing the word, he might himself have been considered sentimental by the enemy officer beside him. The knowledge that he *was* sentimental, that his reason for permitting his prisoner to come on the bridge at all had been to give himself the opportunity of expressing his regrets for the deaths of the anti-submarine trawler's crew, made his discomfort worse. Harding decided not to mention the subject.

The fighters were distant specks now, their engine note lost in the overall drone of aircraft movement, most of that movement a constant stream heading south and east towards the battle raging in North Africa.

'So many,' Schobert said. He sounded subdued.

'Yes.'

'Perhaps you should be not allowing me to see this.'

'It makes no difference,' Harding told him. 'Your agents in Algeciras across the bay will be counting every one.'

'Ah, is true.'

The Rock of Gibraltar brooding, menacing even in the bright sunlight, coming into view beyond the Spanish headland. A light blinking, Yarrow's Aldis lamp clattering a reply and the chief yeoman saying, 'Identification passed, sir,' Harding nodding in acknowledgement.

'Permission to hoist the "Jolly Roger", sir?' Yarrow again.

'No.'

Schobert asking, 'What is "Jolly Roger"?'

With his eyes on Yarrow's, Harding saying, 'Flags "J" and "R". We call them the "joyous return". They mean "request permission to enter harbour".' Yarrow's gaze sliding away from Harding's, colour showing in his cheeks.

'And you do not wish to enter harbour?'

'It is the escort vessel's duty to ask that,' Harding said and lied for the second time in ten seconds.

Neither spoke again until *Trigger* was within three miles of the harbour entrance, then Harding faced Schobert.

'I must ask you to go below now.'

'*Sofort, Herr Kapitän.*'

Harding's earlier decision deserted him and he called out the German's name as he was lowering himself through the upper conning tower hatch.

'*Ja, Herr Kapitän?*'

'I'm sorry about Hans Bodenschatz and the others.'

For countable seconds Schobert stared at some point on the deck beside him, then nodded his head and disappeared down the ladder without looking at Harding again.

'I'm very sorry about that, sir.'

Harding looked at the chief yeoman and said, 'What? Oh, I see. Well don't be, Yarrow. My idiosyncrasies are no responsibility of yours. I didn't want to rub his nose in it, that's all. You can hoist the flag now. No, wait. You do it, Norris. Yarrow, make to the depot ship "Request escort for German officer on arrival".'

Leaning against the side of the bridge, listening to the clacking of Yarrow's lamp beside him, Harding watched Ordinary Seaman Norris several feet above him securing the black flag with its grinning white skull to the after periscope. Then it was streaming in the breeze, revealing the crossed-guns insignia which symbolized the death of *die Königin*, somebody called Hans Bodenschatz and a lot of other men he couldn't even put a name to. As a record of an unmarked grave it seemed less than adequate.

Grunting impatiently at the persistence of an emotion he neither understood nor welcomed Harding turned his back on the flag and scanned the crouching lion shape of the Rock beyond *Trigger*'s bows.

Chapter Thirteen

A woman about half as tall as her name was long and many times prettier than it made her sound had been Harding's companion during his sole previous visit to Gibraltar eighteen months earlier when, as first lieutenant of the submarine *Shadow*, his captain had delivered his exhausted second-in-command into her hands. They had not slept together. It had not been because Harding would not dearly have loved them to have done so. It had not been because she was ten years his senior and something important on the staff of the Governor. It had not even been because she was his captain's aunt, a state of affairs brought about by family planning, or the lack of it, resulting in her being only fractionally older than her brother's son. It had been because, with a forthrightness so startling that it had made him blush, she had announced within seconds of their meeting that sharing his bed had no part in her plans for him.

For all that, the ensuing three days spent in her company had been the happiest he had known, for no other reason than that she was a wonderful person to be with, and he had returned to his ship rested, relaxed and very grateful to her. So it was with enormous contentment that Harding learned on the telephone from a male voice in the Governor's office that she was still in Gibraltar and could probably be found at that hour in the bar of The Rock Hotel. He made his way there immediately and found it almost deserted.

'*Eek!*' Agatha Emily de Vere Charnley-Bulstrode said and launched her slender five foot nothing directly from the bar stool to clasp him round the neck and hang there with her shoes dangling inches from the floor. Harding rocked under the assault, but stood his ground hearing the barman murmur 'Well held, sir,' as though he were a spectator at a cricket match.

'Hello, Peter.'

'Hello, Aggie.'

She slid to the floor then and grinned happily up at him.

'You got here very quickly.'

He blinked. 'How do you know if I got here quickly or not?'

'Well, you don't think I'm the sort of girl who hangs around bars alone, do you? I only left the office to come here after you'd talked to Jeremy on the telephone.'

'Good old Jeremy. He certainly had me fooled.'

'That's what diplomats are for. What do you want to drink? I've already got one, so I'm buying.'

When the barman had served him and moved away, 'Oh, it's so good to see you, Aggie.'

'You too, Peter dear.' She reached out and touched his cheek before adding, 'And please don't be hurt when I tell you that the house rules are as before. I'm still the same chap's mistress. He's away now, but I'm an honest dishonest woman.'

'I didn't know that,' Harding said. 'I mean about your being attached – I mean you never mentioned…' His voice trailed away into silence.

'Didn't I? How extremely remiss of me. You must have thought me a very odd fish.' Genuine surprise in the words.

Harding shook his head. 'No I didn't. It was like having a stunning older sister, although I do admit to some incestuous thoughts. Still, never mind about that. I never was so happy.'

'We had fun, didn't we? Is there time to do it again, or must you sail?'

'There's time,' Harding said. 'I'm not allowed to tell you how much. In fact I shan't know how much until they've finished surveying the ship for storm damage. We ran into some heavy weather on the way down.'

In a very low voice, 'No you didn't,' Agatha Bulstrode told him. 'You ran into an *Oberleutnant* Helmut Schobert on the way down. I've been interrogating him for most of the afternoon.'

Trigger lay in the flood-lit dry-dock, a beached whale under attack by land crabs. Crouching shapes crawled on her, oxy-acetylene torches hissed with violet tongues extended to lick cascading orange sparks from steel. A crane stood sentinel above her like a huge scavenging bird ready to feast on her internal organs as soon as the crabs laid them bare. The crabs were very active and the bird would not have long to wait.

*

Harding lay on a bunk in the cabin allocated to him aboard the depot ship, staring at the deckhead, thinking about Agatha Bulstrode, captivating playmate, lawyer, linguist, interrogator. He wondered if he had ever been as surprised by anything in his life as by the revelations of the evening, decided that he had not, wondered too why he should be surprised as she had to be doing *something* for the war effort. That point recognized he went on being surprised anyway.

He found that he was experiencing pique as well as astonishment, pique that it had not been simply desire for his company that had caused her to make herself so quickly available to him. Forty-five minutes of close cross-examination in a quiet corner of the bar had made that clear enough and left him with the impression that had he not contacted her he would have been sent for.

'Damn,' Harding said aloud to the deckhead and began cautiously to combat cramp in toes which a sudden onset of shyness had curled back under his feet.

*

Helmut Schobert was lying on a canvas cot in a sparsely furnished room without windows which he knew to be somewhere within the great fortress of the Rock itself. He was searching his memory for anything of significance he might have let slip either during the long conversation of the afternoon or the subsequent one which had lasted from just before midnight until two-thirty in the morning. He knew the times precisely as they hadn't taken his watch away, which had surprised him although he wasn't sure why it should.

It was confusing trying to remember because it had all lasted so long. At first he had done nothing more than repeatedly identify himself, which was all that he was required to do under the Geneva Convention, and the small pretty woman hadn't seemed to mind that in the least. She had simply talked on and on in the friendliest way about all sorts of subjects. Sometimes she had done it in slow careful English which made him concentrate, sometimes in fluent German with the harsh accent of a Berliner which relaxed him with its familiarity. At some point he had begun to comment on some of the things she said but, despite his watch, he didn't know when that was, nor did he much care. It was what he had said that he was trying to recall.

There had been harmless things of course. It had been genuinely gratifying to hear that the captain of the undersea boat had reported that *die Königin* had done well during the submerged phase of the operation and fought gallantly throughout the subsequent surface gun action. The lady had looked impressed when she had told him that, so he had described the battle for her from his own point of view. Nothing wrong with that. Nothing wrong with talking about women either.

He couldn't be sure how that subject had come up and at first he had been reluctant to discuss it, but she had seemed so interested in what German sailors did with their time ashore. Rather more than interested he had thought. 'Aroused' was the word to describe her when he had spoken of the facilities provided for the *Kriegsmarine*. No doubt about that at all and although he found the fact a little strange to say the least, he had become excited in his turn and talked on. After all, she really was awfully pretty and might there not be just a chance…? No, it was foolish to think that way. He was a prisoner of war now.

Perhaps it had been a mistake later on for him to have corrected one or two of the statements she had made, but in the face of her amazing knowledgeableness it had seemed only right to set the record straight and the points had been extremely minor. Nevertheless, he decided to watch what he said more carefully in future.

Helmut Schobert sank towards sleep picturing the movement of a small tongue moistening red lips, hearing again the sound of rapid, shallow breathing and the susurration of silk on silk as she moved her thighs against each other when he was describing the brothels.

*

Agatha Bulstrode sat, slouched forward across her typewriter the hands covering her eyes supporting her head. It was aching, her head, and so was her back because the chair she had been sitting on for the two hours since she had left the German was the wrong height for the desk. She yawned so widely that the angles of her jaw made sharp cracking sounds, shook herself as though she were a dog and straightened her spine. Four forty-two the clock on the wall said. Another page or so and she could go outside and watch the sun rise.

'The following points,' she typed, paused, then went on, 'emerge from the foregoing. One. The supply of medium to heavy (i.e. 20mm and above) automatic weapons to small units of the *Kreigsmarine* appears to have dried up. Subject complained volubly about this when describing the action with the submarine (HMS *Trigger*) in which his ship was sunk. His repeated requisitions for an automatic cannon, which he claims would have saved the day for him, have been refused on the grounds that priority had to be given to the *Luftwaffe* and Russian front armoured vehicles. Subject blames Allied bombing for this shortage.

'Two. Subject's confidence having been obtained, the "deliberate mistake gambit" was employed and elicited the response that, as was thought, all E-boats have now been transferred from the Atlantic to the Channel ports.'

Agatha Bulstrode let her hands fall to her lap, closed her eyes and allowed her mind to wander. She had, she knew, rather spoilt Peter Harding's evening the day before. That would have to be put right when she met him at lunch for the afternoon and evening she had promised him. It was a nuisance that she would have to spend the morning at what the local Intelligence people called their weekly prayer meeting because she needed sleep rather badly, but… She shrugged and addressed her typewriter again.

'Three. Subject was initially reluctant to talk about sex, but having been induced to do so became quite lyrical in that regard. It transpires that the area in Quiberon Bay from which he and his anti-submarine group have been operating (see attached water-soaked but still legible envelopes addressed to him and taken from him by Commanding Officer HMS *Trigger* and which Subject confirms show the address of his base) is that covered by RAF Photographic Reconnaissance Unit's (Jeremy, please look it up and fill in serial number, Aggie) showing suspected camouflaged inlet. Subject states that there are three brothels now in operation at the quayside, one for officers and two for other ranks, housing twelve, twenty and twenty-two girls respectively. While it is no part of this Section's duty to analyse in any depth material obtained during interrogation, it is submitted for consideration that the above figures represent altogether too much hospitality for what was a group of three anti-submarine trawlers with a combined complement of only thirty men. Accepting this, it is tempting to speculate on the possibility of the inlet being a temporary base for one of the flotillas of U-boats waiting to be allocated accommodation in the new reinforced concrete pens.'

'Now,' Agatha Bulstrode said to her typewriter, 'you can bomb it, or mine it, or send in the Commandos, or sit on your fat bottoms.' She stood up, stretched, put the typed sheets into a box for a man named Jeremy to collect, locked the box and walked out to watch the sun come up.

Chapter Fourteen

Harding was at breakfast when Gascoigne sat down beside him at the depot ship's long wardroom table.

'Good morning, sir.'

''Morning, Number One. What's the news?'

'Not too bad. They're going to replace the whole of No. 1 battery. It has over thirty cells cracked by the depth-charging, which is too high a proportion for comfort so they're making a clean sweep of all hundred and twelve. No.2 is much less badly damaged and No.3 hardly at all.'

'I see. What about the capstan?'

'Well, sir,' Gascoigne said, 'we seem to have caught them on the wrong foot there. It appears that nobody ever had their capstan blown over the side before, so the need for a replacement hadn't been anticipated.'

There were traces of egg and a small piece of fried bread remaining on Harding's plate. He manoeuvred the two substances onto a collision course with his knife and fork, then transferred the result to his mouth before saying, 'I'll arrange to have one flown out to wherever they send us. How soon do you reckon we can get away?'

'The dockyard wants another two days, then I have to provision ship and get her painted blue, sir. Say three days, give or take.'

'All right,' Harding said. 'That'll do very well.'

During those three days, tidal waves of which he had been the unwitting epicentre were to spread out from Harding. Other smaller waves, little more than ripples, from another source were to lap around him, but he was to be aware only of the latter.

As Harding rose from the breakfast table in Gibraltar harbour the submarine *Tarquin*, sister to *Trigger*, surfaced to the north of Crete to investigate a large caique proceeding eastward under full sail assisted by an auxiliary diesel engine. Within a matter of seconds *Tarquin* was diving again in the face of withering fire from guns revealed only when the side of the caique's long deck-house fell outwards. After one look at his unconscious captain's four bullet wounds, *Tarquin*'s first lieutenant ordered course set for Beirut and medical help which he feared would come too late.

*

With little or nothing he could usefully do with his ship in the hands of the dockyard, Harding strolled along the mole looking at the vessels moored there. He was standing, staring up at the towering side of the aircraft carrier *Intractable* feeling glad that he was no part of such a floating city, when a civilian in an untidy office off Whitehall in London broke the seal of an envelope marked 'Immediate' and read carefully through the long decoded signal it contained. When he had finished he turned back to the first page and looked at the impression of a rubber stamp at its top. There were two lines of abbreviated words, 'Orig. Rel. Fac.' above 'Est. Acc. Inf.' Impressed that the originator should have a pencilled-in reliability factor of 78% and that the estimated accuracy of the information in this particular case had been awarded seven points more than that, he wrote, 'Bomber Command for action soonest' in the margin, added his initials and pressed a bell-push to summon a messenger.

*

It was chilly in the deep shadow on the eastern side of the Rock and, squatting on the sand, Harding drew his knees closer to the front of his shirt. He was trying to think of something to think about other than the small matter of its being cold enough to make him shiver periodically and the far more disturbing one of the figure lying beside him. The first had impinged on his consciousness during the last thirty minutes, but had done little to distract him from the second which had been occupying his mind for over three hours.

For a while he stared fixedly at the darkening horizon beyond which lay the naval bases of Algiers, Malta, Beirut and the waters between them which were to be his world when his ship had been healed, but they seemed so remote; remote and less of a magnet than they had been. Quite quickly he lost interest in the horizon.

She looked so pretty, so defenceless, with his uniform jacket held close up under her chin, the jacket and her skirt rucked around her thighs. He had tried to draw first one and then the other down to cover the beguiling bands of white skin above her stockings, but she had stirred and moaned softly in unconscious protest on both occasions, so he had desisted. Harding was watching the tiny frown on her face, a frown which seemed to state that sleep was something requiring great concentration, when she opened her eyes wide and stared at him.

'What?' Agatha Bulstrode said.

'I didn't say anything.'

'But…' She sat abruptly upright like a puppet controlled by strings, glanced questioningly around, then down at her legs and wailed, 'Oh my God!'

'It's all right,' Harding told her. 'You look just like "Jane".'

Casting his jacket aside, hips squirming as she drew her skirt down, 'I look just like Jane who?'

'Just "Jane". She's the strip-cartoon girl in *Good Morning*. That's the newspaper without any news in it the *Daily Mirror* publishes for the Submarine Service. We take thirty or so editions on patrol with us.'

She was standing now, brushing sand from herself. 'Oh, do they and do you? What does this "Jane" do?'

'Loses her dress several times a week by snagging it on barbed wire or anything else handy.'

'I see. What happened, Peter?'

'We had lunch. We came here. We lay down on the sand. You said "Oh that's nice," and fell fast asleep. Were you up all night?'

'Yes, I was. But that's no excuse. It was very rude of me. And look at you standing there shivering.' Picking up his jacket she shook it clear of sand, then held it so that he could slip his arms into the sleeves. 'Sweet Peter,' she said and the gentle tone of her voice made the words a caress. She took his arm companionably during their walk back along the tunnel through the Rock, but to Harding the contact seemed more than companionable.

*

'Put me through to "Group",' the air vice-marshal said and waited for four seconds with the telephone receiver to his ear before saying, 'Ah, Harry. Sorry to muck you about, but I want you to hold back a hundred planes from the Mannheim show tomorrow night.'

The receiver chattered at him and he shook his head irritably as though he could be seen by the speaker, then broke in curtly, 'Don't argue, old chap. They're wanted for a high priority target and the orders came down from the same altitude, so you'll have to grin and bear it. The crews are to be hand-picked; bomb loads three quarters high-explosive, one quarter phosphorous. Got that?'

The receiver admitted resentfully that it had.

'Right. I'll come down and put you in the picture at 1430 hours tomorrow. You can brief your air-crews immediately after that. 'Bye.'

In a bunker beneath a ploughed field somewhere in the south of England the air vice-marshal replaced the telephone on its rest as Agatha Bulstrode and Harding walked into a restaurant in Gibraltar.

*

'Fireworks with dinner tonight,' Agatha said.

Harding raised his eyebrows at her. 'Why? Does this place have a temperamental chef?'

'Not that I'm aware of. It's a show the Rock puts on from time to time to impress the natives. They'll be opening the windows in a few minutes. I chose this place to give us a good view.'

'It can't be the sun,' Harding said. 'It's nothing like hot enough yet. They must have slipped something into that drink you had at the bar.'

'Just you wait, my lad,' Agatha told him and grinned like an urchin.

Suspecting some privately arranged hoax Harding watched the waiters open the windows, listened to her saying 'It helps to keep glass out of the soup' and allowed himself to be led to one of them. Her words 'Don't jump' registered seconds before the Rock erupted. He jumped violently.

The silence shattered by the slam of countless guns, ripped by the sound of air displaced by streaking rockets and streaming back to fill the vacuums their passage left behind them, the night blasted out of existence by myriad bursts of fire until it seemed as though the sky itself was burning like some huge incandescent bulb. Then, as abruptly as it had begun, it stopped, leaving only an after-glow on the retina and the throbbing of shocked ear-drums. The waiters closed the windows.

'Bloody hell!' Harding said.

'Impressive, wasn't it?'

'Awesome.'

'They say the barrage covers a cubic mile of sky.'

'Bloody hell!' Harding said for the second time and looked down at his small companion. 'And for your next trick?'

She smiled. 'Well, that's a difficult act to follow. Do you have any suggestions?'

'No, I've had enough excitement for one day,' he told her and, to his dismay, flushed scarlet.

Harding saw Agatha Bulstrode back to her flat before midnight and was walking slowly back to the dockyard while the submarine *Tarquin* raced through the channel between Crete and the island of Kásos. When the land was lost to sight in the darkness astern, the first lieutenant ordered all internal ballast water and most of the drinking water supply pumped overboard to give the ship an extra half knot of speed. Fully aware that he was taking a considerable risk by rendering *Tarquin* incapable of diving quickly in an emergency he did it anyway because he wanted to save his captain's life.

That was the end of the first day.

*

It was late afternoon before all the work connected with replacing *Trigger's* damaged battery cells was completed and Gascoigne, torch in hand, a Webley .45 revolver at his hip, was moving along the bottom of the dry-dock from one to another of the big free-flood apertures in the undersides of the ship's main ballast tanks. At each one he clambered up onto the baulks of timber on which *Trigger's* keel rested, put his head and shoulders through the aperture and shone his torch around the tank to ensure nothing was there which should not have been. 'There's a local standing order about possible sabotage attempts by dockyard workmen,' Harding had told him, so as soon as the workmen had left, he, Walker, Randolph, the coxswain and the chief engine room artificer had searched the ship from the torpedo tube space forward to the after machinery compartment at the stern. Others had crawled through the casing above the pressure hull and now he was examining the only places left where some device might have been rigged.

There was no device and he clambered up the stepped side of the dock and shouted, 'All clear, sir!' to Harding on *Trigger's* bridge. Able Seaman Jameson and Ordinary Seaman Norris, he saw, were in position by their machine-guns mounted at each side of the conning tower. Harding's acknowledgement reached him and he walked to the centre point of the gangway linking ship and shore, then stood looking down into the dock, aware that Lieutenant Walker was watching the other side.

A man detached himself from a group sitting on the steps near the dock floor, clambered down to it and began to stroll towards the submarine.

'Back off!' Gascoigne called, drew his gun from its green webbing holster and raised it.

The man walked on, gesticulating and talking in loud Spanish.

'Jameson!' Urgency in Gascoigne's voice.

'Sir?'

'Fire a burst into the air to seaward!'

Jameson's gun made its tearing calico noise, the man stopped, turned and ran for the dockside, shaking his fists and shouting unintelligibly up at Gascoigne.

'And fuck you too,' Gascoigne said, but he said it quietly because he was feeling rather silly as he didn't really believe that the man had had any hostile intent.

A minute later water was surging into the dock, covering its floor, then flowing over the lower steps. The workmen retreated upwards ahead of its rise and Gascoigne put his .45 back in its holster. It was nearly dark by the time *Trigger* was afloat.

*

In the front turret of Lancaster G for George, Flight-Sergeant Ffoulkes fired his guns as well as soon as the bomber crossed the Cornish coast at Padstow heading south and west for the Atlantic. He watched the tracer curving down towards the sea, sniffed appreciatively at the combined fumes of cordite and hot oil, then began softly to sing 'I wish I was a fascinating bitch, I'd never be poor, I'd always be rich. I'd sleep all day and work all night and…'

'Shut up, Double F,' his earphones said.

'Sorry, Skipper,' Ffoulkes answered and went back to sniffing the dying scent of cordite and hot oil. He liked the combination, but not enough to make him want to fire his guns again that night. If he had to do that it would be in earnest, not simply testing them as he had just done. As if there had been no intervening pause, '… have a little cottage with a little red light,' he sang, then realizing what he was doing he stopped doing it before the skipper got angry. Not that he often did that, Ffoulkes thought. In fact he was a pretty good bloke for an officer was Flight-Lieutenant Pyle and had done nothing more than roll his eye-balls in resignation when his crew had named G for George 'The Hurtling Haemorrhoid' and painted the words on the side of the fuselage. Ffoulkes grinned at the memory of Cole asking him afterwards if perhaps the skipper had suffered jokes like that before. Cole was not what you would call bright although they were all very glad to have him in the rear turret, for he was a natural as a tail gunner.

'Skipper, ain't this the way to fuckin' America?' Cole's puzzled voice in his earphones and Pyle's languid reply, 'Now don't you worry your knobbly little head about a thing, Blackie. We'll be turning for fucking France before you're many hours older.'

Ffoulkes grinned again and began to count the long line of dots which were the bombers of the first strike still just visible against the fading gold of the western horizon.

*

'I don't know how to reply to that,' Harding said. 'Obviously command is something every officer wants. Well, I suppose they do but – well, you see…'

A long five seconds of silence followed before Agatha asked, 'Do you think you could stop saying "well" and murdering that potato with your fork for long enough to answer a girl's question. I only wanted to know if you like being in command of your own ship. Of course if that's some sort of privileged information, pretend I never spoke.'

Harding didn't smile. 'I'd like it better if I was better at it,' he told her, 'and if it wasn't such a lonely job.'

Agatha nodded, a long, slow series of nods as though, Harding thought, she had just received confirmation of something she had long suspected. He was almost right.

'Peter.'

'Yes, Aggie?'

'When you came to Gib before with *Shadow*, my esteemed nephew, your ex-captain, dropped you in my lap for me to try to pull you out of the dumps. Remember?'

'No,' Harding said, smiling now. 'I don't seem to have any recollection of that.'

Ignoring him, she went on, 'He told me then that you were first-class at your job and the only things wrong with you, apart from being tired out, which he said was his fault, were that you were too gentle and much too self-critical. I like the gentleness. Not all women would, but I do. Nevertheless, you mustn't let it affect you professionally. That's why I got a bit terse with you yesterday when you said you rather liked Helmut Schobert and I…'

'Knock it off, Aggie,' Harding broke in. 'I got the message. I agree with it. Now drop it. You're not *my* aunt.'

121

He had spoken quietly, but with a firmness she hadn't heard before and his smile was gone.

'Wow!' she said. 'Perhaps you're not so gentle after all. I think I like that too. Right. Lecture over. Actually, I wouldn't have sounded off at all but for that loneliness remark of yours. There must be literally hundreds of thousands of men in command of something or other in this war, so that doesn't rate much sympathy.'

'I wasn't asking for sympathy,' he told her. 'I was answering your question and, for your information, I'm not in command of something or other, I'm in command of a submarine.'

'And that makes a difference?'

'From the loneliness point of view, yes.'

'In what way?'

'Oh look,' Harding said. 'If an army colonel gets a situation all wrapped round his neck he can yell for the brigadier. A fighter pilot has ground control vectoring him onto a target and a flight leader to tell him what to do with it when he gets there. The captain of an escort vessel has the senior officer of the group to order him around. A cruiser captain has his admiral and the admiral himself has his staff to chew things over with. Of course that's an over-simplification. Some of those people are alone some of the time, but we're alone all the time, often for weeks on end. When we're sent information by wireless on the movements of enemy shipping they add the words "attack at your discretion" because only you in the whole wide world know what the set-up is at that particular place at that particular time and there is nobody at all you can ask for advice. As I said, it's lonely. Come and dance.'

Her expression thoughtful, Agatha held his gaze for a moment before saying, 'It isn't like me to overlook the obvious. I must be slipping. Yes please, I'd love to dance.'

*

Ffoulkes could see the glowing exhausts of the four Merlin engines of the Lancaster immediately ahead quite clearly and he kept his eyes on them because it was less frightening than watching the flak bursting all around. 'The Hurtling Haemorrhoid' was shuddering and jerking in the shock-waves of the exploding shells. As if the old cow didn't vibrate badly enough under ordinary flying conditions, Ffoulkes thought, and winced at the sharp rattle of shrapnel striking the fuselage somewhere behind him. He wondered which was worse, the flak or the night-fighters which had intercepted them some miles out over the Atlantic. Two Lancs had bought it there and 'Blackie' Cole had reported that he had hit one of the Ju88s but didn't think he had damaged it much. No fighters now of course, not even the bloody Jerries were stupid enough to send them into their own anti-aircraft barrage. That was why he was watching the Lanc ahead instead of scanning the night sky for them.

Shrapnel clattered for the second time and he winced again, then relaxed at the sound of the skipper's voice in his earphones saying, 'Will somebody please answer that door?' Good bloke Pyle, even if he did have a toffee-nosed accent. Good pilot as well. He was jinking the big bomber right and left now, trying to break away from the sticky finger of a searchlight filling the plane with violet brilliance, succeeding too, leaving only the lesser brightness of exploding flak.

'Come left five degrees, Skip. I can see the flares. Fires too.' That was Munchen talking from the bomb aimer's position just below him in the nose of the aircraft. Everybody called him Munchen. Not so much because he was always eating, which he was, but because his surname was Chamberlain and Munchen was the way the Jerries spelt Munich. 'Blackie' Cole didn't quite get that joke either. To be fair, Ffoulkes thought, he'd had to have it explained to himself because he'd been only fourteen when some prime minister called Chamberlain had gone to Munich and been sold a bill of goods by old Adolf. He looked down to see what Munchen had been talking about.

The four flares dropped by the path-finder Mosquitos were very bright still and close enough to forming a square, allowing for the perspective, which Miss Lister had taught him about in art class at school. Two big fires were blazing inside the square and another off to the right of it, so the bunch of twits in the first wave of Lancs had got most of it right. The flak ceasing abruptly and Pyle's voice in his earphones saying, 'Jock, Blackie, Double F, watch it. Night-fighters coming for sure.'

It was only seconds later that he saw one. At least he didn't so much see one as stop seeing the exhaust flames of the Lane in front which meant that there was something between him and it. He reported what he could see, or rather couldn't see, to the skipper, then fingered the hand-grip of his guns nervously, unable to fire for fear of hitting the Lane. Then he saw it silhouetted clearly against the expanding ball of orange fire which a moment earlier had been a Lancaster bomber and his guns spat a double stream of lead carrying his fury with them. Almost at once the fighter flipped onto its back and dropped away, dragging a shroud of smoke after it.

'Nice shooting, Double F,' Pyle said. 'They'll have to make his Iron Cross posthumous.'

Miss Lister's perspective effect lessening as they neared the target area and the flashes of a stick of an unseen plane's bombs marching diagonally across the square like street lamps being switched on in sequence at dusk. The flak starting up again and Munchen saying, 'Right, Skip. More right. More. Steady. You're bang on.' Ffoulkes nervously whispering his battle hymn under his breath, 'And once in a while I'll take a holiday just to make my customers wild. Oh I wish I was a fascinating bitch and not an illegitimate child.' The cry 'Bombs gone!' 'The Hurtling Haemorrhoid', relieved of their weight, soaring high above the bursting flak. Pyle asking, 'Where did they hit?' A voice replying, 'Just left of centre, Skipper. I've got a good photograph.'

'So I should hope,' Pyle said. 'Without that the bastards wouldn't believe we'd come here at all.'

Ffoulkes began his song again, a little louder now.

That was the end of the second day.

*

Dawn in Gibraltar found *Trigger* turning patchily from Atlantic grey to Mediterranean dark blue under the paint brushes of fifteen seamen plus four members of the engine room staff who had not been quick enough to convince Chief Petty Officer Ryland that they were urgently needed elsewhere. Food in boxes, crates, sacks, cartons, enough to feed seventy men for weeks, moved along a human chain from the great oblong opening in the depot ship's side and down the submarine's fore hatch. A barge crossed the harbour carrying replacements for the few 4-inch shells and larger quantities of 20mm and .303 ammunition expended during the gun action with the anti-submarine trawler. One of its fenders scraped five feet of blue paint from *Trigger*'s ballast tanks and produced some colourful language from Ordinary Seaman Norris who had just finished that bit. In his cabin aboard the depot ship Harding slept restlessly through a sexual encounter with a beautiful woman who was half Agatha Bulstrode and half his American fiancée, Lee Lawrence.

*

Around an inlet in Quiberon Bay, dawn revealed desolation, a wide expanse of smouldering woods, smoking rubble, a ruined jetty, dead people, dead animals. It didn't need the dawn to declare the presence of men and women trapped under collapsed buildings or of animals lying wounded in the fields. In diminishing numbers and with diminishing strength they had been doing that for themselves for hours. Things bobbed on the oil-streaked surface of the inlet. Just things. Most of those left alive were too shocked, too stunned, to care what they might be, but one woman crouched at the water's edge crying for her child and pointing at a floating bundle. She had never had a child. After a little, somebody led her away. A pall of smoke stretching from horizon to horizon and hiding the scene from the sky provided the only decency.

*

Two reports reached Berlin shortly after noon. That addressed to *Oberkommando der Kriegsmarine* was read by *Kapitän-zur-See* Rudolf Dietl.

'Sir,

As instructed I write to confirm this morning's telephone conversation in which I informed you of last night's air raid.

'The attack, which was pressed home with exceptional savagery, by an estimated six to seven hundred English heavy bombers resulted in the sinking of five UA-VII C-class U-boats as listed in the appendix. The remaining U-boat in harbour at the time saved itself by submerging at its moorings and lying on the bottom until the raid was over. The duty officer (see appendix) is to be commended for his prompt action.

'Damage to the temporary port installations is extensive. All but one of the five cranes have been demolished, the jetty rendered 75% useless, the three oil storage tanks completely burnt out, as are the prefabricated offices, sleeping accommodation and the recreation centre. There is at present no supply of either water or electricity and the nearest usable telephones are in the local village which is itself more than 50% destroyed. There is also damage to roads and the sewage system has been breached in places.

'In the absence of leave-records which were burnt with the administration office it is impossible at this time to establish the total number of casualties. So far the bodies of 28 Kriegsmarine and 4 Wehrmacht personnel have been recovered, together with 33 civilians and 11 prostitutes. I have no figure for wounded as they have been dispersed to hospitals in surrounding towns.'

Wondering bleakly what the leutnant who had signed the report imagined prostitutes to be if they were not civilians, Dietl wrote 'Grand Admiral Doenitz to see' at the head of the paper, then added

'Luftwaffe reports indicate that only 200 bombing planes were involved in this attack of which 29 were destroyed by fighters and ground fire. Not that it matters. I have of course ordered this temporary base abandoned'.

The second letter bore the inscription 'Reichssicherheits hauptamt-Amt IV E' because counterespionage and the Gestapo were interested too. It recalled the secrecy with which the U-boat sanctuary had been prepared, the absence of enemy aerial reconnaissance over the immediate area since the inception of the plan and the pin-point accuracy of the assault where saturation bombing of the region would have been more readily understandable. The reader was not at all clear why saturation bombing of the region would have been more readily understandable, and concluded correctly that his subordinate in north-west France had allowed himself to be carried away by his own eloquence. Nevertheless, he agreed with his conclusion that a spy ring existed in the vicinity and with his intention to execute ten Frenchmen daily until it was exposed.

The effect of Agatha Bulstrode's stockinged legs on Helmut Schobert's imagination was continuing to kill people.

*

In Dorset Flight-Lieutenant Pyle awoke at 3.45 in the afternoon, got up, shaved, dressed and walked to the officers' mess to get something to eat. The big room was empty except for a staff officer lounging in an armchair, feet on top of the stove, not reading the paper he was holding.

'Hello, Jim. Nice trip last night?'

'Super,' Pyle said. 'Beautiful weather, matchless scenery, gourmet cooking and music both ways. You should come along some time. How many did we lose?'

'Eleven I'm afraid.'

Pyle stared through the window at the row of Lancaster bombers parked on the far side of the airfield. In that group alone he could see that two of the stands were empty.

'Shit,' he said. 'That's over ten percent.'

'Bloody quick mental arithmetic, old boy.'

'Did we do the job?'

'Blew the whole place to blazes,' the staff officer told him. 'They sent a Photographic Reconnaissance Mozzie over there early this morning to check it out, but there was too much smoke around for it to see anything, so they sent another a few hours later.'

'And?'

'Mm?'

'Oh for Christ's sake, Mac, what did we hit?'

The other dropped his newspaper onto the floor and bent to retrieve it before looking up at Pyle and saying, 'All I can tell from the photographs is that you flattened a fishing village and set a lot of woodland on fire. There's something that looks like a crane there, but there's still a lot of smoke around so it's hard to be sure. Nothing very significant about a crane anyway.' He paused before adding, 'It's occurred to me, Jim, that Jerry put up that camouflage as an invitation to us to attack it and lose a few aeroplanes in the process. What do you think?'

Pyle shrugged, turned away and walked out of the mess. He no longer felt like eating.

*

Harding took Agatha Bulstrode to the Rock Hotel for his last evening in Gibraltar. She was beautifully dressed, very carefully made up, vivacious, amusing and brittle. He waited until they had finished dinner, a dinner she only toyed with, before saying, 'Do you want to tell me what the matter is?'

Whatever reaction he had expected to his question, tight-lipped silence and a stare of wide-eyed panic had not been it.

'Aggie! What on earth…?'

He stopped talking at the violent shaking of her head and the sight of her lips turning inwards until they were all but invisible. Two identical tears detached themselves from the corners of her eyes and traced identical paths down either side of her nose.

For unnerving seconds she held his regard with her appalled stare, then, without taking her gaze from his, ducked down to lift her bag from the floor beside her, remove a sheet of paper from it and thrust it at him. He took it in his hand, saw the clamped lips released for just long enough to whisper 'Damn you' before, with an effort of will, he broke the magnetic eye-contact and looked down at what he was holding.

'I am requested by his wife,' he read, 'to inform you that Lt-Cmdr W. G.

de Vere Charnley-Bulstrode, commanding officer H M Submarine *Tarquin*, has suffered amputation of right leg following wounds received in action. Condition critical. You will be kept informed of any further developments.'

Harding continued to stare at the paper, confusion growing in him because his immediate and overriding emotion was less one of sadness than anger at the dim-witted oaf who had concocted such a heartless message. The words had certainly not been those of darling, plump, plain Sarah, gentle Sarah at whose wedding he had stood as 'best man' for her husband and his ex-captain. He felt his own lips compress, then raised his head to meet his companion's round-eyed gaze again.

'Come and dance,' Harding said.

'Don't want.' The mouth opened only far enough to release the two syllables before clamping shut again.

'Yes you do,' he told her, stood up, gripped her below her shoulders and lifted her bodily from her chair. When she was upright he hurried her across the corner of the dance floor to the tall screen masking the exit. Behind it he took her in his arms. With his head bent forward his nose didn't quite reach her dark curls.

It seemed a long time to Harding before her rigid body melted against his and she began to tremble. He didn't speak.

'Damn you. Didn't mean to tell you.' Muffled words from the region of his chest.

'You're more sister and brother than aunt and nephew, aren't you?' he said.

Her curls nodded their agreement.

'But expect you'd have heard soon enough.'

'Yes.'

Silence and a small nose nuzzling him.

'Peter.'

'Yes, Aggie?'

'How would you feel if I asked you to come to bed with me?'

'Very honoured,' Harding said.

'Then come and be honoured.'

'No, Aggie.'

'Because of Lee Lawrence?'

129

'No. I think she would understand. It's – well, it's because I think you would feel awfully unhappy about it tomorrow.'

Silence again, then what sounded like a small giggle with a break in it. 'It would make me a dishonest honest dishonest woman, would it?'

'Something like that.'

The trembling increased and he found himself supporting more of her slight weight as though the denial of solace had deprived her legs of their strength.

A naval captain and a girl rounded the screen on their way to the exit. They stopped.

'I hardly think…' the captain began and Harding had snapped, 'Possibly not, but…' before he realized that he was speaking. He flushed and added, 'I beg your pardon, sir, but the lady is extremely distressed. If you wouldn't mind just…' The sentence trailed into silence.

'Sorry,' the captain said and again 'Sorry' as he moved away with his girl.

Harding had never undressed a woman before, but found himself having to do so when he got Agatha Bulstrode back to her flat. Agonizing for her he had watched while she fumbled with her necklace, broke its string, tried to unfasten her skirt with fingers which refused to obey her, then collapsed onto the bed having achieved only a scattering of beads on the floor.

'Easy, easy now,' he had whispered and gone to her aid. It was, he discovered, a complex and alarmingly exciting procedure. She lay on the bed, watching him, not helping much until, Harding having got her down to her underwear and decided that enough was enough, she arched her back to give him access to the clasp of her brassière. He went grimly on with his task.

Suddenly, quaveringly, 'This isn't me, you know,' she said. 'I'm really a very tough cooky. It was you seeing through me that did it. I thought I was covering up so well and then you had to go and say…' She sniffed and went on, 'It's my job to see through people, not yours. If you'd kept quiet and…' The words stopped there.

When she was naked, 'Where do you keep your night-dress?'

'I don't wear one.'

The bedclothes he covered her with pushed down to her waist, his hand clasped and drawn between her breasts, the actions without enticement, like a child seeking comfort.

'Stay a little while, Peter.'

'Of course.'

Harding reached out with his free hand and switched off the bedside lamp. It was easier like that.

About twenty minutes had passed, he guessed, when her breathing deepened and her fingers slackened their grip on his. He stood up and moved silently towards the door.

'Damn you, Peter.'

There was something close to desperation in his voice when he said, 'You're doing a lot of damning tonight, Aggie. Please don't make it harder for me. I'm sure I'm right.'

'I didn't mean that, my dear. I was damning you for being so young. Had you not been, I'd have given Lee Lawrence a run for her money.'

Groping for something to say all he could find was, 'Bill's going to be all right.'

'What makes you think so?'

'He's a very tough cooky too,' Harding said and let himself out of the flat.

Walking down to the dockyard he told himself repeatedly that he had 'done the decent thing', but the telling carried no conviction with it. The really decent thing would have been to stay with her, comfort her, even kiss her, but he knew that any of those would have led to sleeping with her. He had reached the dockyard's main gate before he understood that that was exactly what he should have done, that he had failed her, she who had not failed him when he needed help.

The realization brought him to a standstill and he was turning to retrace his steps when a voice asked, 'You wouldn't happen to be the captain of *Trigger*, would you sir?'

He looked at the sentry. 'Yes, I would.'

'Oh good. You're wanted back aboard urgently, sir.'

'Telephone through to tell them I'm on my way,' Harding said and began to run.

That was the end of the third day.

Chapter Fifteen

'Sit down and get your breath back,' Captain Submarines said. 'I want you to sail as soon as we're finished here.'

Harding nodded and subsided onto a chair in the depot ship's operations room, still panting from his sprint through the dockyard and along the mole. He looked from the captain to the lieutenant-commander who was the operations staff officer and back to the captain again.

'The situation is this,' the captain went on. 'There's an Argentinian blockade runner called the *Carlos Roca* which has been carrying cargoes between Spanish Mediterranean ports and Marseilles. Mostly iron ore and foodstuffs. The trouble has been that she stays firmly inside Spanish territorial waters all the way to the French frontier and we've never had a submarine free just for the purpose of catching her during the short trip across the Gulf of Lions. An hour and a half ago I received an Intelligence report placing her in Malaga and probably sailing at dawn. You're to get along there and sink her when she does sail.'

'Inside territorial waters, sir?'

'What territorial waters?'

Harding nodded again, smiling.

'No, actually,' the captain said, 'it's been decided that she's too valuable to the enemy to be allowed to continue with what she's doing and that if we annoy the Spanish and the Argentinians that's just too bad. It'll have to be a torpedo attack of course. No gun action in full view of the Spanish coast. If you do sink her you'd better mark the track chart of your attack as being outside the 3-mile limit for form's sake. Okay?'

'Yes, sir.'

'All right.' The captain gestured towards his staff officer. 'Bob here will give you the rest of your orders. Basically this is just an acclimatization cruise. Poke around the Balearics and as far north as Barcelona keeping your eyes open and getting your crew shaken down. You'll be working out of Algiers after that, so proceed there when you get your recall signal. Good luck with the *Carlos Roca*. She's getting to be a pain in the neck.'

'Yes, sir. Thank you, sir,' Harding said.

*

'All hands aboard. Ship ready for sea, sir.'

'Thank you, Number One.'

Harding looked up at the dark bulk of the depot ship beside him, at the loom of the Rock, then towards the town. He thought he could make out the house where Agatha lay sleeping. At least he hoped she was sleeping by now and felt both regret and thankfulness that he was not lying beside her. The thankfulness was the stronger of the two emotions. The *Carlos Roca*, *Trigger* the only available submarine, and her captain unable to be found because he was in a bed he had no business to be in? The thought made him work his shoulders as if struggling free of imagined disgrace.

'Let go aft.'

Gascoigne relaying the order in a shout to the men on the stern, the splash of the securing line striking water and the rasp of its being drawn aboard.

'All clear aft, sir.'

'Let go for'ard. Slow ahead port. Half astern starboard. Starboard fifteen.'

Harding's orders repeated back to him, telegraph bells chiming, *Trigger* coming alive, trembling, beginning to move away from the depot ship's side, more orders and the diesels coughing, then settling to a steady rumble of power, the ship turning, gathering way towards the lights marking the harbour entrance.

Trigger was passing between them, beginning to roll at the urging of the open sea, when Gascoigne said, 'How's Felicity, sir?'

'Felicity? Who's Felicity?'

133

He glanced curiously at his second-in-command's face, a pale blob in the darkness, too indistinct to read any expression on it, but the surprise was clear enough in Gascoigne's voice when he replied, 'Why, the pretty brunette you go around with when we come to Gib, sir. I couldn't help seeing you both times we've – Oh, I'm awfully sorry, sir. It's no business of mine.'

Harding bent to the voice-pipe. 'Cox'n, port ten and steer 180.'

'Port ten and steer 180. Aye aye, sir.'

Turning back to Gascoigne, 'There's no need to be sorry, Number One. There's no secret about it. I just don't understand what gave you the idea that her name's Felicity.'

'You did, sir. When we came here in *Shadow* you went off to see Lieutenant-Commander Bulstrode's rich old aunt. The one he was always carrying on about. You took her companion out and told us that her name was Felicity.'

'Oh, did I? Yes, now you mention it I remember I did. It *was* a secret then. An unimportant little secret which doesn't matter any longer.'

'Ship steady on 180, sir,' the voice-pipe announced.

'Thank you, Cox'n.'

Depression settled on Harding as he went on, 'He hates his silly long name, so he invented a rich old aunt who threatened to cut him out of her will if he didn't latch her name onto his. She never existed. At least the old and rich bit didn't.'

'Do you mean to say that…?'

'Yes, there was no companion. That was his aunt you saw me with. They're roughly the same age and she isn't feeling too good at the moment because he's been wounded in action and lost a leg. He may die.'

Gascoigne only grunted and Harding was grateful to him for that. It was the approved reaction, the decent thing not to embarrass others with shows of emotion. The decent thing. That phrase again. He frowned, no longer so sure that the decent thing was the best thing and looked back at the receding lights of the town with a lump forming in his throat.

When it had subsided, 'Come round to 060 degrees when we're clear of Europa Point, Number One,' Harding said. 'I'm going below for a bit.'

*

The master of the *Carlos Roca* enjoyed contrast and had been indulging his liking since four o'clock the previous afternoon by drinking alternate glasses of the sweet Malaga wine and Tio Pepe. It was very pleasant, he thought, the way the sharpness of the sherry shaved the sugar from his tongue and the blandness of the wine blanketed the cutting edge of the sherry. He had continued to think that until nightfall after which he hadn't thought about anything much except instructing the cabin boy to bring him fresh bottles. Having had a lot of practice it was not until one in the morning that his conscious mental processes ceased altogether.

The mate, too used to the procedure to feel more than mild resentment, ordered the engine room staff to have steam raised by half an hour before dawn and retired to his cabin.

*

'Diving stations,' Harding said, looked again at the lights of Malaga bright on the port quarter, then ahead at the first trace of day marking the eastern horizon. 'Stop main engines. Out both engine clutches.' The voice-pipe repeated his words back to him, the diesel note faded into silence and *Trigger* ghosted on with only the sounds of the sea for company.

'Crew closed up at diving stations, sir. Both engine clutches out.'

'Thank you. Half ahead together. Clear the bridge. First man through the hatch press the klaxon.'

The sounds of shuffling shoe leather, the klaxon's double blare and the metallic thuds of the main vents in the ballast tanks opening. Alone on the bridge Harding forced shut the two heavy voice-pipe cocks, feeling the spray thrown up by air jetting from the vents drifting down on him, then followed his look-outs and the officer of the watch into the conning tower. The hatch clapped shut above him he dropped rapidly down the ladder to the control room.

'We'll go to sixty feet for ten minutes, Number One. There should be reasonable periscope visibility after that.'

135

'Aye aye, sir.'

Trigger sounded, a great blue whale lying suspended sixty feet below the waves, waiting for the light which would draw her closer to the surface of the sea, waiting for a ship which had broken the rules of neutrality, waiting herself to break the rules of war. Her captain waited too, intensely nervous at the imminence of his first submerged torpedo attack in command, not showing it, concentrating so fully on not showing it that all knowledge of how to do what he had to do seemed to him to have been wiped from his mind. Of the target vessel there was nothing to fear, only of unthinkable failure. Harding stood motionless, thinking the unthinkable.

'Ten minutes, sir.'

'Thank you. Can you hear anything, McIntyre?'

'No, sir,' the chief sonar operator said. 'Quiet all round.'

'Very well. Periscope depth, Number One.'

'Sir.'

He watched the depth-gauge needles moving slowly back round their dials, then gestured with his hand when they showed thirty-eight feet. The forward periscope rose out of its well in obedience, he jerked its handles into the horizontal position, put his eyes to the binocular fitment and waited.

'Thirty-six feet, thirty-five, thirty-four,' Gascoigne chanted and the upper lens lifted clear of the small waves at the last number. Harding turned the periscope in a full circle, saw nothing but water, sky and the Spanish shoreline in the half light, then stopped the movement on the bearing of the port of Malaga.

'Now, that's what I call punctual,' he said. 'I thought we might have to hang about here for ages. She's leaving harbour now. Or, *a* ship is. It's still a bit dark for a positive identification.'

Despite his words Harding was positive enough. It was a big ship, seven or eight thousand tons of it which fitted with the information he had been given, the timing was what he had been told it should be and there was a large pale oblong shape on the side which, in all probability, was a painted replica of the light blue and white of the Argentine flag. He ordered the periscope lowered and looked at the electro-mechanical torpedo data computer known familiarly as the 'Fruit Machine', noting that Randolph had already set the masthead height provided by Intelligence on it. That piece of information was essential if the readings he would shortly take with the periscope range-finder were to be translated into the distance of the target from him.

'Start the attack, sir?' Walker asked.

'Not yet, Pilot. We'll wait until we're sure who she is and she's turned onto an easterly course and reached cruising speed.'

The anxiety that he might mess up the attack was still in Harding, but a precise awareness of what he had to do and how to do it had returned as though it had never been away.

'Up periscope,' he said and the clarity with which he heard its softly hissing rise made him realize how quiet the control room, the whole ship, had become, the breathing of the men near him clearly audible. He swung the periscope in a circle again and, as he did so, saw the rim of the sun top the horizon spilling daylight across the water towards him. It had reached the merchantman by the time he had completed his sweep.

Words poured out of Harding. 'It's the *Carlos Roca* all right. Start the attack. Port fifteen. Steer 360 degrees. I am twenty degrees on her starboard bow. The bearing is *that*.'

Behind him a petty officer wiped grease away from the vertical line etched into the column of the periscope where it passed through the pressure hull, noted its position against the azimuth ring set into the deckhead and called out 'Red 162'.

At the turn of a knurled knob between the finger and thumb of Harding's right hand the image of the ship in the periscope lens became two, one rising until its waterline rested on the tip of the mast of the other.

'And the range,' he said, 'is *that*.'

Peering over his shoulder at the little window of the range indicator the petty officer called out another number and Lieutenant Randolph fed them all to the 'Fruit Machine', then read out its message.

'Range five thousand eight hundred yards, sir. Distance off track seventeen hundred. Target's course 110 degrees.'

'I've got it now, sir. Same bearing as you. I think the sound of our own screws was blanketing it before. Reciprocating engine I think.' McIntyre's voice.

'Thank you, McIntyre.'

For seconds longer Harding stared at the approaching ship, then clicked the periscope's handles upright and watched it sink downwards. Because of its very simplicity he found the situation confusing. He was perfectly placed, had plenty of time and, unless the *Carlos Roca* altered course without reason, nothing much to do. It was quite unlike the 'Attack Teacher' at Fort Blockhouse in England, the submarine simulator set on dry land in which trainee commanders were subjected to images of fast-moving zig-zagging ships, poor visibility, destroyers casting like hounds on a scent and, if they did the wrong things, a barrage of thuds on the floor above produced by the Wren operators of the equipment triumphantly dropping weights. This indicated both depth-charging and the derision of the girls who, having long experience at their job, were often technically superior to the officers who passed through their hands.

Harding grinned fleetingly, nervously, at the memory and two sailors who saw him do it winked at each other. All was well. The skipper was enjoying himself again.

'Ship steady on 360, sir.'

'Thank you, Chivers. Up periscope.'

The day sparkling, the *Carlos Roca*, on *Trigger*'s port bow now, much larger in the lens, the periscope observation following the pattern of the one which had preceded it, but carried out more quickly to lessen the risk of being seen, Lieutenant Walker at the chart table saying, 'The plot suggests target course and speed 114 degrees and 10 knots, sir.'

'Use those figures,' Harding said, put his hands in his trouser pockets surreptitiously to wipe away the sweat gathering on the palms, and added, 'Stand by numbers 1,2, 3 and 4 tubes.'

The finality of the order swept confusion from him, but a sense of unreality replaced it, disbelief that he was about to murder people who were not attempting to murder him and his crew. That phase lasted only for seconds and ended with the acceptance that the blockade-runner was an accessory to murder.

The penultimate periscope observation coinciding with the words, 'Numbers 1, 2, 3 and 4 tubes standing by, sir.'

'Very well. Open bow caps.'

Three paces separated the two periscopes. He took them and stood by the after one with its monocular viewer and much thinner top.

'What's the Director Angle?'

'Red 7, sir. Bow caps open, sir.'

Harding waited, tension returning, fighting it with his will.

'Up 'scope.'

Head angled awkwardly to press the left eye against the monocular viewer, the freighter close, filling the lens.

'Put me on Red 7.'

Hands reaching from behind him to cover his own, edging the periscope to the right.

'You're on Red 7, sir.'

'Thank you.'

Only the merchantman's stem visible now, moving towards the hairline at the lens's centre. He could read the name *Carlos Roca* quite clearly.

'Fire 1,' Harding said.

*

The mate died first. Standing at the top of the bridge ladder, looking back at Malaga through his binoculars, the stunning concussion of the torpedo which struck No 2 Hold hurled him fourteen feet down onto the steel deck below and broke his back. When the second torpedo exploded alongside the engine room its blast killed two of the five men there instantly. The remaining three all had time to scream before the sea raging through the enormous hole blasted in the ship's side engulfed them. The *Carlos Roca* rolled to starboard and kept on rolling, tipping the master from his bunk. He didn't notice. He didn't even notice when he started to breathe water.

*

Harding's skin was tingling. Whether it was doing it from relief, reaction, excitement or anything else, he had no idea at all. It was just tingling.

'Tell the Torpedo Gunner's Mate to come and see what his fish have done,' he said. 'Here, Number One, you take a look, and the rest of you chaps use the other periscope if you want to.'

They wanted to, and man after man took his turn staring at the weed-streaked bottom of the *Carlos Roca* until the sea closed over it. *Trigger* went deep and moved silently seaward away from the small fleet of boats setting out from Malaga.

'Well, congratulations, sir,' Gascoigne said. 'That was a darned good attack.'

'You think so, do you?' Harding replied. 'Then let me tell you something. If, like Helen of Troy, we sink a thousand ships we'll never have an easier attack than that one.'

Momentarily disconcerted Gascoigne recovered quickly. 'Oh, I don't think she actually *sank* any ships, sir. She launched them, or caused them to be launched.'

'It must be wonderful to be so well informed,' Harding said and went to his cabin to work on his patrol report.

At the end of his account he wrote, 'Although this vessel was sunk a mile and a quarter outside Spanish territorial waters in the position recorded above, it is regretted that two of my torpedoes missed their target and ran on to explode on the coast of Spain. I can only hope that my inaccuracy will not lead to any difficulties with the authorities of a neutral power.' Having lied about the location of a sinking which had been only three thousand yards from the coast and having deliberately aimed one torpedo to miss ahead and another to miss astern in case he had under- or over-estimated the target's speed, Harding felt that he had done the best he could for the diplomats on whose plate the problem of placating the Spanish would land.

Harding put the papers away in a drawer and tried to write a letter to Agatha Bulstrode, but the emotional evening he had passed with her, followed by a night spent mostly on the bridge and the conflicting stresses imposed on him in the dawn which followed it, proved too much. Wanting permission to alter course to the east Gascoigne found him asleep with his cheek resting on the desk and his arms dangling. He withdrew quietly and, on his own initiative, told the helmsman to steer 090 degrees.

Fifteen fathoms beneath the surface of the Mediterranean *Trigger* turned in obedience to her rudder, pointing her bows towards a more official war.

Chapter Sixteen

'Welcome to Algiers,' Captain Anderson said. 'Sorry I wasn't aboard when you got here this morning. It isn't often we get a brand new submarine arriving having already got off the mark and flying the "Jolly Roger". I'd have liked to have seen that, but I've been tied up at a Combined Services meeting all day. Sit down.'

Harding sat, looking around him at the big day cabin and the flotilla captain went on, 'Before you say anything which might incriminate you I had better tell you that the Spaniards are extremely annoyed. Indeed, they're so angry about the *Carlos Roca* affair that they've demanded that you be disciplined.'

'Isn't that a little precipitate, sir?' Harding asked. 'I've heard a rumour that she was sunk by a Free French submarine.'

Captain Anderson nodded. 'So has the Foreign Office and they've been trying to sell that theory to Madrid for the past two weeks. No luck I'm afraid. Your departure from Gib was just too coincidental, so consider yourself severely reprimanded and deprived of one minute of seniority as a lieutenant. What about a drink? Gin? Whisky?'

'Gin and water please, sir,' Harding said and smiled faintly. He felt that he was going to like his new commanding officer.

'Your name's Peter, isn't it?'

'Yes, sir.'

'Fine. What did you do after the *Carlos Roca* business? I haven't seen your patrol report yet.'

'Thank you, sir,' Harding said, took the drink handed to him, then went on, 'We went up to Barcelona first and did a lot of submerged practice attacks on Spanish shipping. Didn't see anything else until we found an Italian anti-submarine trawler to the east of Minorca. The crew abandoned ship as soon as we surfaced and shot off in a motorboat, so I put a party on board to collect papers and things. There were a couple of code books which may or may not be of any interest. I gave them to the red-headed lieutenant-commander in the staff office, sir.'

'Yes, that's "Ginger" Donaldson.'

'Well, after that we stood off and sank it with the 4-inch, sir. I could have set it on fire of course and saved ammunition, but I wanted to exercise the gun's crew.'

'Fair enough.'

'Oh, we did take one prisoner from the trawler, sir.' Harding added. 'Name of Benito. At least, that's what we called him until he had six kittens on the way here. I suppose it will have to be changed to Benita now. Anyway, the whole family has been transferred to your chief petty officers' mess.'

Captain Anderson laughed and said 'Fair enough' again.

*

A sack of mail for *Trigger*'s crew had been delivered aboard minutes after she had secured alongside the depot ship that morning. The Navy was very good about that. Of all the things it took a struggle to extract from authority, mail was not one. A letter with the recipient's name on it was delivered to him quickly, somehow, somewhere. Harding was well aware of this from personal experience, but was astonished on emerging onto the quarter-deck from Captain Anderson's day cabin to be given an envelope bearing his name and inscribed 'By hand of officer'. He was more than astonished to see that the officer wore United States Air Force wings on his tunic and eagle insignia on his shoulders.

'Thank you, Colonel,' he said. 'Where did this come from?'

'Gibraltar, Lieutenant. I flew in from there a half hour ago.'

'Really? Well, come and have a drink, sir.'

'Gladly,' the colonel told him, 'but maybe you should read it first.'

The sun had set and when Harding had ripped the envelope open he held the letter out under the arc lamp illuminating the quarter-deck gangway. The first lines told him that Bill Bulstrode, ex-captain of *Shadow*, ex-captain of *Tarquin*, was going to live and he read no further.

'It's very good news, Colonel,' he said and put the letter in his pocket. 'Now, let's go to the wardroom and have a drink and something to eat. I certainly owe you that.'

The evening passed pleasantly, the American admitting to an ulterior motive in not entrusting the envelope to one of his junior officers. His never having seen the inside of a submarine was easily remedied, and when he walked with him to his jeep two hours later Harding had acquired a new friend. Now he was sitting in the cabin allocated to him aboard the depot ship reading the letter for the third time feeling bemused, embarrassed and very guilty.

'Dear Peter Harding,

Aggie wishes you to be told immediately that Bill Bulstrode is out of danger having undergone a successful amputation of his right leg. Other wounds to his neck and chest are no longer a matter of concern. I received her news by signal from Beirut where I recently arranged to have her flown (rank hath its privileges) and hasten to pass it on to you as she requests.

You will, no doubt, be wondering why I should employ such a complicated method of communicating with you when a signal would have sufficed. The reason is that I am the person she described to you as her 'chap' and, certain difficulties having been disposed of, shortly to become her husband.

Now, as you know well, an Aggie in distress is not only so unusual as to be a virtually unique manifestation of the improbable, it is also, such is her metal, an affront to nature. Bill Bulstrode, to my mild envy, is closer to her than anybody else on earth, taking the place of a brother so much older than she. This you surmised and I would ask you to accept the thanks of an older man for what, when she thought he was dying, you did and did

143

not do for her. Having listened to her detailed description of the
incident (that's Aggie for you) the latter can't have been easy.
    Please do me the further courtesies of destroying this letter and
refraining from acknowledging it.
    Yours ever,
    Charles Chandos.'

'Bloody hell,' Harding whispered to himself, hearing again the voice of
the sailor at the dockyard gate in Gibraltar saying, 'You wouldn't happen
to be the captain of *Trigger*, would you sir?' the voice which had stopped
him going back to Agatha Bulstrode's flat and, inevitably, into her bed.

Slowly he tore Admiral Sir Charles Chandos's letter into tiny pieces and
dropped them into the waste basket then sat, staring at nothing, disturbed
less by an error narrowly avoided than by being credited with a degree of
probity he did not believe he possessed. He had forgotten all about his
agonized search for 'the decent thing'.

After a little he stopped thinking about himself and found pleasure
flowing into him from outside, gladness that Bill Bulstrode would live,
delight that Agatha Bulstrode would soon be Lady Chandos and the wife
of a national hero. That, to him, seemed eminently fitting.

*

'I simply can't understand how anybody could ever go down in one of those
things,' the girl said. 'I'd have absolute kittens!'

Gascoigne watched her, thinking that she really was rather attractive
sitting there in her white dress across the pavement café table from him.
Not beautiful, but attractive. Comfortable too with nice curves in nice
places even if there was a little too much of her. Yes, 'comfortable' was the
word. Comfortable and bouncy.

'We liberated a cat recently,' he told her, 'and it did just that.'

'Did just what?'

'Had absolute kittens. Six of them.'

'Oh, do be serious. Don't you get the most awful claustrophobia?'

A sensual mouth, Gascoigne thought, and a welcoming bosom. Very welcoming. Try for bed? No, don't rush this one. Only met her an hour ago. Where did one go in Algiers anyway?

'No we don't,' he said. 'If we did we'd have to leave and do something else.'

'But why do it at all? It must be frightfully dangerous. Please don't say "Because somebody has to". You're all volunteers, aren't you?'

'Yes. Well, nearly all of us.'

She looked genuinely interested, even concerned, so Gascoigne decided against the standard flippant reply about the pay being good.

'It's exciting,' he went on, 'but I suppose that the biggest attraction, for officers at least, is that it's the quickest way of getting command of a powerful warship. My own skipper is only twenty-four and a half.'

Eyes attractive as well, particularly when their lids drooped in that compassionate way.

'That's sweet,' she said.

'*Sweet?*' Voice startled, nettled.

'Oh, don't misunderstand me, John. I didn't mean your captain being so young. I meant the half. Like a small boy telling you he'll be five and two months next Tuesday.'

The expression on Gascoigne's face told her that she had gone altogether too far and she added hastily, 'So the lure of command is enough to make you go through all that awful depth-charging and everything, is it? It's incredible what men will do!'

Mollified, as he was meant to be, 'Depth-charging isn't too bad if it doesn't go on too long,' Gascoigne said. 'There are worse things.'

'Like what?'

He thought about that for a moment before saying, 'Bad weather. The things are designed to go under the water, not on it, so in a storm it's essential to hold on to something every step you take, or you're liable to break a bone. Gets a bit tiring after a bit, particularly as if you aren't soaking wet to begin with you will be when your soup lands in your lap. It wouldn't be so bad if you were actually going somewhere with a harbour at the other end, but just staying in the same place for three weeks waiting for something to happen is very boring.'

'Goodness! I can believe that!'

'The chaps have a saying,' Gascoigne went on. 'If you're thrown off the lavatory it's rough. If the thing's moving about too much for you to sit on it in the first place it's very rough.'

He had hoped to get a little of his own back by shocking her, but all she did was laugh happily.

Yes, Tessa Brown told him, she would like to see him again the next day. No, he need not see her home. She'd take a gharry from the rank at the end of the road if he'd walk with her that far. Pleased with himself and the world in general, Gascoigne went with her, wondering if her surname was really Brown. She had hesitated a little before saying it. He smiled, enjoying the small touch of conspiracy.

*

From inside a bar along the street Chief Petty Officer Ryland and Chief Yeoman Yarrow watched Gascoigne pass.

'"Jimmy the One" ain't wasted no time findin' 'imself a piece of 'omework,' Ryland said.

Yarrow nodded. 'Nice-looking slice of crumpet too. Not up to the standard of that half-pint pocket-size Venus the Skipper had in Gib, but nice. Talking of pints, would you like some more of this slush, 'Swain?'

'No, Lofty, I wouldn't,' Ryland told him. 'Bloody foreign muck. Still, as we don't 'ave no option I'll try to gag another down.'

Nodding again Yarrow stood and made his way carefully to the bar counter to collect their eleventh beer.

*

'How soon can you sail, Peter?'

Still blinking sleep from his eyes, feeling silly standing barefoot in the staff office wearing pyjamas and dressing-gown, Harding looked at his watch.

'Not for another three and a half hours, sir. Some of my crew were granted all-night leave. They won't be back aboard until 0800.'

Captain Anderson almost smiled. 'You won't have to leave in quite that much of a rush. I only wanted to know if you'd fuelled, embarked torpedoes, stored ship and had no major defects.'

'Yes to the first three and no to the last, sir. We're ready. What's up, sir?'

Without speaking the flotilla captain walked to the bulkhead and drew aside the curtain covering the big wall-chart there. It showed the central Mediterranean from Sardinia in the west to Sicily in the east and from Tunisia in the south to Genoa in the north. Known and suspected minefields were marked on it, hatched in red. Submarine patrol areas were shown too, each containing a flag with a name on it indicating the submarine's estimated position at midnight. *Tarn, Tarantula, Tusker, Tiger-shark, Tornado*, Harding read, spread from the Franco-Italian border to the west of Sicily.

'The S-boats and the U-class from Malta are covering the rest,' Captain Anderson said and drew an oval with his finger enclosing an area from the Straits of Messina to the Tunisian Gulf of Hammamet, then asked, 'Got the picture?'

'Sir?'

Anderson glanced at his staff officer. 'Yes, Ginger?'

'Peter spent all of yesterday in here reading other boats' patrol reports, but we didn't touch on the military situation. Didn't seem much point as *Trigger* wasn't due to leave for five days.'

'Of course. Silly of me,' Anderson said. 'Listen to me, Peter. We're on the verge of a stunning victory. It's the end for the Germans in North Africa. 8th Army has smashed through Rommel's Mareth Line here and taken Sousse, the Anglo-American Free French forces in the west have reached this arc and a quarter of a million Axis troops are being compressed into this area.' His finger prodded the chart as he spoke. 'Those troops are to be permitted neither to be evacuated nor reinforced by sea, hence this particular deployment of our submarines.'

'It looks a pretty tight net to me, sir.'

The flotilla captain made slow affirmative movements with his head as though considering the statement before saying, 'So it was.' He paused there, then added, '*Tarn*'s gone and *Saurian* too. We've only just heard.'

*

Harding watched the massive semi-circular ends of the seawall seeming to slide past to either side of *Trigger*'s conning tower just as they had done less than twenty-six hours before, but in the opposite direction now. When they met the open sea the bows reacted not at all to the little waves of the Mediterranean spring day, simply parting them to swirl aft along the ballast tanks in translucent slicks of white water. Beside him Yarrow's Aldis lamp clicked out the letter 'R'.

'Depot ship says "Good luck", sir.'

'Make "Thank you".'

The clicking again, the words 'Message sent, sir' and the sound of a shuddering yawn. Harding looked at the chief yeoman, noted the pallor of his face.

'Are you all right, Yarrow?'

'No, not really, sir,' Yarrow said. 'The Cox'n and me made pigs of ourselves drinking the local battery acid last night. We wasn't expecting to sail this morning. Leastways, not into a screaming gale like this.'

'Never mind, Chief Yeoman. We'll be diving shortly and you can get your head down.'

'Not me, sir,' Yarrow replied. 'My old mum will want to hear that I died on my feet.'

Harding grinned.

Four miles from the coast, columns of spray soared up from *Trigger*'s main vents and the sunlight played rainbows with them until they vanished. Then there was only the sea and the sky and the gulls.

Chapter Seventeen

Across the length and breadth of London the eerie monotone wail of the sirens announced the 'all clear' and Harding tried to stretch his cramped legs, but could not because of the girl's weight. It didn't matter. Nobody had restored electric power to the air raid shelter and it was very pleasant there in the darkness with his arms round her and his hands, where she had guided them for comfort when it seemed the bombing must destroy them both, cupping her breasts inside her clothes. Darling Lee Lawrence. Beautiful golden American girl.

The shelter was no longer jerking to the concussion of exploding bombs and no bits of ceiling were falling on them, but the vibration was very noticeable, which was strange as the anti-aircraft guns had fallen silent and…

'Christ Almighty!' Harding said and rolled out of his bunk onto the deck, the fading note of the ship's almost ultra-sonic alarm still sounding in his ears. He was only halfway to his feet when his cabin door slid open and banged against its stops.

'Cap'n to the bridge, sir!'

'Coming,' he said.

Men pushing past each other in both directions on the way to their stations in the narrow passageway outside, someone shouting, 'Gangway there! Make way for the Captain!' shouldering a path into the dimly red-lit control room, cannoning into somebody, ridiculously saying 'Sorry', grasping the sides of the conning tower ladder, beginning to climb with the down-draught of air feeding the racing diesels flattening his hair about his face and the brass rungs hurting his bare feet. It seemed a very long climb to the top.

Drifting rain and nearly total blackness met him when he pulled himself through the upper hatch onto the bridge, then sidled between an unidentifiable look-out and the forward periscope standard to its front. The officer of the watch very tall. Must be Gascoigne.

'What's up, Number One?'

'Destroyer we think, sir. Another ship too. They came out of a rain squall around the north side of Levanzo Island. I've turned stern on.'

'Right. After look-outs, any sign of them now?'

'No, sir.' Two voices almost in unison.

'Who made the sighting?'

'Chivers, sir,' Gascoigne said.

'Any impressions, Olivers?'

Still not knowing who was who in the darkness, in which direction *Trigger* had turned, or on what bearing the enemy had been seen, Harding jumped when Able Seaman Chivers spoke from directly behind him.

'Not very clear ones, sir. Two dark shapes, longish. Different sizes, sir, like a big ship and a smaller one. At least I think so because I'm pretty sure the smaller was nearer and that it turned towards us. The silhouette shortened like, sir. A lot, sir. Not like a zig.'

'Could it have turned away?'

There were several seconds of silence before Chivers replied, 'I don't think so, sir. That would have had it pointing almost straight at the bigger feller which don't make sense, sir.'

'Well done, Chivers,' Harding said. 'Tell them to warm up the radar, Number One.'

Night vision improving, but not much to see in the rainy night with its negligible visibility. Brain activity improving too, the drug of sleep and the other vision, the female one, releasing their hold. The Italians reported to be almost totally ineffectual at detecting radar transmissions. So use radar. Damn. Mind not clear yet. That decision already taken on the assumption that *Trigger* has been sighted, therefore electronic silence pointless with his presence already known. Which way would the enemy have been heading? From Sicily to Tunisia? The other way? Probably the first, but…

'Radar standing by, sir.'

'Tell them to transmit for just long enough to give us the picture, then switch off at once.'

Hearing his orders repeated into the voice-pipe, drizzle constantly clouding the lenses of his binoculars, wiping them clear with tissue. Nothing to be seen. Feet cold.

'Tell somebody to bring up my shoes and socks, Number One.'

Gascoigne surprised, saying 'Good heavens!' relaying the message, adding, 'And send up a towel and an oilskin as well.'

'Radar-Bridge!'

'Bridge here.'

'Targets bearing 260 to 270 degrees, sir. One large blip and three small ones. The nearest is a small blip bearing 265 range 3,200 yards. The big blip bears 270 range 4,800. I didn't wait to range the other two, sir, but they're further away.'

Harding let his near-useless binoculars dangle from the strap about his neck, turned and bent to the voice-pipe. He had more efficient eyes now.

'Thank you, radar,' he said. 'Stand by to transmit again at my order.'

'Aye aye, sir. Sir! I'm getting hostile transmissions from their bearing now!'

'That means we haven't much time,' Harding murmured to nobody in particular, then more loudly, 'Port 20, Cox'n. Steer 290.'

Trigger swinging fast, her stern appearing to skid sideways across the flat sea, the rain stopping, starting again, Harding drying his feet, pulling on socks and shoes, ordering another radar scan, Ryland's voice saying, 'Steady on 290, sir,' more ranges, more bearings from the radar operator.

'Stand by numbers 1, 2, 3, 4, 5 and 6 tubes,' Harding said and began to chew his lip, remembering the theory he had expressed to the flotilla captain in Scotland that in poor visibility like this a submarine commander's proper place was at the radar set, not putting it into practice because it would be unfair to expect Gascoigne to handle emergencies of which he had little experience. He frowned at the thought, wondering what made him think that he was any better equipped to deal with them himself, but made no move to leave the bridge.

'Cap'n, sir?' The voice-pipe.

'Yes?'

'Navigator here, sir. The plot suggests that the enemy is steaming due west to pass north of Marettimo Island at a speed of nine knots. Their disposition seems to be a large vessel with a smaller one ahead and a smaller one on either side. Sort of arrowhead formation, sir, with the port flanker nearer to us than the starboard one. That's probably the destroyer that turned towards us, but it seems to have turned back to rejoin the others now. You're overtaking fast, angled twenty degrees to starboard of their track.'

'Thank you, Pilot,' Harding said. 'Course to rejoin their track for an attack from directly astern of the main target about 265 degrees?'

'Make it 260, sir. You're getting very close.'

'Very well. Cox'n steer 260. Are those tubes standing by yet?'

'Steer 260. Yessir, they are. I was waitin' until you and the Navigatin' Officer 'ad finished chattin' to tell you.'

A feeling of mild amusement coupled with slight irritation, the amusement gaining the upper hand because Ryland didn't know what sarcasm was and had simply been stating a fact. A feeling of positive pleasure at having socks and shoes on his feet recognized as a trick of the mind to distract it from its fear of a situation about which he knew too little and which was developing too fast. A feeling that the enemy's radar could not possibly be as ineffective as it appeared to be, that this was some sort of trap, pushed aside as nonsense for they would have done something about it had they been aware of his presence.

No longer willing to deprive *Trigger* of her eyes even should their gaze be felt, 'Set permanent radar watch,' Harding said. 'Use relative bearings, not compass.'

Almost immediately, 'Large blip bearing Green 5, sir. Range 1,400 yards. Nearest small blip Red 50 at 1,200 yards. Another on Green 45 at 1,800. Can't see the third escort, sir. Probably shielded by the ship ahead.'

'Very well,' Harding replied. 'Update that information every thirty seconds, or immediately if you suspect an alteration in course. Control room, steer 265 and open bowcaps.'

The vibration, the hiss of the sea swirling along the ballast tanks, the rain, heavier now, sweeping out of the darkness straight into his face, all added to Harding's impression of speed and to his sense of urgency, urgency now becoming extreme. A vessel, presumably a destroyer, close to port. Another further away to starboard. A third somewhere ahead of the invisible target ship *Trigger* was careering after. The voice-pipe talking almost constantly, telling him that the bowcaps of the torpedo tubes were open, telling him what the navigating officer's carefully pencilled lines and figures on the chart assessed the situation to be, telling him what radar knew of the ranges and bearings of his adversaries. Only his slitted eyes seemed incapable of telling him anything even with the help of his powerful Barr and Stroud binoculars.

For a few moments he closed his mind to the influx of information, ears alert only for a change of tone in the tinny voice which might indicate alarm. During those seconds he considered firing blind by radar with the assistance of a check-bearing from Petty Officer McIntyre's sonar set, but abandoned the idea. There had been too little time to establish the enemy's course accurately and without that a bearing alone was insufficient to ensure a hit. The alternative was clear enough. Break away at once, speed ahead of the little convoy throughout what was left of the night, dive at dawn and carry out a standard submerged attack by periscope. That lengthened the odds against him because the target had a formidable number of escorts and their sonar was likely to be much more effective than their rudimentary radar, but he had to accept those odds.

Harding was bending towards the voice-pipe to order the pursuit abandoned when the starboard forward look-out said, 'Darkened ship bearing dead ahead! Budge over a bit, sir!'

Surprised at the words, but doing as he was told, Harding surrendered the exact centre of the bridge to the sailor, listened to him say, 'Yeah! I reckon our bow is exactly bisecting his arse, sir!'

It was then that he ordered the first torpedo fired. When five more had followed it towards a ship that only Able Seaman Chivers and radar had seen, *Trigger* began to swing in a great arc towards an opposite course, away from a vessel about to die and the thousands of men who would die with her. Harding didn't know about that yet. Not quite yet.

Trigger's turn was little more than a quarter completed when the flat, unemphatic boom of an explosion reached his ears over the hiss of rain and sea and the throb of the diesels.

'Sharp underwater explosion, sir. Possible torpedo,' the voice-pipe told him.

'Thank you,' Harding said. The detonation would, he knew, have been far clearer down below as the sea carried sound more effectively and much faster than the atmosphere, but it was with alarm and a momentary total lack of understanding that his eyes registered the second hit before its sound came to him, a tall column of water, brilliantly illuminated, rising above an already listing ship.

It resembled a theatrical set, he thought. A single actor pinned by flood-lights to a darkened stage like a butterfly to a collector's board, except that this specimen was under attack by hordes of ants spreading across it in a remorseless tide.

'Second underwater explosion, sir.' The voice-pipe again.

'Yes, we see it,' Harding answered, then added, 'Radar, we've all had our night vision ruined up here. The destroyers have their searchlights trained on the target. I want to cover as much distance on the surface as possible, so you're our only eyes. Understood?'

'Understood, sir. The blips appear to be converging on each other at the moment, sir, and the big one's getting bigger.'

'Yes, well keep watching them and everything else too.'

'Aye aye, sir.'

The target blip would certainly be showing bigger on the radar screen, Harding knew, with the bows of the stricken ship lifting clear of the water, rising higher and higher as the stern settled. The carpet of ants moving faster as the angle increased, the tiny figures of soldiers, hundreds upon hundreds of soldiers, sliding, rolling, tumbling across the decks and dropping into the sea, more replacing them, appearing through hatches and doorways in steady streams. The scene momentarily obscured by the black shape of a fast-moving destroyer silhouetted against its own lights, then revealed again in time for the six men on *Trigger*'s bridge to witness the final act of submission with their quarry, hurrying now as if anxious to be done with the play, sliding downwards, vanishing from their sight. A collective sigh came from them.

'The big blip's gone from the radar screen, sir,' the voice-pipe said. 'Ship steady on 090 degrees, sir,' Ryland's voice added. Harding said 'Thank you' twice and that was when the searchlights blinked out one after the other and the depth-charging started.

'Oh no,' Harding whispered, then speaking sharply, 'Radar, are the three destroyers still in the same position?'

'Yessir. They seem to be milling about on our starboard quarter. Range and bearing are…'

'It doesn't matter,' Harding broke in. 'Just keep an all-round watch for the next five minutes, then switch off. We'll have our night vision back by that time.'

He turned and stared at the blackness astern, aware once more of rain in his face, rain he hadn't noticed for long minutes, hearing and feeling the sea erupt under successive patterns of depth-charges.

Almost but not quite under his breath, 'The rotten, panicky, bastard Wops,' he said.

'Sir?'

Harding glanced at Gascoigne's tall figure beside him, then away again.

'They don't know what the hell's going on, Number One. They don't have the least idea where we are, so they've persuaded themselves that they've got a sonar contact on a submerged submarine and are blasting away at a figment of their imagination to salvage their stinking pride. They make me want to vomit!'

'Yes, sir.'

'Yes, sir! Yes, sir!' Harding said. 'Don't you realize that there are hundreds of German soldiers in the water back there? Don't you know what depth-charges do to swimmers? I'll tell you what they do! The lucky ones are having their spines snapped! The unlucky ones are having their stomachs burst open! All right, so it's our job to kill Germans but I wouldn't wish that on them even if they are our worst enemy, not done by their own side I wouldn't! Those destroyers should be doing their utmost to pick them up and…' He paused there, then added quietly, 'I'm sorry, Number One. At least it'll save 8th Army the trouble of killing them.'

'There's always that, sir,' Gascoigne replied, 'but I entirely agree with what you've said. I was a bit too excited to think of it for myself.'

155

Lieutenant Walker's voice saying, 'Cap'n, sir. Urgent signal for us.'

Harding bent to the voice-pipe. 'Read it, Pilot.'

'Yes, sir. "7,000-ton ship escorted by three destroyers departed Trapani, Sicily, at midnight for Tunis carrying 4,400 troops. Do utmost intercept and destroy. Advise situation by 0500 for benefit *Tiger-shark* to the south of you". That's all, sir.'

Tiredly, 'Very well, Pilot,' Harding said. 'Reply "Your signal number so-and-so. Troopship sunk by torpedo". Add the time and position. All right?'

'Yes, sir.'

Trigger turned to the north and her crew left their action stations, but her captain stayed on the bridge for another half an hour before clambering slowly down the ladder to the control room. When he got there he stood, trying to recall what it was he had left undone. After a moment he remembered and walked through the ship to the torpedo stowage compartment forward. Men got to their feet when he entered it.

'No, sit down everybody' Harding said. 'Is Chivers around?'

'Here, sir.'

'Ah, Chivers. That was extremely well done.'

'Oh. Thank you, sir.'

'I shall report it of course.'

'Thank you very much, sir.'

Harding nodded and left.

In his cabin he sat for a long time staring at the bulkhead before suddenly whispering, 'Four thousand four hundred. Dear God.' Then he frowned at the words he had used. Harding had decided that if God existed he, personally, didn't want to know Him.

Chapter Eighteen

'All in all,' Harding wrote, 'this must rank as one of the most "By guess and by God", hit or miss submarine attacks of the war and the entire credit for its success belongs to Able Seaman Chivers.'

He paused there, chewing his pencil, before writing, 'Finally, I have to record my disgust at the criminally hysterical behaviour of the escorting destroyers whose panic reaction to the loss of the ship in their charge resulted in…' Then, grunting impatiently, Harding obliterated the lines. Nobody would be interested in his disgust.

Six days had gone by, six days during which *Trigger* had patrolled the waters to the west of Sicily. Only two things of interest had happened in that time, the interception of a 900-ton coaster off Marsala which Leading Seaman Peters and his gun's crew had reduced so effectively to scrap-iron with the 4-inch that Harding had not bothered to remain in the vicinity to see it sink, and the pin-pointing of an enemy radar station on the island of Marettimo. The latter came as a relief to Harding who had been unable to understand how the destroyers in company with the troopship had so utterly failed to detect his presence however embryonic their radar might have been. Now it was reasonable to assume that they had been maintaining radar silence and that the transmissions *Trigger* had intercepted had come not from them but the island. He amended his patrol report accordingly.

Now, with *Tiger-shark* recalled to Algiers to rest, *Trigger* had replaced her off Cape Bon, the easterly arm of the Gulf of Tunis. It was a lovely day in the fourth week of April when the strange planes appeared above the northern horizon. Randolph sighted them. Walker identified them.

157

Harding and Gascoigne witnessed their execution.

'Jameson, ask the Captain if he'd come here for a minute,' Randolph said.

When Harding arrived from the direction of the wardroom, Randolph stepped away from the periscope and gestured towards it.

'Mind taking a look, sir?'

It was hardly an orthodox way of reporting a sighting and Harding glanced at him curiously before approaching the periscope, adjusting the binocular to suit the distance apart of his own eyes and looking through it.

'Well I'll be damned. What on earth are they?'

'I'll be as damned as you, sir. I haven't got a clue, but Walker might. Aircraft identification is a hobby of his.'

'Send for him.'

Waiting for his navigating officer Harding watched the stately advance of sixteen of the largest aircraft he had ever seen, vast high-wing monoplanes propelled by six engines which, from their altitude, appeared to be having difficulty in keeping the enormous machines in the air.

'Sir?'

In his turn Harding stood back from the periscope and said, 'Indulge your hobby, Pilot, and tell me if you know what these gigantic things are.'

Five seconds later, 'That's what the Germans call them, sir. "Gigants",' Walker told him. 'The official designation is Me323. Messerschmitt built them as towed gliders first, then they stuck on those six French Gnôme-Rhône radial engines. They have a crew of twelve and are the biggest aeroplane in the world, sir, except for the Russian Tupolev ANT-20 which…'

He stopped talking at Harding's quiet, 'All right, all right. I did ask, but I don't actually need to know their tyre pressures. What are they? Troop-carriers?'

'Yes, I think so, sir.'

'Okay, let me have another look.'

The aerial juggernauts were closer now, flying about five hundred feet above the sea directly towards the submarine. Gascoigne wandered into the control room and asked what was going on.

'Take a look through the after periscope, Number One.'

Gascoigne signalled for the periscope to be raised, swung it onto the bearing, looked and said 'Good grief! What are they?'

Walker told him.

'I see. Sir, they seem to be moving awfully slowly. What about surfacing and letting Chivers have a crack at them with the Oerlikon?'

'They each carry at least ten machine-guns, Number One.' Walker sounded surprised that Gascoigne did not have that fact at his fingertips and added, 'That makes a hundred and sixty machine-guns altogether.'

'There you are, Number One,' Harding said. 'The Pilot's amazing talent for mental arithmetic seems to answer your question.' He began to make a careful all-round sweep of the horizon, searching it for enemy shipping, then suddenly froze and murmured, 'Oh boy. Just look at those fighters.'

The Spitfires came out of the south, almost skimming the surface of the sea, arrowing towards the enemy planes, cannon-fire sparkling along the leading edges of their wings. Harding just glimpsed the roundels of the RAF as the fighters flashed past and he jerked the periscope round to follow their progress. Quick as he was he was still too slow to witness the first encounter. The Spitfires had disappeared from his field of view and five expanding balls of orange fire met his astonished gaze, balls that grew like exploding suns until they filled the periscope lens. He heard the sound of breath expelled between teeth and realized that it was his own.

The burning suns dipped down to the water, reached it, flattened like collapsing balloons, spreading, joining to form one long, unbroken line of blazing sea. Four other Me 323s descended less spectacularly, trailing smoke, broad splashes marking where they struck. The remains of the air armada, its pattern broken, separated slowly, lethargically, as though despairing of each other's company and of life itself.

'Here come the Spits again!' Gascoigne said.

The fighters were in pairs now, not in the precise echelon formation of their first strike. Five more suns lived briefly, then the Spitfires were streaking back the way they had come like hornets reacting to a queenly command from their nest leaving, as though beneath contempt, the last two Gigants wallowing in the air.

'Petrol,' Harding said. 'Petrol for the *Wehrmacht*. Not troops. That's what they were carrying.' He watched the two periscopes slide down into their wells before turning to Walker.

'So much for your hundred and sixty machine-guns, Pilot. I don't think any of those Spits were even dented.'

'Oh, I agree, sir,' Walker replied. 'They're no use against fighters. That's exactly what the US 8th Air Force has been finding out with its unescorted daylight raids over Germany. Awful losses. You need fighters to oppose fighters. All I meant was that Chivers might have found it a bit much.'

Harding smiled. 'Point taken. You seem to know a lot about aeroplanes.'

'That's thanks to my uncle, sir. He's a "commode". I mean he's an RAF air commodore and he sends me loads of gen about planes.'

'Isn't that secret information?'

'Our own and American stuff is secret, sir. He doesn't tell me about that, just what's generally available on the enemy.'

Nodding, Harding stared at the deck for a moment, the after-image of the fire-balls still alive on his retinas. He felt no distress at the memory of the massacre. Those Germans had died at the hands of their opponents, not of their own side, and that made it all right.

'Come round to starboard onto 045,' he said. 'We'd better see if there are any survivors from the ones that didn't blow up.'

Like the head and neck of some strange rigid water snake, the periscope moved through patches of floating debris and oil. There was no life to be seen on the surface of the sea and it was sixteen miles away and twenty-one hours later before *Trigger* found any.

*

More water slopped over the side of the rubber dinghy to join the pool swirling around in its bottom and the man with the sodden cigar in his mouth muttered, 'Great. Just great,' took off his cap and began to scoop it back into the sea. The other two watched him morosely. One of them had dropped the bailer some hours earlier and it had sunk before they could retrieve it. Now they took turns using the man with the cigar's cap as only he had one and he put it straight back on his head as soon as the job was done.

The man who had dropped the bailer said, 'Why don't you take that goddam cigar out of your face, fatso?'

Still scooping water, 'Because it fits my image, that's why,' the other replied. 'Intrepid air ace battling with the elements.'

'Jesus, what elements? I've seen it rougher than this on the lake in Central Park. The Air Force never figured on guys like you when they designed these rafts. If you weren't so goddam fat we…'

'Cut it out, O'Halloran.'

The third man had spoken with quiet authority.

'Sure. Sorry, boss.'

'You keep on the way you've been going the past five hours and you'll be a darned sight sorrier when we get ashore. If you must talk keep it pleasant or…'

'Boss! We have company!'

Both looked at the man with the cigar, followed the direction of his gaze and saw the periscope, a white wake marking its passage through the sea.

'Jesus! A goddam U-boat!'

'Not necessarily. Could be one of ours.'

'No way. They're all in the goddam Pacific.'

'A Limey boat then!'

'Cut it out,' the quiet man said for the second time. 'We'll soon know.'

A prolonged rumbling, the dinghy quivering as if in anticipation, then a great dark-blue shape rearing out of a sea suddenly churned into foam. Men appearing as if by magic even before the water had drained from it, clambering down to the long deck, running forward. A heaving-line snaking through the air and dropping across the rocking dinghy. An English voice shouting, 'Don't sit there like a collection of ruptured ducks! Somebody grab hold of that line!' The quiet man grasping it, making it secure. The dinghy pulled alongside, hands reaching down, gripping. Another voice saying, 'Up you come, mate.' Feet scrabbling for purchase on wet sloping steel, not finding it, but going upwards anyway drawn by the wrists. 'I've got him, Norris. Grab the next one.' A third voice. Legs rubbery from hours of crouching in the dinghy, but a man to either side taking the weight. A confused impression of clambering up the side of a vertical tower, then into a hatchway and down a long brass ladder into a compartment filled with dials, levers, brass columns and men. A fourth voice saying, 'Come this way, please.' Following him and sinking thankfully down onto a padded seat, the other two joining him. 'Well, how about that?' Lieutenant-Colonel David Furness said.

All of them standing again, stripping off wet clothing, when a sailor arrived with an armful of towels, sweaters, trousers, underwear and socks. Others followed with pairs of shoes, about a dozen of them. 'You might find something that fits in that lot, sir.' Somebody else ladling soup into mugs, handing them round. An officer pouring whisky into glasses.

'You shouldn't have gone to all that trouble, Colonel.'

Furness looked at the grinning bearded face of a man wearing grease-stained khaki slacks and a shirt which bore no badges of rank.

'How's that again? What trouble?'

'Delivering letters "by hand of officer". You needn't have paddled all this way in a dinghy. I could have waited until we got back to harbour.'

Incredulously, 'Well, how about that? *How* about that?' the colonel said. 'It's Harding! Peter Harding! I didn't recognize you with all that fur on your face! And if that outfit you're wearing is a British Navy uniform it's a new one on me!'

Shaking the hand held out to him, 'Not many of us bother to shave on patrol,' Harding told him, 'and we wear whatever is comfortable.'

'How about that?' the American said yet again. 'Boy! Am I glad you happened by. And that goes for these two cretins here as well. Their names are Winnick and O'Halloran, both entitled to describe themselves as lieu-tenants on account of some administrative foul-up back home. Gentlemen, this is Peter Harding, captain of His Majesty's submersible craft *Trigger* which I have had the privilege of visiting before. I can tell from the naked dames on the lampshade, even if the skipper is in disguise.'

It was twenty minutes later when, clothes changed, soup and whisky drunk, the man called Winnick with the chewed remnants of a dead cigar still clenched between his teeth addressed himself to Harding.

'Cap'n, I'd appreciate it if you'd give us the word before you crash-dive this thing. I've seen it done on the movies and it looks mighty scary. You know, just so I can hold my breath and maybe the Colonel hold my hand.'

Harding smiled and said, 'There's no such thing as a crash-dive. That's newspaper talk. All dives are carried out as fast as possible.' He jerked a thumb in the direction of the wardroom depth-gauge behind him and added, 'Anyway, don't worry about it. You've had thirty feet of water over your head for the last half an hour. We didn't sound the diving klaxon in case it made you jump. It's rather noisy.'

Winnick glanced at the gauge, angled his cigar upwards, leered at O'Halloran and asked, 'How about this one, Pat? Intrepid submariner withstanding colossal pressure.' O'Halloran made no reply and Winnick went on, 'If that isn't the darnedest thing, Cap'n. I'd never had known if you…' He stopped talking at the sight of Harding's rapidly retreating back and shrugged before adding, 'Guess my image must have scared him.'

'Why'd he take off like that, boss?' O'Halloran wanted to know.

'I think I heard somebody call for him. Captain to the control room or somesuch.'

'Oh.'

Within seconds the words 'Diving stations. Diving stations,' came metal-lically from the Tannoy public address speaker and the flyers listened to the stamp of feet and watched sailors hurrying past the gap in the wardroom curtains. Then all movement ceased and there was only the faint hum of the ventilation system to be heard.

'What the hell's with this diving stations bit?' O'Halloran said. 'The kid told us we were already under water.'

Winnick nodded in puzzled agreement.

'It's their expression for "battle stations",' Furness told the two lieuten-ants. 'He explained that to me when I was aboard in Algiers. And don't call him "the kid". He may look like one, but he's still the captain.'

The empty soup mugs and whisky glasses on the wardroom table began to quiver, then to rattle.

'Now what?'

'Speeded up, I guess. Flank speed, or whatever they say in the Navy.'

'Yeah. Hear that water rushing past outside? We're deeper too. That gauge is reading sixty.'

A man put his head round the curtain.

'Colonel Furness?'

'Here.'

'Cap'n says to tell you we're attacking a tanker, sir. It's got an escort of two destroyers. He'll keep you informed.'

'Thanks, sailor.'

The vibration easing, ceasing. Harding's voice quiet, reaching them faintly from the control room. Something about ranges and bearings. Other voices answering him and the vibration building up for the second time. It lasted for three minutes before the voices came again.

'I'm beginning to get it,' Furness said. 'They make their periscope observations, close the range with a burst of speed, slow down and look again. That way they build up a picture of what the enemy ship is doing and figure the angle for firing torpedoes. Like our gunners firing ahead of Me109s. Like shooting duck for that matter.' He paused, grinned and added, 'That guy calling us a bunch of ruptured ducks. I liked that.'

Winnick smiled. O'Halloran did not. Neither spoke. Twice more the sequence of vibration and stillness repeated itself then, quite clearly they heard Harding say, 'Fire 1! Carry on firing by stop-watch. Two hundred feet.'

Each felt a slight jolt and momentary pressure on the ears, none of them knowing that the pressure came from compressed air, which had expelled the first torpedo from its tube, venting back inside the ship so that it should not escape to the surface and make tell-tale bubbles. The jolt and the pressure came three more times, then the vibration began again.

'Shut off for depth-charging. Shut off for depth-charging,' the public address system said and almost simultaneously the messenger reappeared.

'That's just a precautionary order, Colonel sir. We've fired four torpedoes at the tanker and now one of the destroyers is in sonar contact with us so we're trying to make ourselves scarce. It may get a bit noisy in a minute, but the Cap'n says to tell you that it sounds a lot worse than it is.'

Furness smiled faintly. 'That's a mighty comforting thing to hear, sailor. Tell the Cap'n "thanks", will you?'

'Aye aye, sir.'

A solitary sharp cracking explosion making the airmen jump and Furness and Winnick grin nervously at each other. Another following six seconds later.

'Ash-cans?' Winnick asked.

Furness raised his shoulders and dropped them again. 'Dunno. I never heard one.'

'I can't help feeling,' Winnick said, 'that we might have been better off if we'd stayed on that raft.'

A savage whisper of 'I don't give a single goddam for what you can't help feeling!' from O'Halloran and Furness saying, 'Cool it, Pat.' The tinny voice of the Tannoy ordering complete silence throughout the boat and the vibration dying away. Winnick's eyes fixed on the depth-gauge needle pointing steadily at the figure 200 and a flailing noise like a threshing machine coming from above their heads. Vibration increasing rapidly and the sailor, tense-faced now, telling them to hold onto their hats.

Long dragging seconds, then thunder beyond belief and instant darkness, their bodies jerking to the repeated concussions, the mugs and glasses swept from the table to shatter on the deck neither seen nor heard. Light returning, dimmer light, but bright enough to show each the white faces of the others. The detonations ceasing, but their reverberations living on, eventually to fade leaving only the sound of blood pulsing in shocked ears.

The Tannoy seemed to have acquired a booming tone when it ordered, 'All compartments report damage.'

'I heard that instruction,' Winnick said. 'It must mean we're still alive.'

'Speak for yourself,' Furness told him, wiped sweat from his forehead with the back of his hand and added, 'I wonder what it's like when it gets *worse* than it *sounds*. I just hope I get a chance to ask Harding *that*! I could do without a demonstration.'

Men passing with torches, peering into corners the emergency bulbs left in shadow, a different sailor replacing the bulb in the shade with the pin-ups on it. 'Cap'n thought you might like a spot of light, sirs.' The American flyers not knowing that theirs was the only one to be replaced, as it would be pointless to renew them all and have them smashed by the next depth-charge attack. Somebody saying, 'Tell the control room there don't seem to be no special damage in the accommodation spaces.' The vibration falling away. Total silence. Even the ventilation system switched off. Not that their hearing had recovered enough to detect the fact, only the absence of cooling air currents on their skin betraying it.

'Bully for the accommodation spaces,' Winnick said. 'You suppose all the other bits dropped off?'

Furness telling him to keep his voice down, Winnick nodding his head solemnly as though considering some profound statement, O'Halloran swallowing repeatedly as though trying to prevent himself from vomiting, the renewed juddering of speed and the messenger returning to say, 'Sonar reports they're coming in for another go, sir.'

The second underwater bombardment as terrifying as the first to three men without the experience to know that the charges had exploded significantly further away and considerably above them, men who knew nothing of the submarine's evasive tactics, its variations in course, speed and depth, men who also knew nothing of the element they were in and who, not many hours before, had come close to death in the one they were familiar with 16,000 feet over Naples before nursing their wounded plane to within a few miles of the North African coast.

'Hello. I'm the navigator. The Skipper says if you'd like a spot of Scotch or something please help yourselves. It's in the locker you're sitting on. Here's the key.'

Tired-eyed, grey-faced, they looked up at the young officer, indistinguishable from anybody else they had seen on board.

'Why now, that's mighty considerate of him,' Furness said. 'I suppose with you being on duty you can't join us.'

Walker sounded quite shocked when he replied, 'Oh, the ships officers *never* drink at sea.'

'In that case neither do we,' the colonel told him. 'But thanks all the same.'

It went on for six minutes short of seven hours, the game of cat and mouse. For varying periods of time the cats lost the mouse, then found it again. There was disagreement amongst the flyers as to whether sixty-eight or seventy-one more depth-charges were dropped on them, increasingly resigned argument about whether a pattern exploded nearer or further away than the one which had preceded it, unanimity that it was the most unpleasant experience of their lives. None of them noticed that the wardroom light bulb had not broken again. Had they done so it might have provided them with a yard-stick and lessened their fear of the unknown.

When, for only the second time, the threshing sound of a destroyer's screws passed directly over their heads and memory screamed a warning at them of what was to come, it was Winnick who broke. He did nothing hysterical, just sat with his arms folded and tears trickling down the sides of his nose. That it should be Winnick surprised Furness, but what surprised him the more was to hear O'Halloran say, 'Take it easy, fatso old buddy. I didn't enjoy seeing Hank's guts splashed all over the bomb-bay either. It's been a goddam crummy day, so maybe it just has to get better from here on out.'

Speaking gruffly, aware of it, embarrassed by it in case he should be thought theatrically paternalistic, but unable to stop it, Furness said, 'What the hell's everyone so steamed up about? We three made it through the flak, dropped our load, knocked down at least one night-fighter, survived a ditching in the sea because I'm a darned good pilot and get picked up by a Limey submarine. What more do you want? Molasses on it?'

He doubted if either of his surviving crew members heard him, locked as they were, as he so nearly was, in near-screaming suspense with their imaginations tracking the descent of the pattern of depth-charges which was likely to finish it all. Unable to think of anything else to say he slid closer to joining them in their trap, then did so at the sound of a wailing cry from the direction of the control room, a cry abruptly cut short. Furness wiped sweat from his face again and waited.

'That seems to be it, gentlemen. I'm reliably informed by my chief sonar operator that they're buggering off home. Sorry to have put you through all that.'

One after another they raised listless eyes to look at Harding standing in the gap in the curtains.

'What?' Furness said. 'I mean – that guy ran right over the top of us like the first time. He didn't drop any ash-cans?'

Harding shook his head. 'Their passing over us was pure chance this time. They'd lost contact with us and didn't have any idea where we were. We were lucky enough to find a temperature layer which deflects their sonar transmissions and we're sitting under it.'

As he had done once before Harding jerked his thumb in the direction of the wardroom depth-gauge. Furness glanced towards it, read its message of 365 feet and said, 'Jesus! One for each day of the year.'

'Oh. I hadn't thought of that,' Harding answered vaguely, and called, 'Pilot, come here and open up the booze locker. Our guests could do with a shot of something about now.' Then he frowned on hearing Furness's formally spoken words, 'No thank you, Lieutenant. We don't need courage out of a bottle.'

Had he been less shaken himself, or known Harding better, Furness might have recognized strain in the younger man's voice when he said, 'Now don't you start giving me that "Into the wild blue yonder" crap and don't "Lootenant" me in my own ship either. I'm the Captain and if I prescribe medicinal alcohol that's what you'll get. Just take a look at each other's faces and…'

Harding stopped talking, sat down and rested his forearms on the table before going on, 'Listen. That wasn't the worst depth-charging anyone ever got, not by a mile, but it was rather a prolonged affair and bad enough to make one of my own chaps lose control. The First Lieutenant had to lay him out with a spanner. None of you has experienced it before, on top of which you'd just been shot down or whatever happened to you. Not really your day what with one thing and another and by the look of you you're all a little shocked so…'

He stopped talking for the second time when Furness grinned tiredly, gestured for silence and said, 'It was your navigator saying you guys never – oh forget it. I guess we'd be glad of a drink.'

Nodding, smiling, Harding stood, turned away, then back again.

'We're pretty sure we sank the tanker,' he told them. 'The running time was right, hydrophone effect ceased on the bearing and we heard breaking-up noises afterwards.'

'Great. Just great,' Winnick said for the second time that day and began to laugh, then quelled the outburst by holding his breath. Most of Harding's statement about the tanker had meant nothing to him and he had forgotten hours earlier that it had ever existed.

Chapter Nineteen

'They really were terribly good, sir,' Harding said. 'I didn't know until later what a time they'd had before we picked them up. Half the plane's crew dead and all that. Then when they thought they'd got away with it – well, it must have been like a bad dream.'

Captain Anderson nodded. 'It must indeed. And a recurrence of it the following night I see from your report.'

'Yes, sir. I don't know where that destroyer materialized from, but it forced us to dive and worked us over for a bit. Nothing like as badly as the previous lot, but badly enough for our guests. That's why I let one of them man a machine-gun when we sank that armed tug the next day. He was jolly good too. Said it was like shooting fish in a barrel compared with firing at Messerschmitts.'

'There's nothing about that in your report, Peter.'

Harding noted the anticipated frown on the flotilla captain's face and said, 'It seemed best to leave it out, sir. I know it was highly irregular and I'm only telling you now because the story was bound to reach you eventually. They tossed a coin when I offered them the chance, Lieutenant Winnick won and was visibly happier about life after he'd helped to sink an enemy vessel. The others got some vicarious satisfaction out of it too and when they discovered we would be at sea for another week all three volunteered to stand watch as surface look-outs.' He paused, then added, 'That makes Winnick the only American flyer to engage the enemy from the bridge of a British submarine and *Trigger* the only submarine in the world to have had a colonel and two lieutenants as look-outs.'

Smiling diffidently, Harding was thankful to see his superior officer smile back at him and to hear him say, 'All right, Peter. I expect you knew what you were doing. Anyway, I'm not about to cavil at success. Four sinkings with both the troopship and the tanker being vital targets makes for a fine patrol. Good show.'

'It seems little enough in three weeks, sir.'

'Oh dear me, you new boys,' Captain Anderson said. 'You really do seem to have difficulty in grasping the strategic picture.' He glanced at his watch and added, 'I'm nearly late for a meeting ashore so you'll have to excuse me. You listen while Donaldson here reads you Lecture 4b, or whatever it is, on the availability of targets.'

Donaldson and Harding both got to their feet while the flotilla captain put on his cap and left, then, 'What did he mean, sir?' Harding asked.

'Just call me "Ginger". All the other submarine captains do,' the operations staff officer replied, took his pipe out of his pocket, polished the bowl absently and put it away again. As though that had somehow arranged his thoughts for him he began to speak.

'The basis of Lecture 4b,' he told Harding, 'is that if you think you are going to run up big scores like the Germans and the Americans you've got another think coming. Look at it this way. When war was declared our naval superiority was such that enemy merchant shipping simply vanished from the world's trade routes. Well, it stands to reason, doesn't it?'

Answering his own rhetorical question Donaldson went on, 'Any time any of them might have thought of sticking their noses out of harbour they knew that they could run straight into anything from a motor torpedo-boat to a battlewagon, so they stayed put and that, apart from an occasional blockade runner, was the end of international trade for them and, surely, the chief reason for Hitler's invasion of Russia and the Balkans. He had to have the oil and the grain and – well, you know.'

Harding, who for a long time had thought of very little other than submarines and a girl called Lee Lawrence, said, 'Yes, Ginger,' as though he *had* known.

'Good. So where does that leave you? It leaves you with the old "seek out and destroy" thing, which is why you have to spend so much time hanging around off heavily defended enemy harbours instead of sitting in the middle of the Atlantic like the Germans waiting for *their* enemy to go lumbering past in huge numbers, or the Americans rampaging all over the Pacific knocking off largely unprotected Jap ships by the dozen. It's a different war here in the Med. Single enemy merchantmen with sometimes as many as three escorts as you've already found out, clear water that aircraft can see you through down to God knows what depth – well ninety feet anyway – and all the rest of it. For all that, you chaps have been a major factor in old Rommel's imminent departure from North Africa because you've destroyed the Afrika Korps' supply lines and…'

Donaldson cut himself off in mid-sentence, stood up and said, 'Oh, for heaven's sake, that's enough of that. Let's go to the wardroom and have a drink before lunch.'

Following him out of the staff office Harding found himself to be trembling slightly. He frowned in quick perplexity, but the tiny spasm had passed before they reached the bar and he forgot about it.

When he had eaten, Harding wandered out into the warm spring sunshine and leant on the depot ship's rail looking down at *Trigger* lying alongside. The umbilical cord of a heavy metal-ringed fuel pipe connected her to her mother ship now, diesel oil replacing that burned during almost a month at sea pulsing through it. A smaller hose was in the process of being fixed to the fresh-water connection. Men came and went in endless succession readying the ship for a hurried departure should that be required of her. As if to offset that possibility Leading Seaman Peters had scraped the blue paint from the muzzle of the 4-inch gun and was burnishing it as though making ready for an admiral's inspection. Leading Seaman Peters liked his gun functional at sea and smart in harbour even if the rest of the submarine looked as though it had contracted some skin disease with its paintwork worn patchy by the elements. Harding smiled. He liked it that way too and Gascoigne would have the rest of *Trigger* up to Peters's standard soon enough.

Only when he was satisfied that all went well with his command did Harding look about him at Algiers harbour and the city beyond. He had barely had time to glimpse them on his previous brief visit. The port itself was crowded with warships and merchantmen of many kinds, all of them in their wartime livery of grey, although he noticed two destroyers with their upperworks coloured a strange mauve hue. A passing officer told him that that was for rapid identification during the naval and air mêlée which was expected to occur when the Axis attempted to evacuate its armies from Tunisia.

The white and pastel shaded buildings of the city with their back-drop of lush green hills climbing into the Atlas Mountains seemed to doze in the afternoon light. It was a serene setting and not one he found easy to picture as the base of the Moslem Barbary corsairs who had preyed upon Christian commerce in the Mediterranean until little more than a century before. Then his gaze dropped to the skull and cross-bones flag fluttering from the after periscope of his own ship. Algiers was still keeping faith with history.

Harding turned away and walked to the staff office. There was a mass of Intelligence material and other people's patrol reports he had set himself the task of reading.

*

Tessa Brown's eyes as well as her bosom looked welcoming to Gascoigne when he met her at the pavement café they had visited before. He was relieved about that because both time and security had made it impossible for him to warn her of *Trigger*'s precipitate departure for patrol and of his inability to keep his date with her.

'You needn't have worried,' she told him. 'Yours was the only submarine in the harbour that evening and when there wasn't one there the next day I knew you had gone. Do you have to go back aboard tonight?'

Even aware as he was of his attraction for women the abruptness of the question, with its obvious implication, startled Gascoigne, but he contrived a casual enough reply.

'No. I've got four days' leave. There's a villa along the coast reserved as a sort of rest camp for submarine officers. It can take about six of us at a time. Perhaps you could get a day off and visit us down there. I'm told the swimming's very good. I could drive you there tomorrow, but that's probably too short notice.'

'We'll see,' she said and the sensual mouth formed itself into a smile he was unable to read but would never forget.

Over dinner, 'Where does one go in Algiers?' he asked. 'At night?'

'One goes,' Tessa told him, 'to a flat I have the use of.'

For a long way the horse-drawn gharry followed the boundaries of the old Arab quarter surmounted by the fortress, the Casbah, from which the area took its name. When they got out of the ramshackle vehicle there was still another hundred yards or so to walk up a steep narrow alleyway to a green door set in an almost windowless high white wall. Tessa took a key from her handbag and let them in. The stairs inside were narrow and steep as well, leading to a room which, Gascoigne guessed, had once been two, their levels split to the height of three steps where the ancient building followed the contours of the hill.

Furnished in the Moorish style the flat, Gascoigne thought, had everything required of a love-nest with its concealed lighting, boldly coloured rugs and the good-looking naked black girl lying face-down, reading a book on one of the low divans. Excitement mixed with trepidation flickered in him.

'This is Maxine,' Tessa said. 'She goes with the flat.'

The black girl looked Gascoigne up and down with no particular expression on her face before saying, 'He'll do. You'd better give him a drink, Tess. He's going to need it.' Then she returned to her book.

Trying to decide whether to stay or go, wondering if going could be accomplished without the use of physical force, Gascoigne stood, holding a half-finished drink, looking from one to the other of two women who appeared to have forgotten his existence. Neither had spoken again and, unable to think of anything to say, nor had he. Indecision held him motionless, speechless, until the black girl moved. As though having reached some convenient stopping place she closed her book, got off the divan, walked up to him and began to unfasten his tie. Tessa Brown took the glass from his hand, then knelt and unlaced his shoes.

'Look,' Gascoigne said, 'I think I'd better…'

'Hush, baby,' Maxine told him.

Gascoigne awoke in daylight in a deserted flat. There was blankness for a moment before memories and physical sensation flooded in on him.

He groaned, eased himself gingerly to the floor and stood slowly upright, chafing his wrists, stretching his spine. It took him a full ten minutes of frantic search before he would admit to himself that his clothes had gone.

It took him longer than that to understand precisely what his situation was. There was food in the small kitchen. Plenty of it. He wasn't interested in food. There was a view, when he got the slatted shutters of the single window open, of the blank wall of the Casbah a few feet away across the alley. By leaning out he could even see a few Arabs at the bottom of it. There was a wardrobe and drawers full of female clothing, none of it the slightest use to him. There was no telephone. As if to underline his helpless state neither the flat door nor that leading to the alley was locked.

With a towel around his waist Gascoigne considered the options open to him. Walking for miles barefoot with another towel under his arm trying to look like a returning swimmer? Through the centre of a city? Stupid. And there were the marks on his back to conceal. Use sheets to simulate Arab dress? The thought of having to explain that to the officer of the watch and his minions on the quarter-deck of the depot ship made him wince. He would be the laughing-stock first of the flotilla and then of the Navy. There were the marks on his wrists to conceal too and only his uniform could achieve that.

His face had been in close contact with Tessa's so welcoming bosom when, before he knew what was happening, Maxine had drawn his arms behind him and strapped them there so that they could treat him as they wished. What they wished had been bizarre, bringing him both pleasure and pain. Towards dawn they had given him a drink and he had known no more until he woke alone.

Gascoigne's thoughts turned to the Arabs passing in the alley outside, but did not stay with them for long. Without money or the ability to make himself understood there was nothing for him there. Even their second language, if they had one, would be French and he had very little of that. Marginally more than his German, he thought ruefully. Overpowering the two women was, he concluded, his only course of action. It was when he realized that should he succeed in doing so it would bring him no closer to recovering his clothes that he became seriously afraid.

The day dragged, nervous second following nervous second. He ate a little, drank rather more than he would have liked and cut himself twice shaving with a tiny razor he found in the bathroom. It was 5.32 by the clock on the wall when the girls returned together from their jobs.

'Any callers today, darling?'

It was the ordinariness of Tessa Brown's question, the certainty it carried with it that he would be where he was, that added to Gascoigne's alarm. He shook his head.

'Good,' she said and twitched the towel from his hips as she passed him saying, 'I don't think we need that.'

Those were the last words spoken to him for two hours, two hours during which he drank the cocktails and ate the food he was given, feeling totally vulnerable in his naked state seated between the fully clothed women. They talked quietly across him and looked at him with mild surprise on the three occasions when he spoke, then went on with their conversation as though he didn't exist.

When the dishes had been cleared away the good-looking negress crooked a finger at him, the strap dangling from her other hand.

'No,' Gascoigne said.

'It's entirely your choice, baby,' Maxine told him. 'This, or we bundle you out into the street.'

'With me in *this* state?'

'With you in *that* state.'

Gascoigne approached her, turned and crossed his wrists behind his back.

It was on the fourth and last day of his leave, the fourth day of his imprisonment, that for the first time he found the girls still with him when he awoke. They were dressed, ready to leave.

'I've put your watch and wallet in that desk, darling,' Tessa Brown told him, 'and a boy will return your clothes in half an hour.' She gave him a friendly smile and walked out.

The girl called Maxine said, ''Bye, baby,' winked and followed her.

The Arab boy was punctual and about twelve years of age. He grinned, put a cardboard suitcase on the floor inside the door of the flat and said, 'You have nice long good time, mister? Lotsa guys have nice long good time here.' Then he held out his hand.

When he had examined the contents of the case Gascoigne took a note from his wallet and gave it to him.

*

'Hello, Number One,' Harding said. 'Nice to see you back. Did you have a good – I say, have you been sitting up with a sick friend again?'

Gascoigne grimaced. 'Touch of "gyppy tummy", sir.'

'Oh. Bad luck.'

For half an hour they discussed *Trigger*, then Harding watched his first lieutenant walk away, wondering why he did it so stiffly and why he had declined to sit down during the conversation.

Wherever he went a sense of desolation surrounded Gascoigne like a bubble he could see and hear through, but whose membrane he could not pierce. He felt directionless, lost, fragmented. Part of that, he supposed, could be attributed to the physical punishment he had undergone, punishment he had in no way earned, punishment which had increased in subtlety and the rigorousness of its application as dreaded night succeeded dreaded night. The interminable days between had been terrifying in their shortness, the hands of the clock seeming to stand motionless as he watched, and race round the dial when he took his eyes from them. That had unbalanced him too and further diminished his ability to think constructively. Not that there had been anything constructive to think about, he knew. Whatever action he might have taken would, at the very least, have resulted in ridicule; and ridicule would have ended his career as soon as the end of the war made his services no longer essential.

In retrospect he recognized the quiet ritual of the cocktail hour and the dinner which followed it as the most erosive of whatever courage the day had left to him. Murderous thoughts had come to him then, and only the knowledge that their fulfilment would amount to self-destruction drove them away. Now he wondered if he had made the right choice. To have been so effortlessly reduced to an object was an experience crippling for a man who had never been short of prideful satisfaction with himself, and Gascoigne was not sure that he could support the memory.

He went about his work automatically, his expression blank, his temper short, snapping at some people, totally ignoring others. Harding, almost a permanent feature of the staff office in the depot ship, engrossed in the study and analysis of submarine warfare, content to leave the day-to-day management of his ship to his second-in-command, noticed nothing.

Two women, one white, one black, were coming close to bearing the responsibility for the sinking of *Trigger*.

*

'Yes, I don't mind if I do,' Chief Petty Officer Ryland said. 'Thanks, Lofty. Good drop of stuff this is.'

Chief Yeoman Yarrow regarded him pityingly. 'I knew it, 'Swain. I knew it.'

'You knew what?'

'That you'd go native. You should have heard yourself talking about this beer before last patrol.' Yarrow grinned, stood up and took their glasses to the bar.

'Lofty! Come 'ere quick!'

'What's the matter, 'Swain?'

'I've just discovered what's the matter with "tall, dark and 'andsome". Somebody's nicked 'is piece of 'ome-work. That's what's upset 'im so bad.'

Through the window they watched a gharry carrying Tessa Brown go by. There was an army officer at her side.

*

Trigger had put a hundred and forty miles of sea between herself and Algiers before the first lessening of darkness to the east proclaimed the approach of day.

'Tell the Captain it's beginning to get light,' Lieutenant Walker told the voice-pipe. Seconds later, 'Cap'n says to dive the ship, sir,' it replied.

Trigger submerged rapidly and continued to drop with a sharp bow-down angle.

'Open "A" inboard vent. Pump from for'ard,' Gascoigne said.

'Belay that order! Shut main vents! Blow numbers one and two main ballast!'

Heads jerked towards Harding at the sharpness of his voice, then high-pressure air was roaring into the two forward tanks. The depth-gauges read eighty feet and falling.

'Blow number three main ballast.' Harding again.

Slowly the angle came off and the submarine began to rise.

'Stop blowing.'

Trigger broke surface moments later and porpoised three times. It took nine minutes to get her resting level at periscope depth and twice as long as that for Harding to reach the decision to say nothing about the incident to Gascoigne.

That it had been a very poor showing on the first lieutenant's part there was no question. To have so badly miscalculated the position and quantity of ballast water required to keep the ship level and at neutral buoyancy was serious enough, but could possibly be explained by an arithmetical error, or a misreading of the numbers given to him by the petty officer responsible for the level of the water in the trimming tanks. What was worse was Gascoigne's failure to recognize an emergency when confronted by one.

Harding sat in his cabin frowning at the memory of his second-in-command's order, an order which would have had not the slightest effect on a submarine obviously many tons too heavy plunging downwards out of control. Not knowing how right he was, 'The silly ass must have been day-dreaming,' he muttered to himself.

Two things decided Harding to take no action. The knowledge that the lesson had been so clear that there was little but possible resentment to be gained by underlining it for a man who was not, in truth, a silly ass, and the fact that he was blaming himself. He should, Harding was well aware, have dived the ship to check its trim immediately after leaving harbour, not waited until they were well into enemy waters, but so accustomed had he grown to Gascoigne's normal proficiency that he had not bothered to do so.

*

178

'With the thanks of the United States Air Force,' the unsigned message had read, then gone on, 'However, three of its members ask that the next time you see them sitting on a raft you leave them be, on account of a lift home comes too expensive for the nervous system.' Seventy-two very large T-bone steaks had accompanied the note, one for every man of *Trigger*'s crew, and there was a party atmosphere on board when they were served for dinner on the second night out of Algiers.

Gascoigne carved his into small pieces which he tried to hide under cabbage leaves, then put down his knife and fork.

*

It had been a copy-book attack and six miles to the west of Cape Spartivento, the southernmost point of Sardinia, Harding had seen both ships of the little convoy struck by one each of the four torpedoes he had fired. Their single escorting destroyer had reacted busily, but ineffectively, dropping a number of depth-charges, none close to the submarine and at no time was sonar contact detected. Hydrophone listening conditions were not good and *Trigger* crept away from the scene of the double sinking at a depth of one hundred and eighty feet, the sound of the destroyer's screws intermittent and fading.

That had been just before sunset.

Two hours later Harding ordered *Trigger* brought to the surface and within sixty seconds he himself sighted the phosphorescent bow-wave of the destroyer, the vessel itself indistinguishable against the bulk of the land behind it.

'Dive! Dive! Dive!' he said.

Closing the conning tower hatch above his head, clipping it in place, then dropping rapidly down the ladder he wondered how the enemy had contrived to be lying stopped, soundless, so close to his ship, ready to come in and ram as soon as it emerged from the sea. He was wondering too, with a bleakness he had not experienced before, if this was the end for him and his crew. The bow-wave had been very close.

He was standing in the control room saying, 'Shut off for depth-charging,

179

shut all water-tight doors,' watching the depth-gauge needle creep from figure to figure, hesitate, then resume its slow progress. The periscope standards were, he knew, still showing above the surface.

'Did you flood "Q" when we surfaced, Number One?'

Gascoigne said, '*Jesus*!' leapt to the diving panel, grasped the metallic blue lever of the emergency quick diving tank and jerked it. Water roared into the tank and *Trigger*'s descent quickened.

Afterwards, Harding concluded that it was the enemy's excitement which saved them all. The destroyer passed directly overhead, the sound of the propellers close, very close, as loud as a railway train, but it had dropped its depth-charges too soon. Everybody was shaken by the detonations, nobody was hurt. It was after three in the morning when *Trigger*, alone at last, could surface again.

*

Norris, rated up to Able Seaman now, put his head round the wardroom curtain and said, 'Cap'n wants to see you in his cabin, sir.'

Gascoigne nodded and rose to his feet.

'Close the door, Number One.'

'Aye aye, sir.'

They stood, facing each other, only a few feet apart in the tiny cabin, Gascoigne looking white, strained.

'I'm sorry about forgetting "Q" tank, sir. Very sorry.'

Harding stared at him for a long time before asking, 'What's the matter with you, man?'

'Nothing, sir.'

'Nothing? You've been in a bad temper for days, you aren't eating, when we dived for the first time after leaving Algiers you'd worked out the trim so badly that we might have been on a roller-coaster, now tonight's performance which came near to killing us all and you say there's nothing wrong.'

Licking his lips, Gascoigne gave a small, helpless shrug, but didn't say anything.

'Sit down,' Harding said and when Gascoigne was seated in the only chair added, 'Now take it slowly and tell me.'

After a moment, staring at the deck between his feet, Gascoigne began to talk. Not once throughout the recital did Harding speak or move from his position propped against the wash-basin, his entire concentration centred on his second-in-command's faltering words.

'Then I came back to the ship, sir,' Gascoigne ended.

'You poor old chap.'

The quiet voice brought Gascoigne's eyes sharply up to meet Harding's. The words, the tone, were the last things he had expected to hear.

'Sir?'

'It's all right, it's all right,' Harding said. 'It's over now, but why on earth didn't you tell me before?' He paused there, frowned and added, 'Don't answer that question. It was a damn silly one. I admire you for telling me now.'

Gascoigne sighed softly. 'It's been an enormous relief, sir. Living with it alone has been almost as bad as being in that place. Like being a – a nothing, sir. I think I know now what it must be like for a woman to be raped.'

'That and a lot more, from the sound of it,' Harding told him. 'It's the most twisted thing I ever heard of.'

In his turn he stared at the deck wishing ridiculously that either Lee Lawrence or Agatha Bulstrode could be transported aboard by telekinesis to comfort his first lieutenant. Just to read a letter from Lee was, he thought, like being stroked and, despite her recent agonizing over her brother, the company of Agatha Bulstrode refreshed the soul. Well, she was Lady Chandos now, but that didn't make…

'Sir?'

Gascoigne's voice brought Harding out of his pointlessly rambling reverie.

'Yes, Number One?'

'I'll be all right now. Now that you know. Honestly.'

Harding looked at the still pale face before him, but a face from which the lines of strain were already dissolving.

'I know you will,' he said. 'Now bugger off and find me something to sink.'

For the first time in days Gascoigne smiled.

Chapter Twenty

'Are you busy, Cox'n?'

Chief Petty Officer Ryland swung round on *Trigger*'s casing at the sound of Harding's voice, saluted and said, 'Regular old bee-'ive I am, sir.'

'Then do you think you could stop buzzing for a little while and come for a stroll. I want to talk to you where we can't be overheard.'

'Right, sir.'

The coxswain followed his captain across the narrow plank between *Trigger*'s bows and the sea wall, then fell in at his side. Harding waited until they were well clear of the two other submarines moored there before he spoke again.

'Cox'n.'

'Sir?'

'A great wrong has been done to somebody and I'm going to need help in putting it right and preventing it happening to anyone else. I'm going to ask you for that help, but the enterprise will be highly illegal and you are to refuse at once if you can't see your way to joining me. Understood?'

'I shouldn't bother your 'ead about that, sir,' Ryland said. 'I sold me soul to the devil when I nicked two fenders from *Tarantula* to replace those what we'd lost.'

Harding nodded, smiling slightly. He had spent a lot of time during the passage back to Algiers thinking about what he was going to do and rehearsing what he was going to say. Now he began to say it. Apart from an occasional muttered 'Bloody 'ell', Ryland heard him out in silence.

Then, 'You're on, sir,' he told Harding. 'The lads would do anythin' for you.' He paused before adding with heavy emphasis, '*And* for the First Lieutenant.'

Halting in mid-stride Harding faced him.

'What's the First Lieutenant got to do with it, Cox'n?'

Ryland shifted uncomfortably, stared out to sea and said, 'I just figured it out, sir. 'Im not bein' 'imself like. And the timin', sir, and the way 'e looked when 'e come back from leave, and – Sir?'

'Yes?' Harding's voice sharp, anxious that the coxswain had so easily torn away the shroud of security.

'I think Yarrow and me saw 'im with one of the bitches just before it all started, sir. In a gharry they was, drivin' towards the district you told me about, sir.'

'I see. Would you recognize her again?'

'Yessir. Tasty, sir. Voluptuous like.'

'I see,' Harding said again, then stood chewing his lip, frowning.

'Don't worry about this goin' any further,' Ryland told him. 'It won't, but we'll 'ave to think up some story for the lads we use as a flyin' wedge.'

'A flying wedge?'

'Oh, maybe you 'aven't been told the form, sir. The Casbah is out of bounds, but some bloody fools goes in there anyway after Ayrab bints. That's askin' for trouble, sir, and there's been a knifin' or two. Anyway, when the duty guard ship 'ears of trouble they lands a flyin' wedge, sir. Officer in the lead, men formed up be'ind him like a – well, like a wedge, sir. They carry pick-'andles and go through a bunch of Ayrabs like a dose of salts, grab whoever's in trouble and bring 'im out.'

'I see,' Harding said for the third time, 'but I don't think we need create that sort of disturbance. The place isn't in the Casbah, it's just outside the walls. Anyway, that would mean involving far too many people and blowing the whole thing wide open, but we will want one other chap. Who do you suggest?'

'Lofty Yarrow, sir. 'E'll come like a shot and 'e won't talk.'

Harding nodded and began to walk again before saying, 'You know, Cox'n, I wouldn't touch this with a barge-pole if there was any other way. It's a job for the provost-marshal or the police really, but nobody would jeopardize his reputation and career by giving evidence against them. That's where they've been so clever. Or they were,' he added grimly, 'until they nearly sank *Trigger*. They can't be permitted to endanger anyone else so this is what we'll do and we'll do it tonight before the First Lieutenant gets back from the rest camp.'

The discovery on the steps of the main police station of two sacks informatively labelled and each containing a struggling naked woman painted red from head to toe was a nine-day wonder in Algiers.

*

'I ain't never seen the Skipper really angry before,' Chief Petty Officer Ryland said, 'And when we busted into that flat I thought 'e was goin' to…'

'What flat was that then, 'Swain?'

The coxswain looked at the chief yeoman, then nodded. 'You're quite right, Lofty. Not even between us. 'Old on while I get us a refill of this excellent ale.'

The subject was never mentioned again but, for a long time, the faces of the two men wore an expression of grim satisfaction. They were still wearing it when *Trigger* again sailed for patrol.

No believer in coincidences of such a nature, Gascoigne had guessed something of what must have taken place immediately upon his return from the rest camp, but for the remaining days in harbour and a further day at sea he said nothing. Then he went to Harding's cabin.

'Come in, Number One.'

'Thank you, sir.' Gascoigne slid the door shut behind him before going on, 'I just wanted to say…'

'Ah, the past tense,' Harding broke in quickly. 'I never was very good at history. All that boring stuff about the Corn Laws and the Factory Acts, or was it the Corn Acts and the – well, never mind. I'm glad you came along. It's time I briefed you on this particular mission.'

He turned away, took a chart from a drawer and spread it out on his bunk. Gascoigne half smiled, half shrugged and peered over his captain's shoulder at the chart. Harding's message had been clear enough.

*

'Return Algiers at best possible speed diving by day. Signal ETA', the deciphered message read.

'What do you suppose that's about, sir?' Lieutenant Walker wanted to know.

'I haven't the remotest idea, Pilot,' Harding told him. 'Ours not to reason why. Tell the officer of the watch to reverse course, work out our estimated time of arrival and cipher it ready for transmission as soon as we surface tonight.'

'Aye aye, sir,' Walker said.

Harding climbed into his bunk and lay back with his hands behind his head, a little troubled at finding that he was glad that *Trigger* had been recalled before she had covered half the distance separating her from the patrol area to which she had been assigned. The trembling he had first noticed aboard the depot ship had recurred several times since then, all of them unpredictable, and he wondered why that should be, why he felt physically tired.

1943 was, he supposed, quite a long way from 1939 and a lot of the ride had been bumpy, but so had it been for very many people. He thought about the early months in a cruiser and about being first the navigator then second-in-command of *Shadow*. Quite a lot had happened in *Shadow*. Then had come a period in an obsolete L-class submarine when nothing had happened at all. Nothing was meant to happen other than that he should learn the basics of command. That he had done and been given *Trigger* to take to war. That he had done too, but the exhilaration with which he had done it had been dampened by the breakdown of Maddox and the first gruelling patrol in the Arctic. Harding moved uneasily in his bunk at the memory of Maddox's failure which he still obscurely saw as his own.

When he had pushed that unease away from him his thoughts turned to Helmut Schobert and *die Königin*, to the *Carlos Roca* and the tanker he had torpedoed while the American airmen had been aboard. There were the two ships sunk in a single attack as well and the near-ramming which followed it, the destruction by gunfire of smaller vessels, the...

His thoughts became confused as he sank towards sleep. Agatha Bulstrode's distress. The periodic cataclysmic jarring thunder of depth-charges. An Me109 with cannons spitting explosive shells at Walker and himself. The memory of the destruction of the ship carrying so very many men so callously murdered by their comrades forced out of his brain to be replaced by the recollection of the rush up the stairs with Ryland and Yarrow at his heels. The women spitting like the Me109. Lonely thing, command.

Thank God for such people as Ryland and Yarrow – and Gascoigne. An excellent officer, Gascoigne, and a bloody fool too. Why did he have to…?

Harding slept.

*

'Come in, Peter,' Captain Anderson said. 'I'm sorry to have brought you rushing back like that.'

Harding hesitated between 'That's all right, sir,' and 'It was no trouble, sir,' decided that neither statement was worth making and settled for silence and an enquiring expression.

'*Tiara* was sunk two days ago,' Anderson told him.

'I'm very sorry, sir.'

It was the least and the most Harding could say. He had liked Commander Jacoby and his officers, but one simply did not voice extravagant sentiments, so he waited to hear in what way the loss of *Tiara* affected *Trigger*. The waiting lasted a full ten seconds with the flotilla captain apparently lost in contemplation of the blue and white ribbon of the Distinguished Service Cross beneath Harding's left shoulder. He had been awarded that in *Shadow*. 'For courage, resolution and skill' the citation had read. Harding shifted uncomfortably.

Then, 'You've done four patrols, haven't you Peter? In command I mean.'

'Yes, sir.'

Anderson hummed tunelessly to himself for a moment before saying, 'Jack Jacoby was a very experienced officer. Obviously you are less so, but four patrols make you practically a veteran in these crazy times and I'm going to send you on a job he died trying to do.'

'Very well, sir,' Harding said. 'What does it consist of?'

His superior's reply was oblique. 'Rommel's done for, Peter. In fact we believe he's been flown home and, apart from mopping up a few pockets of resistance, the war in North Africa is over. That's a very telling victory for us as you can imagine and it puts the Germans on the defensive everywhere. It's the first time they've been in a crisis situation and when we land in southern Europe, in say Sardinia or Sicily, Italy itself or perhaps Greece, there's a chance that they may panic and do something stupid.'

186

'Like what, sir?'

'Well, you know how Hitler's always ranting on about secret weapons, things like the magnetic mine which was supposed to cripple us but didn't, don't you?'

'Yes, sir.'

'Right. Now, there's a school of thought which believes that one of those weapons may be gas and that they might resort to its use if they've really got their backs to the wall. It's not just mustard or phosgene or whatever was used in the last war, but something that does nasty things to the nervous system.'

Harding nodded and Captain Anderson went on, 'Intelligence reports indicate that the stuff is being manufactured in a number of places and one of those places is believed to be to the north of Bastia in Corsica. That locality may have been chosen because of its isolation.'

'Believed to be, I think you said, sir.'

'Precisely, Peter. Believed to be, but now the time has come when we have to be sure, so that the RAF or somebody can do something about it. Apparently the only evidence available at the moment is that quantities of farm animals are taken into the area and end up dead. They aren't eaten, they're burned in piles. That seems to indicate experimentation, and that sort of experimentation indicates a source of production close at hand. *Tiara* was carrying a mixed bag from the Special Operations Executive and the Commandos whose job it was to have pin-pointed the place. She never got there.'

'Do we know what happened to her, sir?' Harding asked.

'Yes,' Anderson told him. 'She was depth-charged to destruction by the "First Eleven" out of Spezia. You haven't been up that way yet. They're the only truly efficient Italian anti-submarine force. That's why we call them the "First Eleven". German equipped and trained probably. We don't know how they happened to run across *Tiara*.'

That didn't surprise Harding. What did surprise him was that the flotilla captain should know by what means *Tiara* had been sunk, for the submarine could have had no opportunity to transmit a signal while it was being hounded to death under water. He thought about secret agents with wireless transmitters and might well have guessed right. He thought, too, of asking, but decided against it, not knowing that to have done so would have

187

got him nowhere. Captain Anderson, like most people, had never heard of Bletchley Park, with its radio intercepts, its cryptographers and 'Ultra' which ingested enemy codes and spat them out again in plain language.

Harding said, 'When do I sail, sir?' and Anderson replied, 'As soon as the replacement SOE team gets here from England. I'll keep you informed.'

*

May came, bringing with it summer and white uniforms. It brought Sir Charles and Lady Chandos as well and, to Harding's wincing embarrassment, an invitation to dine with them. But that he had had no call for misgivings emerged as soon as he entered the crowded foyer of their hotel and Aggie threw herself into his arms shouting 'Rapist!' Bemused, pleased, relieved, he held her, looking over the top of her head at the grinning face of the admiral. Harding had heard it rumoured that admirals had been known to smile and thought he had witnessed a hint of that phenomenon in the past, but was quite certain that he had never seen one grin before.

Emboldened, 'Good evening, sir,' he said. 'Is this female anything to do with you?'

'Not a thing, Harding. I suggest that you have her ejected by the hall porter. Her speech and behaviour are in keeping neither with the dignity of this establishment nor of the uniform we wear.'

It was a happy three hours for Harding, with the admiral a good talker, a good listener too, and his wife a captivating companion to them both. He rose to leave their presence with regret, thanked the admiral, stooped to kiss Aggie's cheek, then felt a restraining hand on his arm.

'Good luck off Bastia, young fellow. This is an important one. Do your best.'

It was the first time a Service matter had been touched upon.

'I know it is, sir. And I will,' Harding said.

When he reached the quarter-deck of the depot ship, 'Captain Submarines wants to see you in his cabin,' the officer of the watch told him.

'Okay.'

He walked there, knocked and let himself in. A large man in Royal Marines uniform was talking angrily to the flotilla captain.

'I beg your pardon, sir,' Harding said and turned to go.

'No, that's all right. Come in, Peter. This is Colonel Buckton who'll be leading your Bastia party. Colonel, this is Lieutenant Harding, captain of *Trigger*.'

Captain Anderson's face was flushed and the source of his anger being obvious, Harding merely inclined his head towards the Royal Marines officer.

'Where have *you* been all evening?'

The colonel's question had been harshly, rudely put and Harding turned away from him to face Anderson.

'You wanted to see me, sir?'

Amusement blending with irritation in the flotilla captain's face he nodded and asked, 'How was the Admiral?'

Having already detected conflict, Harding was able to recognize a cue when he was given one.

'Most helpful, sir.'

'And his orders?'

'Explicit, sir.'

'Good,' Anderson murmured, and again, 'Good', as though he had just received a piece of information he had been expecting, but was thankful to have had confirmed.

'Which admiral is this?'

They turned and looked at the colonel.

'Sir Charles Chandos,' Anderson told him.

'I thought he had been invalided out of the Navy.'

'You thought wrong,' Anderson replied. 'Since he recovered from his wounds he's been Director of Naval Intelligence.'

To Harding, who had had no knowledge of Aggie's husband's position, the statement came as a complete surprise but, playing out the part he had assigned himself, he moved his head in ponderous affirmation.

'This is getting beyond belief!' Colonel Buckton said. 'Every Tom, Dick and Harry seems to know about this operation. We'll sail at dawn before we're all completely blown!'

'No, I don't think we'll do that.'

Buckton's head jerked towards Harding.

'Why?'

Ignoring the question, Harding asked one of his own.

'Have you and your party ever manned canvas canoes from a submarine at sea, Colonel?'

'Not to my knowledge. Does it matter?'

'It does to me. I'm not going to sit around on the surface in enemy waters while you practise. With Captain Anderson's permission we'll spend tomorrow doing that. Then we'll do it all again tomorrow night to make sure you can manage it in darkness. After that I'll take you to Corsica.'

'Captain Anderson, are you going to stand there and allow…?'

'Buckton!'

'Yes?'

'Have you ever flown by RAF Transport Command?'

'Of course. That's how I got here.'

'In that case,' Captain Anderson said, 'you will be familiar with the notice on the door to the flight-deck stating that regardless of the rank of any of the passengers the pilot is in sole charge of the aircraft. The same applies to Harding here. It doesn't matter to him whether you are a corporal or a field-marshal. He is in full command and now that you have heard his orders I will bid you good-night.'

When the door had closed behind Buckton, 'How'd you feel about a night-cap, Peter?' Anderson asked.

'I'd feel very warmly towards one, sir.'

'In that case pour me a bloody great whisky and pour yourself a bloody great whatever you like. What a bloody man.'

Pouring the drinks, 'He's no Royal Marine, sir,' Harding said. 'They know the form as well as we do.'

'Of course he isn't,' Anderson replied. 'He's some hot-shot from SOE they've dressed up to look like one. I'm told that he's very good at his job, but I don't envy you having to watch him do it.' He paused before asking curiously, 'Did Admiral Chandos really give you any orders?'

'Oh yes, sir,' Harding told him. 'I was instructed to do my best.'

The flotilla captain took the drink held out to him, subsided onto a chair and began to laugh.

Chapter Twenty-One

Harding smelt Corsica before he saw it, the fragrance of the flowering undergrowth which had led to the wild mountainous land being called 'the scented isle' wafting far out to sea. *Maquis* was the French word for the undergrowth and that, he supposed, had provided their resistance movement with its name as it gave excellent cover. It, the mountains and the partisans were all crucial to Buckton's assignment. Those and, according to Buckton, the Marines, although Harding questioned their value. It was his private view that five commandos could contribute little more than increase the risk of detection five-fold, but he kept his opinion to himself. He kept himself to himself too, spending long hours alone in his cabin away from Buckton's abrasive presence.

The man from the Special Operations Executive had gone through the canoe-manning exercises both in daylight and darkness with a grim dedication to perfection, but without any of the enthusiasm and occasional humour displayed by the Marines. When the time taken for the three fragile craft to be manhandled onto the casing, placed in the water alongside and manned had been reduced to two minutes, from opening *Trigger*'s fore hatch, Harding had ordered that the canoes be deliberately and simultaneously capsized. The passage of only seven minutes to redress that mock disaster satisfied him and the dripping landing party retired below with their dripping boats, the hatch thudded shut above them and *Trigger* swung to the east of north, the diesels thrusting her towards the Ligurian Sea.

Throughout the nights she ran fast across the surface of the Mediterranean and by day dawdled beneath it, conserving the power of the batteries so that little time need be wasted in recharging them when darkness came again. Throughout the nights Buckton slept, doing it noisily. Throughout the days he held planning conferences with Marine Lieutenant D'Arcy and Marine Sergeant Cranmore. He did that noisily too, demanding suggestions and shouting them down when they were made. North Africa was only eighteen hours astern when D'Arcy sought out Harding in his cabin.

'My Marines need something to do,' he said.

D'Arcy looked languidly handsome, but faded. His tan was faded, his khaki slacks and shirt were faded and so were his blond hair and green beret. The ribbon on his chest with a rosette at its centre denoting a double Military Cross was faded too, but suggested that he himself was far from being so. Harding liked him but, irritated by Buckton's presence on board, his reply was curt.

'What do you expect me to do about it? Organize a football match?'

The Marine Officer shook his head. 'No, you've got too many planes parked on the flight-deck for that. I thought perhaps they could be lookouts. They've all got eyes like lynxes.'

'That's very kind,' Harding said. 'My people will be delighted at having an extra hour in their bunks.'

'Nothing kind about it,' D'Arcy told him. 'I just don't want their bottoms expanding in direct proportion to the amount of food they shove into their faces. They won't get much in the way of exercise standing on the bridge, but at least they'll be in the open air and not eating for a little while.'

Harding grinned. 'All right. I'll have the Cox'n include the four of them in the roster.'

'Five, including me. And don't say that that's no job for an officer because Gascoigne tells me you had an American half-colonel doing it on a recent trip. The poor old sod must have been at least thirty-five, so if he could do it I reckon I can too.'

Grinning again, 'Five,' Harding said, then asked, 'How's it going generally?'
'With Buckton?'
'Yes.'
'Badly.'
'I was afraid of that. Is he a nut case?'

D'Arcy looked vaguely round the cabin then back at Harding before saying, 'No, he's not a nut case. In fact I think he's very clever in his own way and totally committed to what he's doing. The trouble is that he's a born loner. The operation should never have been mounted this way.'

Harding almost said, 'That's what I thought,' but changed the words to, 'Could you explain that?'

'Yes, I think so.' D'Arcy looked around him again before unexpectedly asking, 'Would it be construed as mutiny on the high seas if I called you "Peter"?'

Harding shook his head, smiling.

'Good. I'm Percival, but try not to let it depress you too much.' Then as though there had been no digression the Marine went on, 'The operation should never have been mounted this way because the chaps and I are a combat team and a good one. I don't have any false modesty about it because it's the truth. Sergeant Cranmore could fill my slot, Marine Hamlyn could fill his and I could fill Hamlyn's – who's just as important as the Sergeant and me. The same goes for the other two. Buckton doesn't understand that. If he can't be on his own, he's a stickler for chain of command and the links in the chain must follow his pattern exactly. He's explained that to Cranmore and me several times. Not in so many words of course, but in effect. We're supposed to pass that on down the line because he's not interested in talking to three ordinary Marines and they don't like that as we've always chewed everything over together before an "op". That's really the main reason for my asking you to give them something to do. They're feeling left out. Christ, what a long speech. Sorry about that.'

'Sounds like pretty bad casting to me,' Harding said. 'I wonder how that came about.'

'*Force majeure* probably,' D'Arcy told him. 'The group that went down with – with…'

'*Tiara.*'

'Yes, *Tiara*. They may have been better balanced, but I can't say because I didn't know them. Anyway, when she was sunk they had to do something in a hurry and came up with us. My lot don't need any explanation. We're just the strong-arm boys. Apart from whatever professional qualifications he may have, Buckton has the advantage over us of speaking the lingo. He lived there for some years before the war.'

Frowning, 'Oh come on. So do hundreds and thousands of other people,' Harding said, saw the negative jerk of D'Arcy's head and listened to him saying, 'Apparently not. Outside of Ajaccio and Bastia they speak a strange Italian dialect all of their own. Not an easy thing in which to discuss the map references of a poison gas factory with peasant partisans.'

'I see. Is there anything I can do?'

'No. You asked me what the situation was and I've described it. I'll bear my own cross.'

'He's no more a Colonel of Marines than I am,' Harding said. 'Obviously *you* know that.'

'I know that and you know that,' D'Arcy told him, 'but his papers and his uniform say we're wrong. Let me know which watches you want us to stand when we surface tonight.'

He smiled a faded smile and left the cabin. Harding watched him go, wondering why the Marine should have sought permission to use his Christian name and then not once done so.

*

Trigger rounded the cape called Corse at the northern tip of the island and turned south, her captain worried by the sense of friction in his ship and frustrated because, the day before, he had had to allow a fine 5,000-ton enemy freighter and its single escorting destroyer to pass by unmolested. To have attacked it would have been to place the mission in jeopardy. To lessen the mutual dislike of D'Arcy and Buckton he knew to be beyond him, so he didn't attempt to intervene in their wrangling beyond insisting that acrimony be set aside at meal-times.

Harding took periscope bearings of identifiable points on Corsica and the island of Capraia, then told Walker to do the same thing. Their observations were identical and told Harding precisely where he was. Locating the small bay chosen for the landing almost mid-way between the towns of Rogliano and Bastia was more difficult, but Harding thought he had pin-pointed it a few minutes before the sun set. He called D'Arcy and Buckton to the periscope.

Moments later, 'We'll go in tonight,' Buckton announced, then blared, '*Why the hell not?*' at the sight of Harding shaking his head.

'We'll do it tomorrow night,' Harding told him quietly. 'I need a full day's reconnaissance to make sure that that is the right place and that I can find it again when I come back to collect you next week. I want to know more about the depth of water nearer the shore and what volume of traffic there is along the coast both at sea and on land. It's really far too short a time for us to establish a pattern if there is one, but it's better than nothing.'

D'Arcy's 'Makes sense to me' brought a scowl from Buckton, then Harding went on, '0130 should be the best time. There'll be a quarter moon over the island by then, so you'll be able to see what you are doing without being silhouetted by it. Us too.'

Buckton grunted and Harding ordered *Trigger* to seaward. When it was fully dark she surfaced and began to recharge her batteries, gliding slowly across the smooth black water. About her the scent of the *maquis* hung heavily.

*

For some days the British naval attaché in Madrid had been making *démarche* to the Spanish Ministry of Marine to recover papers which had been in a black briefcase chained to the wrist of Major Martin. Major Martin was neither his rank nor his name and he had been dead for a long time when the Spaniards recovered his body from the Atlantic near the port of Huelva where it had been removed from a container of dry ice aboard the British submarine *Seraph* and lowered into the sea together with a capsized aircraft dinghy.

The papers were letters, their signatures authentic, their contents misleading. One, addressed to the Commander-in-Chief Mediterranean Fleet, bore the name of Admiral Mountbatten. The other signed by the Vice Chief of the Imperial General Staff was supposed to be destined for General Alexander. Both, in their different ways, indicated that the next Allied thrust would be towards the Greek islands and reduced the likelihood of an invasion of Sicily to the status of a cover plan. The additional evidence of authenticity found on Major Martin's body was so comprehensive and the Spanish so intrigued that it was some time before the British naval attaché's increasingly forceful demands for the return of the letters were acceded to. The Spaniards had needed that time to remove the documents from their envelopes without breaking the seals, analyse their message, copy them for the Germans and place them back inside their original covers.

As they were meant to do the Germans treated the information as genuine and made their plans accordingly.

Colonel Buckton knew nothing of Major Martin, or of his posthumous participation in a classic deception plan. He knew only of his own mission, which had nothing whatsoever to do with poison gas factories real or imaginary, and grew increasingly afraid.

*

'The landing party's ready to go, sir.'

Into the voice-pipe Harding said, 'Thank you, Number One. Stop both motors. Turn out the fore planes.'

'Aye aye, sir.'

Trigger ghosted on, losing momentum, pointing directly at the little bay and less than a mile from it. The moon painted the hills ahead black and silver, and drew a wavering path across the water towards the submarine.

'Fore planes turned out, sir.'

There was enough light for Harding to see them jutting outwards like stubby wings to either side of the ship's bow, almost touching the surface of the sea because he had reduced *Trigger's* buoyancy nearly to diving point. He had done that to simplify the launching of the canoes, to reduce the ship's silhouette and the time required to submerge in an emergency. He hoped he hadn't overdone it, for if the bow should dip under with the fore hatch open… No, they were safe from that on such a calm night.

'Very well,' Harding said. 'Who've you got standing by the hatch?'

'The Cox'n, sir.'

'Good. Open it and get the Marines away, Number One.' The black and silver land looked close enough to touch and, although he knew that to be an illusion, he added, 'I want to get out of here as soon as possible,' immediately wishing he hadn't as it was so obvious.

'Aye aye, sir.'

The thud of the fore hatch opening and Able Seaman Norris shooting out of the aperture like a jack-in-the-box. The light not good enough to recognize him at such a distance from the bridge, but Harding knowing who it was because Norris was always sent for when the manhandling of objects or people was called for. Others following him, then the long cigar-shapes of the canoes. D'Arcy's voice giving orders quietly, the words indistinguishable to Harding. His own voice saying, 'Keep your eyes on your sector, Jameson. The Marines are no concern of yours.' The look-out replying, 'Sorry, sir.' The canoes resting on the hydroplanes, then on the water, men easing their way into them, two to each. Paddles dipping. *Trigger*'s men disappearing back inside the hull. Another thud and the voice-pipe announcing, 'Fore hatch shut and clipped, sir.' The speeding canoes already smaller with distance.

'Full astern together,' Harding said.

*

It wasn't difficult to hide the canoes in countryside which for centuries had hidden bandits from the authorities and feuding clans from each other. When they had done that, spacing them half a mile apart for greater security, D'Arcy's Marines positioned automatic radio transmitters at four locations in an arc around the bay and set the controls which, several weeks in the future, would bring the homing devices to life. After that they ate, then four slept while two kept guard. Dawn was still an hour away.

There was no question now that they were D'Arcy's Marines, not Buckton's. There was no more talk of rank or chains of command. Buckton dropped his hard image and tried to make himself generally useful without getting in the way. The change appeared to surprise nobody.

For three days the men lay in hiding, doing little more than eat, sleep and time the appearance of German and Italian patrols along a coastal road which was scarcely better than a track. The Germans, they found, were predictable in their punctuality. That surprised nobody either, but it did please them because it was a German patrol they wanted to ambush and they intended it to be the last of the day which passed from north to south just after sunset. Only a night patrol would have pleased D'Arcy more, but it seemed that the enemy was unwilling to risk those in the area through which partisans passed freely.

When they were neither eating, sleeping nor timing patrols the men competed to be the first to spot *Trigger*'s periscope. Nobody won. Having no desire for a chance encounter with the 'First Eleven' anti-submarine group out of Spezia, Harding had withdrawn to the south of Pianosa island to record the movements of shipping he was not allowed to attack. It was dusk on the third day when he returned to the pick-up point. He was prepared to wait for the Marines where he had dropped them, every night for two weeks if necessary, but they didn't keep him waiting at all.

*

The canoes had been retrieved from their separate hiding places and now lay together in cover within easy reach of the water's edge. Colonel Buckton lay in cover too, well out of harm's way, his nerves screaming at him. D'Arcy and his Marines flanked the path, prone, waiting, two on one side, three on the other. The Germans arrived on schedule, eight watchful men with their guns at the ready because this was partisan country and sunset the most dangerous time.

Seven of them died simultaneously, cut down by machine-gun fire and hurtling grenade splinters. The eighth hurled himself sideways into the *maquis*.

'Fuck it!' Lieutenant D'Arcy said. 'Sergeant, take everybody and get that man!'

The eighth German died within seconds, but not before he had cut Sergeant Cranmore almost in half with a prolonged burst from his *Schmeisser*. D'Arcy heard, but didn't see. He was loping along the track, a *Luger* automatic taken from a dead German in his hand. Two hundred yards from the scene of the fire fight Colonel Buckton rose white-faced out of the undergrowth to face him, then fell, shot at close range through the right thigh, a second bullet ploughing a furrow across the outside of his upper left arm. D'Arcy dropped to his knees beside him.

A minute later, 'The bone may be chipped a bit, but there's nothing broken, George,' D'Arcy told Buckton. 'I promised you I was good with hand-guns, didn't I? Here, let's get some morphine into you and then we'll move you closer to the scene of the action. This has to look right.'

Through clenched teeth, 'Stop telling me things I know and get on with it,' Buckton whispered. 'You haven't got a lot of time before they come to see what all the noise was about.'

It was fully dark before D'Arcy had everything arranged to his liking.

'Got to go now, George.'

'Then bugger off, Percival. I wonder what in the world persuaded your parents to give you a name like that.'

'God knows,' D'Arcy said. 'They came up with "Algernon" for my middle one. Good luck, old chap.'

*

Moonrise was some hours away and the night overcast when *Trigger* surfaced close to the little bay. The glassy calm had given way to small, steep waves and the scent of the *maquis* borne on the off-shore breeze came to Harding's nostrils as soon as he opened the conning tower hatch. He pulled himself round the still dripping periscope standard to the front of the bridge and started in quick alarm at the sight of a dim flashing light fine on the starboard bow.

Jerking the voice-pipe cock open, 'Gun action stations!' he said. 'Oerlikon and machine-gunners to the bridge! Leave the fore planes turned out.'

The voice-pipe repeated his words back to him, then transmitted the sounds of running feet and the clang of the magazine cover being removed. In front and below him the gun tower hatches thudded open and he was aware of men gathering around the 4-inch, but did not take his eyes from his binoculars.

'Target is a flashing light bearing Green 15. Do *not* open fire,' he told them.

'I think it's Morse, sir.' Walker's voice from beside him.

'So do I, Pilot, and I think it's probably coming from a canoe,' Harding said. 'Difficult to read with the waves obscuring the light half the time. We'll watch for a bit. Could be a trap. Chivers, get up top and tell me what you can see.'

Only seconds later the able seaman spoke from the top of the forward periscope standard.

'Three canoes, sir, and one of them is flashing da-dit-dit pause dit-da, whatever that means, sir.'

'Thank you, Chivers. It's DA, Lieutenant D'Arcy's call sign, but stay up there and watch. It could still be a trap. Control room, steer ten degrees to starboard.'

There was no trap. *Trigger*, her long shape unaffected by the small sea, closed rapidly on the tossing canoes, then turned and stopped, placing them in the calmer waters of her lee. Except that they and Able Seaman Norris, standing on the starboard hydroplane to lift them aboard, all got very wet, there was no difficulty in recovering the four Marines.

*

'How soon can you transmit that?' D'Arcy asked.

'The moment it has been ciphered,' Harding replied. 'It's what we came for after all and we'd look a bit silly if we got sunk before we had passed it on.'

He glanced once more at the message D'Arcy had written reporting the map co-ordinates of the non-existent poison gas factory, describing the surrounding terrain and the probable appearance of the mythical camouflaged building from the air, recording the deaths in action of Colonel Buckton and Sergeant Cranmore, then he pushed it across the wardroom table to Randolph.

'Cipher that and get it sent off, Guns,' he said.

All that night *Trigger* ran fast to the south across the Tyrrhenian Sea, but little more than an hour of it had passed before the signal she had sent was placed on the desk of Admiral Sir Charles Chandos in London. The description of the terrain, after reference to a note-book, told him that his agent had been successfully delivered into enemy hands in reasonable physical condition. The rest of the message he ignored. Apart from the death of the sergeant it was just padding. That death moved him not at all, it was a mote in a galaxy of killing, but he found himself experiencing disquiet at the necessity to deceive, to use, Harding. He had developed a liking for the young man which was not solely dependent on either gratitude or his wife's opinion.

After a moment he grunted impatiently and put the signal into a drawer. No longer fit for sea service he had been offered the job of deception, had accepted it and would deceive anybody and everybody his duty required him to.

*

'You appear to be determined to make things as difficult as possible for yourself, Colonel.'

Buckton looked at the *Abwehr* major through sunken, bloodshot eyes, trying not to think about the pain. It was everywhere from his head to his swollen hands strapped to the arms of the heavy wooden chair, from his wounded arm to his wounded leg. He didn't say anything.

'Won't you try to be reasonable?' the major asked and, as if to underline the existence of a question, the second man brought the ebony ruler down hard across the knuckles of Buckton's left hand. The sound of a bone cracking and his scream came together.

In the nine days Buckton thought he had been in Berlin, although the number was less than half that, the *Abwehr* major had not once touched him. He had been courteous, amicable, seemingly almost concerned for his victim. Buckton hated him and his perfect English with a loathing far deeper than his fear and hatred of the men who tortured him while he watched, or the sentries who burst into his cell and slapped him into wakefulness every time his eyes closed. He didn't know it, but it was his hope of killing the major that was keeping him alive.

As though struck by an original thought, 'I tell you what,' the major said. 'Let's go over some of it again.'

'Let's go over some of it again,' Buckton repeated, the words slurred by exhaustion and the gaps a truncheon had produced in his teeth.

'Good for you, old boy!' The major sounded delighted. 'Now, when I told you that we had found two wireless homing devices obviously intended to guide ships to the landing beach in Corsica you agreed that that was their purpose, did you not?'

'Yes,' Buckton said.

'But you neglected to tell me that there were actually four of them.'

'Yes,' Buckton said.

'That was wrong of you, wasn't it? We Germans have a reputation for thoroughness and when we find a wounded English full-colonel in a place where he has no right to be, we look at the situation very carefully indeed.'

'That's exactly what you were meant to do, you perverted little sod!'

Had he spoken the words aloud, or had it only been his brain shouting? Did it matter? No, it didn't matter and he hadn't spoken anyway because the major was still looking at him enquiringly.

'Yes,' Buckton said.

'Good, good. So we are still agreed, but I am afraid that we must continue to be thorough. You see, your withholding that small piece of information led me to doubt the veracity of some of the statements you have seen fit to make which have indeed subsequently proved to be inaccurate.'

The major took a small notebook from a pocket of his uniform and consulted it before going on, 'When I asked you why an officer of your rank and seniority should have been employed on such a simple task you replied that your presence on the island was for the purpose of acting as "beach master" when the landing took place. Not very plausible, Colonel. A "beach master" lands with the invasion force and with full knowledge of its composition and a prearranged plan for its disposition.'

The voice droned on and Buckton's mind drifted away on a cloud of pain and exhaustion wondering for how long these seemingly endless reiterations could continue. So tired. So very tired. Tired of pain, tired of the fear, tired of being alive. Perhaps they would let him die soon. That would be nice. No, he mustn't die because he had to kill the major first. Silly. How could he possibly achieve that. Stupid even to dream about it and it wasn't even the real reason for staying alive. That was much more important. Something he had to tell them. Something they would believe because they would have extracted it from him under conditions of extreme affliction and because they would want to believe it. No, he mustn't die before…

Agony exploded in his hand again, then faded and the interrogation room faded with it.

Buckton was dripping wet when he recovered consciousness and opened his eyes just as the man with the ruler threw another bucketful of water in his face.

There was only mild reproof in the major's voice when he said, 'I really must ask you to pay attention when I am addressing you. Now, as I was saying, after we had applied electric current to your tongue and private parts you were kind enough to concede that your puerile Corsican venture was nothing more than a deception plan and that an invasion of the island had no place in Allied strategic thinking. After further treatment I asked your opinion on the true target and you suggested Sicily. In fact you became increasingly emphatic on the point as the day drew on. I have it all down here in this book. Tell me again. Why did you say it was Sicily?'

In little more than a whisper, 'Because it's the truth,' Buckton told him. 'Sicily is a stepping-stone to Italy and only a hundred and fifty miles from Tunis and Bizerta. Malta's right on the doorstep. It's – it's so logical, so obvious.'

'Perhaps a little too obvious, Colonel?'

Buckton didn't speak and the major went on, 'We have very strong indications from a certain source that Sicily is not the target. So strong are they that I have reached the conclusion that you were shot by your own people and deliberately left for us to find so that you could mislead us into believing that the Anglo-Americans intend to invade Sicily.'

'That's utterly absurd,' Buckton said.

'Is it, Colonel? Is it not a desperate attempt on the part of the British to recoup something lost in Spain by a colleague of yours, a certain Major Martin?'

'I know nothing of him or of what you think he's lost.'

'Ah well, no matter,' the major said. 'Let us forget about this man

Martin. The target's the thing and if you have temporarily forgotten what that is, we can help you. I know from witnessing the procedure that the introduction of high-pressure air into the body by way of the rectum is a quite remarkable aid to the memory.'

It took several minutes to make the arrangements, but no time at all for Buckton to start screaming. When they desisted he gasped out the words 'Greece! Greece! We're going in through – Greece to – join up with the Russians!'

The *Abwehr* major nodded, satisfied, picked up a telephone and spoke into it.

'The "Martin Papers" are genuine. Target Greece,' he said. When he had replaced the receiver he gestured towards Buckton and added, 'Take him outside and shoot him.'

They didn't take Buckton outside and shoot him. He was already dead.

During the ensuing weeks plans made earlier were implemented, the reinforcement of Sicily was reduced, some troops were sent to Sardinia as a precautionary measure and sizeable portions of the *Wehrmacht* were dispersed uselessly around the Dodecanese.

Sicily was ripe for plucking.

Chapter Twenty-Two

During the hundred hours it had taken Colonel Buckton to die, *Trigger* had sectored most of the patrol area assigned to her and found nothing to attack except a 20-ton craft of doubtful use to the enemy but, as it was flying the Italian flag, Harding had decided that he should sink it. He had done so by surfacing, inviting the five occupants by gesture to take to their lifeboat, then ordering Lieutenant Randolph to go aboard and set it on fire with pieces of rag soaked in oil.

Later, Chief Yeoman Yarrow had asked him how the sinking should be recorded on the 'Jolly Roger' and Harding's dislike of the black flag had shown when he had snapped, 'Chalk "Arson" on the damn thing in capital letters!' Then he had added, 'Sorry, Yarrow. I didn't mean to shout at you, but it was hardly a famous victory, was it? Anyway, the chaps wouldn't be too pleased if you got their precious flag laughed at.'

His small outburst had upset Harding out of all proportion to its significance because it showed that the malaise affecting his men had touched him as well. He recognized, without fully understanding why, that submarine sailors who could contemplate with fair equanimity the prospect of their collective death, the form of death they were most likely to meet, became inordinately depressed at the loss of individual members of the crew. Neither Colonel Buckton nor Sergeant Cranmore had been a member of the crew but, however briefly, they had belonged to *Trigger* and *Trigger* had lost them, her first fatalities since Able Seaman Roberts had vanished in the icy waters of northern Norway all that time ago. Now tempers were short and spirits low.

One decisive action would, Harding knew, have dispelled the general mood of gloom in an instant, but no action worthy of the name had presented itself, with the exception of Able Seaman Norris's clash with Marine Hamlyn. In a remark never intended to contain malice, Norris had said in Hamlyn's hearing that he was sorry for the two Marines, but that the unpopular colonel had probably only got what was coming to him. Knowing that Colonel Buckton had been deliberately wounded and left for the enemy to find, not knowing why, but having been sworn to secrecy by Lieutenant D'Arcy, Hamlyn had made the only reply open to him.

Hitting Norris in the face had been a bad idea and noticeable damage had been done to some of the ship's fittings in the torpedo stowage compartment before others present succeeded in separating the two men. Harding had had no choice but to sentence both to unproductive, time-wasting punishments which pleased neither him, them, nor anybody else.

The atmosphere in the wardroom was bad too. D'Arcy looking more faded than ever, taciturn, almost monosyllabic, lost in a reverie Harding was in no position to guess at. Gascoigne, with only routine to occupy him, was also withdrawn as though emulating the Marine officer. It was much easier for Harding to guess where his first lieutenant's thoughts lay and his sympathy in that direction was waning rapidly. Walker's and Randolph's desultory attempts at conversation never lasted long in the face of their seniors' abstraction. Only Lieutenant Menzies, the engineer officer, appeared unaffected by the prevailing mood but, as he spent most of his time in the engine room as he had always done, his comparative cheerfulness affected the situation hardly at all.

Frustrated by inaction and angry for almost the first time with his second-in-command Harding retired to his cabin and sent for him.

As soon as the door was closed, 'You're falling down on the job again, Number One,' he said and raised a hand when Gascoigne opened his mouth. 'No, just you keep quiet until I've finished. You can say your piece then, but right now you'll listen to me. The crew are in a rotten frame of mind, probably partly because they're a sentimental lot, certainly partly because you are setting them a very bad example by retiring into your shell instead of doing something about them. When we commissioned this ship you introduced the practice of all the officers standing when I came into the wardroom. I remonstrated and you reminded me that you were in charge of discipline on board and that, as we were all lieutenants, you wanted some differentiation in my case, so I acquiesced. I would now remind *you* that discipline and morale go hand in hand. If you're in charge of one you're in charge of the other.'

Harding wasn't very good at speeches and, although he had rehearsed this one, he needed time to collect his thoughts. To gain it, 'Do you understand that?' he asked.

'Yes, sir. Of course, sir.'

'Good, then we'll start with the wardroom. The rest of us are wilting under the clouds of gloom coming from you and D'Arcy and that's got to stop! What the hell's the matter with him I have no idea. I can't imagine a man with two Military Crosses going broody because two of his companions are killed in action, but in your case I know exactly what you've been doing. You've been reliving your time in that flat with those blasted women, haven't you?'

'It's a difficult memory to shake off, sir.'

'Fiddlesticks!' Harding said. 'The only thing they really hurt was your vanity. Their's has since been hurt a lot more and that's to be an end to the matter. I will not have my ship put at risk by a case of injured pride! Is that perfectly clear?'

'Yes, sir.'

'In that case get to work. I want the crew occupied and entertained. Arrange lectures by anybody who knows anything about anything. Set up inter-mess competitions. Offer prizes for the best essay on "Why I volunteered for submarines" or "Butterfly collecting" or – Oh, use your imagination. Put on a funny nose and tell jokes if you can't think of anything better!'

Harding felt his anger translate itself into the onset of the now too familiar trembling, but he steadied himself with a physical effort and went on, 'I want D'Arcy occupied as well. Something more than just standing watch as a look-out. I don't think there are any in our area, but I want him and the Pilot to go over the charts with a fine-tooth comb looking for railway lines near the coast he and his Marines could cut, or bridges they could blow up. He's to report on his findings to me. Now get on with it!'

'Aye aye, sir,' Gascoigne said, reached for the sliding door, then let his hand drop to his side again.

'Sir?'

'What is it now, Number One?'

Gascoigne hesitated for a moment before saying, 'I don't deny that I've been thinking about those girls, sir, but there's something else.'

'Well?'

There was a longer pause before Gascoigne said in a flat voice, 'I've been trying to decide whether or not to tell you, sir. I think – Sir, I think D'Arcy killed Colonel Buckton.'

The incipient trembling vanished from Harding's frame leaving him steady but cold as though the temperature in the cabin had dropped sharply.

Very quietly, 'Why do you think that?' he asked.

'He talks in his sleep, sir.'

'Ah.'

'Yes, sir. He's got the bunk above mine and twice I've heard him say, "Get over here, Hamlyn. I've shot the Colonel, but he's too heavy for me to carry alone". Then quite often he mutters something about making it look right and being good with hand-guns. I…' Gascoigne shrugged and fell silent.

'Oh Christ,' Harding said.

For a full ten seconds Harding stared at his twenty-two-year-old first lieutenant and Gascoigne stared back at his twenty-four-year-old captain. Despite their youth both were professionals skilled in war, but of law they knew little or nothing and there was mutual recognition of the fact that they were out of their depth.

Gascoigne broke the silence.

'Will you convene a Board of Enquiry, sir?'

'I suppose I'll have to,' Harding replied. 'Hell, this is really grim.' Then, grasping at straws, he added. 'I suppose you're absolutely certain about what you heard.'

'I'm afraid so, sir.'

'Yes, you wouldn't have spoken of it if you weren't.'

Staring at the deck now, Harding listened to the faint sounds of the ship coming to him through the closed door of the cabin. He could hear Lieutenant Menzies's quiet Scots voice saying something to the officer of the watch in the control room and was tempted for a moment to seek his advice because, at twenty-eight, the engineer officer was the patriarch of the wardroom. Then he shook himself irritably. The course to be taken was a command decision and nobody could help him with that.

Harding raised his head to meet Gascoigne's worried gaze and said, 'Tell D'Arcy to come here, Number One.'

The Marine lieutenant looked as languid as ever, but there was a watchfulness about his faded eyes when, moments later, he stood in front of Harding.

'You want to see me?'

'Yes,' Harding told him, 'I do. I also want to know what happened to Colonel Buckton.'

There was no flicker of the eyes at the demand, but one brow raised itself into an enquiring arc.

'It's all set down in the report I gave you. He was caught by the same burst of *Schmeisser* fire as Sergeant Cranmore. What else do you want to know?'

Not answering the question, Harding breathed in slowly, silently, before saying, 'I have reason to believe that you killed him yourself.'

'Jesus,' D'Arcy said. 'You must have an annual subscription to the *Police Gazette* to be able to say things like that. As it happens I have three witnesses to vouch for the fact that your reason has deserted you. I killed some Germans and nobody else.' He sighed and added, 'Are you under the impression that I go around killing people just because I don't get on with them?'

Not answering that question either, Harding quoted in a toneless voice, 'Get over here, Hamlyn. I've shot the Colonel, but he's too heavy for me to carry alone.'

The mask of languor slipped from the Marine's face, giving way to a look so venomous that, for a moment, Harding thought that he was about to be physically attacked, then the sudden blaze died.

'Hamlyn never told you that,' D'Arcy said. 'Nor did the other two.'

'No, you told us yourself in your sleep. More than once.'

'I see.'

'I'll have to place you under close arrest, D'Arcy. Your Marines too. Obviously they're implicated.'

D'Arcy scratched himself reflectively under the armpits and sighed again.

'I wouldn't do that if I were you, old son,' he said. 'That way you would have the entire ship's company asking questions which would be a totally unacceptable breach of security. The whole operation would almost certainly be blown. It's bad enough you having to be told. You and whoever it was overheard me. Who was it, by the way?'

'Gascoigne.'

'I hope to God he was the only one. You'd better get him in here.'

It was very crowded in the tiny cabin with the three men standing in it. Gascoigne took up the most room and Harding told him to sit in the only chair, then looked at D'Arcy.

'Well?'

'The operative word in what you tell me you heard me say is "shot",' D'Arcy said. 'I *shot* Colonel Buckton. I did *not* kill him.'

'Why did you shoot him?'

'Because I had been ordered to do so by a very senior officer.'

Harding stared at him incredulously for several seconds before asking, 'Was Buckton a traitor?'

'Far from it.'

'Then you're one of those people prepared to carry out unlawful commands, are you?'

Harding thought he detected the palest of smiles on D'Arcy's face before listening to him say, 'Well, you don't have to sound so damned righteous about it. That's exactly what you do every time you sink an undefended merchantman without warning. At least *I* had my victim's permission. Not, I might add, that that made it any the more enjoyable.'

'You had Colonel Buckton's permission to…'

'Peter.'

The name had been quietly spoken, but its use silenced Harding because it was the first time D'Arcy had used it despite asking if he might do so days before.

'Yes?'

'Let me tell it my way, will you?'

'All right.'

'There never was any poison gas factory,' D'Arcy said. 'Not in Corsica anyway. That was just a cover story, so it follows that we didn't bother to go looking for one. We just hid in the *maquis* for long enough to give the impression that we had searched the area. Then, on the last evening, we ambushed that German patrol to attract attention from the main garrison and Sergeant Cranmore was killed in the action. That was when I shot Buckton as arranged and we left him for the relief column to find. It had to look right, you see.'

'No, I don't see,' Harding told him. 'What had to look right?'

'Their capture of Buckton. He wanted to be captured.'

Harding was far from lacking in imagination and he suppressed the urge to ask why, confining himself to saying, 'It seems we might be getting into rather deep waters here, so I won't press you for any more details. If Hamlyn confirms what you've already said I'll let the matter drop.'

D'Arcy was more than glad to be questioned no further and stood silent for a moment thinking sadly that the only other details available to him were that Buckton was a very sick man who had wanted desperately to do something useful with what was left of his life and that Harding had come close to killing him with the long canoe-manning exercises he had insisted upon before sailing. Those facts he decided to keep to himself, but there was one thing left to be said.

'Leave Hamlyn out of this, please. Having been sworn to secrecy by me it would place him in an intolerable position. That goes for the others as well.'

Harding shook his head. 'I can't help that. This is all too…'

'Yes you can,' D'Arcy broke in. 'Leave it for now and send a cipher to my boss when we get back to Algiers. I won't run away.'

'Who's he?'

'Admiral Sir Charles Chandos. He flew out from home to set it all up, whatever *it* was. He briefed Buckton personally I believe, then sent for me and told me what I had to do.'

'Oh,' Harding said. 'That's what he was doing in Algiers, was it? In that case let's forget the whole thing. All three of us.'

Both men nodded and left the cabin without speaking again. Harding watched them go, his expression thoughtful. He was thinking that this was a particularly nasty war and wishing that he had been nicer to Buckton.

Chapter Twenty-Three

'I'll 'ave your attention, please gents,' Chief Petty Officer Ryland said, 'while you cop an earful of my prize-winnin' entry.'

The others present groaned in unison and winked at each other.

'Thank you,' the coxswain went on. 'Now listen – "Why I volunteered for submarines" by Chief Petty Officer H. F. Ryland, DSM, MID.'

'What's MID, 'Swain?' Petty Officer Selby wanted to know.

'Mention in Despatches of course.'

'But you can't put that after your name. It isn't a medal.'

'You please yourself, Selby. I always 'ave and I always will. Now then, where was I?'

The coxswain returned his attention to his sheet of paper, but the Tannoy calling 'Diving stations, diving stations,' relieved the other members of the petty officers' mess of listening to his reasons for volunteering for submarines. All rose as one and left in a controlled rush.

In the control room Ryland nodded when Leading Seaman Barr said, 'Thirty-four feet, 'Swain,' and surrendered the after hydroplane operator's seat to him. As he slipped into it and put his hands on the control wheel he heard the captain say, 'I think I can see six masts now. You might as well shut off for depth-charging right away, Number One.'

The first lieutenant's murmured 'Aye aye, sir' came from directly behind him as did his arm seen by peripheral vision reaching for the Tannoy microphone.

Ryland could tell from the position of the hydroplane indicators that the ship was a little bow-heavy and knew that that was caused by the men now gathered in the torpedo tube space right in the bows. A moment later he knew that the first lieutenant had spotted it too because as soon as he had said his piece about depth-charging into the microphone he gave the orders for water to be pumped aft out of 'A' internal ballast tank. A good officer Gascoigne, Ryland thought. Not so good as the skipper of course, but then nobody was that, nobody in the whole Navy. That he was acquainted with only a tiny proportion of the officers in the Navy made no difference to Ryland, nor was he making a declaration of faith. It wasn't necessary to do that with facts. He nodded at the depth-gauge in front of him as though sharing again a mutual discovery made long ago.

The first lieutenant had got it right, he saw. The pointer steady on thirty-four feet, both hydroplane indicators level, the bubble in the inclinometer dead centre. Spot on with the trim Lieutenant Gascoigne was, except for that once when he had got it badly wrong, then didn't seem to know what to do about it and the skipper had had to take over. Could have been sunk if an enemy warship had been in sight. It had been puzzling, alarming too, at the time, that and him forgetting to flood 'Q' tank the time the destroyer nearly had them cold, but the skipper had bowled out the trouble a bit sharpish and taken action even quicker. That had been a night that had, and no mistake. Those women!

Behind Ryland's right shoulder the forward periscope hissed upwards. No word had been spoken and he knew that the skipper had gestured to Petty Officer Selby at the control levers. Selby never took his eyes off him during an attack. Not that an attack had been started yet, but Selby watched the skipper anyway. Good bloke Selby.

The skipper asking, 'Can you distinguish anything more, McIntyre?' and the chief sonar operator replying, 'Not really, sir. Sort of clanking noise is all I'm getting. No propeller sounds.'

'I see. Well, we'd better take a closer look. Sixty feet. Group up. Full ahead together.'

Ryland wound his control wheel, putting five degrees of dive on the after hydroplanes, glanced automatically towards his second coxswain on the fore planes and saw that he had done the same thing. Good. Never put too much angle on, or the screws would set up a wash on the surface the Eyeties could see. The pointer moving round the dials. Forty feet.

Forty-five. Fifty. The hull vibrating, making the crockery in the wardroom pantry tinkle softly. Levelling off at sixty feet. Nothing to do for three minutes which was the time the skipper normally used speed for between periscope observations. His hands moving the control wheel fractionally this way and that without conscious effort on his part, Ryland's thoughts wandered again. He felt no particular curiosity about whatever it was they were chasing after. That was the skipper's problem which, he fully realized, was only one of many and that knowledge made him thankful that he was not an officer, let alone the captain. In a rare flash of intuition it occurred to him that it must be worrying and rather lonely to be the captain, with the enemy and the sea and the ship and everybody aboard to worry about. Ryland shook his head sympathetically at the depth-gauge.

'Something bothering you, Cox'n?' The first lieutenant's voice at his back.

'Just remembered I forgot to record the rum issue this mornin', sir.'

The first lieutenant saying, 'We can't all be perfect all the time,' and that making Ryland think about Gascoigne's lapse again. The buzz around Algiers was that the white girl had been flown home to England and the negress deported to Egypt and serve them right too. He didn't hold with women, except for his wife of course of whom he was dutifully fond and wrote to once each patrol ending his letter with 'Your affectionate husband, Chief Petty Officer H.F. Ryland, DSM, MID.' That was the way it should be. There was nothing weird about Mildred. Not like those…

'Periscope depth. Group down. Slow ahead together.'

The vibration ceasing, *Trigger* lifting towards the surface, the hiss of the periscope, the skipper saying, 'Come up another two feet, Number One. I still can't make out – Oh yes I can. You can go back to patrol routine. It's just a bunch of small trawlers getting their nets in.'

And that was when Petty Officer McIntyre said, 'Hydrophone effect astern, sir. Sounds like reciprocating engines and turbines.'

Trigger quivering again to the thrust of her screws, the red numbers of the illuminated gyro repeater tape in front of the helmsman marching across the oblong screen as she turned to port, the skipper saying, 'The target is a convoy of two freighters and one tanker escorted by two destroyers. Course about east. Heading for Naples probably,' pausing, then adding with untypical irritability, 'Fuck it! If we'd stayed where we were instead of frigging around with those bloody trawlers we'd have had them cold!'

Ryland grinned briefly. It always amused him to hear the officers using lower deck language, especially the skipper.

'Any chance of catching them now, sir?' The first lieutenant's voice.

'Might get in a long range shot at them, Number One. Depends on the speed they're making. Chivers, steer 065. Pilot, how long to sunset?'

'Um – forty-eight, no, forty-six minutes, sir.'

'Right. Cox'n, take us up fast when we go back to periscope depth, but be careful not to stick the periscope standards out of the water.'

'Aye aye, sir,' Ryland said, a little worried by the last words because it was unlike the skipper to say unnecessary things and that meant he was tense. Stick the periscope standards out? As if he would.

Two minutes later Ryland brought *Trigger* fast and immaculately to thirty-four feet, hearing the periscope go up before that depth was reached, hearing the skipper begin to talk as soon as the upper lens rose out of the sea. His worry dissipated at the sound of the calm voice speaking of bearings, masthead heights, ranges, angles on the bow, all the jargon so familiar to him and so little understood. His lack of understanding worried him not at all. It sounded right and making sense of it was the responsibility of Lieutenant Randolph at the 'Fruit Machine' and Lieutenant Walker at the chart table. Then he was back in business himself guiding the submarine at high speed down to sixty feet again.

Minutes after that the sequence repeated itself. More ranges, bearings and the rest of it. Something called the 'Distance Off Track' seemed to be causing concern amongst the officers and Ryland groped in his memory for an explanation of that he had once been given. It wasn't the range to the target, it was more the distance to where the target would be when the torpedoes got to the same place, if they did. Yes, that was about the size of it, and seven and a half thousand yards was a lot of distance off track. Nearly four miles of it when you figured it out. The ships wouldn't look very big so far off and they would seem even smaller half turned away from *Trigger* which was what the skipper meant by calling for a course for a 130 track. A 180 track would be dead astern of them. He wondered if there was any point in firing torpedoes at all.

'Stand by numbers 1, 2, 3, 4, 5 and 6 tubes.'

So, Ryland thought, the skipper didn't have any doubts, not knowing that Harding had very grave doubts indeed and had been vacillating between a token attack with two torpedoes and a full bow salvo of eight and could not readily have explained how he had arrived at a compromise of six.

'This will be a firing observation. Periscope depth.'

Ryland turned his hydroplane control wheel.

'Group down. Slow ahead together. Open bow caps.'

Voices repeating the orders and the telegraphs to the motor room tinkling. *Trigger* rising towards the surface like some gigantic blue whale.

Out of the corner of his eye Ryland saw Harding grasp the periscope handles as soon as they rose out of the well at his feet, rise with them until he was upright and turn the periscope through a full circle. That done, he steadied it at an angle fine on the port bow.

The skipper's 'Fire 1' and the slight jolt as compressed air blasted the torpedo from its tube came almost simultaneously and Ryland's eyes flicked towards the inclinometer and the forward hydroplane indicator. He was fully alert now, anxious that he and the second coxswain should anticipate any orders the first lieutenant might otherwise have to give to counteract the tendency of the submarine's bows to rise before water could rush in and compensate for the loss of the weight of the torpedo. All was well and continued to be so throughout five more quietly abrupt commands immediately followed by five more jolts spaced six seconds apart. Then the waiting began with *Trigger* swinging to starboard to distance herself from the point of origin of her own torpedo tracks. Somewhere around five minutes of waiting, Ryland thought, for even with the sleekly shining fish boring through the sea at near fifty land miles an hour they still had a long way to run.

The seconds dragged themselves into minutes and the minutes grudgingly became two, three, five. Nothing. Nothing at all.

'How's the running time looking, Pilot?' The skipper's voice, languid, almost uninterested and Ryland knowing that he was neither of those things.

'They should have crossed the track by now, sir.'

216

'Yes, I was afraid of that. Oh well. We'll surface and chase them as soon as it's dark. Have the tubes reloaded as quickly as…'

A single sharp detonation and the periscope rising. The skipper saying, 'Got it!' and Ryland feeling pleased for him rather than the war effort and without knowing what 'it' was. The first lieutenant asking, 'Which one, sir?' and being told, 'The tanker, Number One. One hit right aft. I just caught the last of the spray when I looked. They must be bigger ships than I thought and further away. That's why it took the fish so long to get there. We'll try to close in and finish if off on the surface when it's dark.'

The counter-attack when it came was protracted, violent and would, Chief Petty Officer Ryland decided, have been very unpleasant indeed had the two destroyers not been engaged in blasting great holes in the Tyrrhenian Sea at least two miles from the submarine. He took a piece of chalk from his pocket to record the number of explosions on the rim of the depth-gauge as was his practice, then he put it away again unused. With them so wide of the mark it would be cheating to add them to the chalk lines already there.

Standing behind him Gascoigne noted the action, understood it and smiled, but the coxswain didn't know that his thoughts had been read.

*

Aboard the depot ship in Algiers harbour Captain Anderson was enjoying the single gin which his ulcer and the surgeon-commander permitted him to drink each day, when Lieutenant-Commander Donaldson followed his own knock into the big cabin and said, 'Enemy report from *Trigger*, sir.'

'Go on, Ginger.'

'She's attacked a small convoy fifteen miles to the east of Tavolara Island and sunk a big tanker. One hit from submerged stopped it. Flooded the engine room Harding thinks. Two more hits after dark on the surface finished it off. He's puzzled about the ease of that, sir, because the two escorting destroyers dropped a lot of depth-charges on nothing in particular then made off to the east to overtake the rest of the convoy. That's two freighters of about 5,000 and 3,000 tons.'

'Just abandoning the tanker, eh?'

'Exactly, sir.'

'What size was it?'

Donaldson glanced down at the pink signal paper in his hand and said, '10,000 tons and fully laden.'

'Curiouser and curiouser as the girl said.'

'Quite. Harding has kept his transmission as short as possible for obvious reasons and apart from plain facts his only comment is "Peculiar. Interrogative freighters vital".'

'Is he still in contact with them, Ginger?'

'Yes, sir. Tracking at long range while he charges his batteries. He has six bow and three stern torpedoes left.'

The flotilla captain nodded, staring at his half-finished drink, thinking that it *was* extremely peculiar. Logic called for one of the destroyers to have kept *Trigger* occupied while the other took the damaged tanker in tow back a mere fifteen miles to anchor it in shallow water or beach it on Tavolara Island or the coast of Sardinia just beyond. The freighters could have gone with it and sheltered in one of the many coves there until either the submarine menace had been eradicated or additional escorting vessels sent for. Neither of those things had been done and for a moment Anderson toyed with the idea that this was simply another example of Italian incompetence but, with thoughts of poison gas intruding, he abandoned that simple solution.

'Interrogative freighters vital' Harding's signal had asked and the question fuelled his imagination, drawing for him a picture of the merchantmen embarking their awful cargo at Bastia, following the Corsican coast south to Sardinia, then turning east on the shortest sea route to Naples.

'Nonsense,' Captain Anderson said quietly. 'Bastia to Leghorn is a fraction of the distance.'

The statement meant nothing to the operations staff officer, but 'Ginger' Donaldson made no comment, aware that his superior was talking to himself and Anderson brooded on, questioning the possibility of the enemy choosing to risk the longer sea passage in preference to transporting such a dangerous consignment by road or rail down most of the length of Italy. The desertion of the valuable tanker by its protectors appeared to enhance the value of the remaining ships, and the notion of gas took a firm hold in his mind. The now inevitable Allied invasion of southern Europe was just such a circumstance as might persuade the Axis powers to resort to gas warfare.

Harding, Gascoigne and D'Arcy could have told him that gas was not involved in the equation, but they were in the Tyrrhenian Sea. A number of others, including Admiral Chandos, could have told him the same thing, but they were in London. An Italian destroyer commander could have told him of a firm submarine contact obtained by his sonar operator shortly after the torpedo struck and of his devastating underwater bombardment, of the disappearance of the echo, of his signal reporting the destruction of the submarine and requesting a tug to assist the tanker which had not caught fire and was in no danger of sinking. What the Italian could not have told him about were the millions of dead fish, fish from the same great shoal the trawlers had been working on. When his depth-charges had killed them and they had floated upwards to form a silver carpet on the surface of the sea it had been too dark to notice them from the bridge of the speeding destroyers and it would have taken sonar operators with greater experience as well as better equipment to have differentiated between an echo obtained from a submarine and a big shoal of fish in the first place.

With none of this information in his possession the flotilla captain considered the options open to him. He could leave it to Harding who had proved his capability, but that seemed to be placing too much of a load on one pair of shoulders if the cargo turned out to be what he was becoming more and more convinced it was. He could order *Tornado* patrolling to the south of Naples to move north-wards and intercept, but that could lead to a disastrous clash between the two submarines. He could…

A rap on the cabin door and the entry of a young lieutenant came together.

'Sorry to barge in, sir. There's another signal from *Trigger*.'

'Read it to us, Bartlett.'

'Aye aye, sir. It says, "Radar indicates three additional ships converging on convoy from north. Their speed of advance suggests destroyers. Battery still low, but shall be in attacking position again well before dawn." He's added the latest position, course and speed of the enemy, sir.'

The apparent reinforcement, more than doubling the convoy's escort strength, settled the matter as far as Captain Anderson was concerned and he chose his third option.

'Ginger, I want an air strike against that lot. I'm not allowed to tell you why, but it's very important. They'll want to know who the hell I think I am asking for that sort of thing, so use Admiral Chandos as authority. Secret orders and all that which, as it happens, is quite true. If you have any trouble, get back to me at once and I'll go through the C-in-C.'

'Aye aye, sir.' Lieutenant-Commander Donaldson said.

*

It felt more than strange to Harding not to be on the bridge when his ship was in visual contact with the enemy. It felt totally unnatural, even criminally irresponsible and he experienced the weird sensation of having physically to prevent his legs carrying him away from the radar screen and towards the conning tower ladder. His legs obeyed him and he stayed where he was, putting into practice the theory he had developed off Norway so long ago that it seemed like some other existence.

That the theory so far made sense was clear enough. On the bridge Gascoigne could see a single dark smudge on the horizon and nothing else at all. Harding himself could see seven ships represented by quivering green 'blips' on the glass of the cathode-ray tube in front of him. It was the three approaching from the north he was most immediately interested in as they appeared to be steering not towards the convoy but directly at *Trigger*. He doubted their ability to detect his radar transmissions, but doubt was hardly certainty.

'Switch off,' he told the operator. 'We'll take another look in a moment or two.'

When transmission was resumed the only change was that the range had shortened. The bearing had not, which meant that the three vessels were on a collision course with him. Regretting the necessity both for interrupting the battery charge and losing distance on the convoy to the east of him, 'Dive the ship, Number One,' he said into the voice-pipe and was answered in turn by Gascoigne's 'Aye aye, sir', the double snarl of the klaxon and the roar of the diesels fading into silence. *Trigger* slid under water.

At ninety feet, 'Can you hear them, McIntyre?' Harding asked.

'Yessir. Fast turbines bearing Red 95.'

'Any sonar transmissions?'

'No, sir. None.'

'That's nice,' Harding said.

McIntyre tracked the speeding destroyers, reporting them passing ahead of *Trigger*'s bow, then continuing on to the south with no interruption in their progress. Thankful for that, thankful too for the technology which had enabled him to observe unseen in two elements, Harding ordered his ship taken back to the surface.

With two-thirds of her engine power devoted to driving life back into her still-depleted batteries, *Trigger* idled through the black night in the wake of the convoy, barely matching its speed. It was lost to the sight of the men on the bridge but, on command, radar stretched out its electronic finger and found it for them.

*

'Yeah, sure we can do that,' Lieutenant-Colonel David Furness told the telephone. 'The guys have been sitting on their butts for a week. All I need is authorization from the "brass". General Eisenhower or your man Montgomery will do just fine.'

Furness grinned at his own joke and listened to 'Ginger' Donaldson's voice in the receiver saying, 'That's a bit too heavy for me, Colonel. I can only offer you Admiral Chandos. You've probably read about him in the newspapers.'

'Who hasn't?' Furness said. 'More to the point I've talked with him and acted as his mailman. If he's picking up the tab that's okay by me. Give it to me in detail, Commander.'

Donaldson gave it to him.

Chapter Twenty-Four

Trigger was not idling any longer. Her batteries as fully charged as the time factor permitted them to be, she was racing across the flat sea with white water swirling aft along the ballast tanks on either side to join in a tumbling wake astern.

It was Marine Hamlyn who re-established visual contact, and Harding abandoned the radar set to clamber rapidly up the conning tower ladder and onto the bridge, then stood waiting for his eyes to adjust to the darkness, feeling the deck vibrating beneath his sandals. His hair and beard had grown over the days and although there was little wind the speed of the ship's advance was enough to make his forelock flutter about his face interfering with his vision. He spoke into the voice-pipe.

'Send up a pair of scissors, please.'

The helmsman's 'Aye aye, sir,' reached him clearly and less distinctly the words, 'Norris, the Skipper wants to clip his toenails. Take him up some scissors,' an inaudible response then, 'No, honest. Hop to it.'

When, a minute later, Harding had chopped off the offending lock he handed the scissors back to the able seaman.

'Thank you, Norris.'

'Thank you, sir. I'm glad to see what you done. We was wondering what you had in mind.'

'Were you indeed? Then I suggest you go back down below and hack some of your own off. You're beginning to look like an Old English Sheepdog.'

'Oh. Aye aye, sir.'

Harding could see the nearest ship now, a darker smear against a dark horizon. He was glad of the overcast, which the weather reports expected to dissipate by dawn, because it helped him more than an enemy whose formation was already known to him from the radar screen. The vessel he was looking at was one of the destroyers with beyond it, hidden from his eyes by the darkness, the two merchantmen and the second destroyer, all in line ahead. From his point of view it was the worst grouping they could have adopted, which was obviously why they had adopted it. Whatever angle of attack he chose he was likely to be sighted by one or other of the escorts and there was nothing he could do about it. Harding muttered angrily and looked carefully all around him. There was certainly something he could do about it. The horizon was appreciably darker in the southern sector and he could strike from there with less chance of being silhouetted.

'Starboard 15, steer 135 degrees,' he said into the voice-pipe, then added, 'Ask the Engineer Officer to work up to maximum revolutions.'

With the vibration so intense that some part of the after casing set up a persistent bell-like thrumming, *Trigger* ran far out on the convoy's flank, the one ship which had been visible quickly lost to sight. A brief radar scan told Harding that neither the configuration, direction nor speed of the enemy vessels had changed and he gave the order which sent the submarine curving in towards them. From down below at the 'Fruit Machine', Randolph gave him the firing angle. He cranked it onto the torpedo night sight. *Trigger* steadied on her attacking course.

One moment there was nothing, the next the ships were there. All four of them. Indistinct against the overcast, but there.

'Stand by,' he said and the voice-pipe answered, 'Standing by, sir.'

The binoculars uselessly clipped to the night sight, the vibration reducing their image of the enemy to a meaningless blur. Harding unclipping them, using the naked eye, hesitating, then saying, 'Fire 1!' A slow count of seven and 'Fire 2!' Counting again, reaching three and something attracting his attention, something silver, something which vanished and reappeared, vanished and reappeared in repeated explosions of spray.

'Stop the attack,' he told the voice-pipe. 'Starboard 30, steer 180 degrees.' That had been said tonelessly, but there was resignation in his voice when, addressing nobody in particular, he went on, 'We might just as well have sent them a telegram.'

As if in confirmation of the statement, the siren of the stern escort began to whoop a frenzied warning of the approach of the wildly porpoising torpedo and a flashing light reinforced its message. The line of ships turned away and, with attacker and attacked on diverging courses, was quickly lost to sight.

'We had a malfunction of the depth-keeping mechanism in the fish from Number 2 tube,' Harding told Gascoigne down the voice-pipe. 'The bloody thing went cavorting off like a steeplechaser and couldn't have attracted more attention if it had been playing a brass band. Set intermittent radar watch and let me know as soon as you've established what they're doing now.'

It was nearly a quarter of an hour before Harding got his report.

'Sorry to have been so long, sir,' Gascoigne said. 'They've been milling about all over the place, but seem to have settled down now. They're steering east at about eight knots again and in the same formation.'

'Didn't either of the destroyers search in our direction?'

'One followed us for about a couple of miles, sir, then changed his mind and went back again.'

'All right,' Harding told him. 'Come to port onto 080 degrees. We'll run ahead of them and attack again at dawn.'

*

Near the small town of Menzel-Temime in Tunisia, ten B-17 bombers lumbered around the perimeter track of the makeshift airfield. It was less than two hours to first light and they had three hundred miles to fly. When the lead plane turned onto the illuminated runway, 'Let's go,' Lieutenant-Colonel David Furness said and the four big Pratt & Whitney engines bellowed at the night.

*

In response to a radio signal ordering added protection for a convoy under submarine attack, one of the three destroyers *Trigger* had dived to evade

224

earlier in the night reversed course and increased to full speed. The ship was out of Spezia and a member of the group known to the British as the 'First Eleven'.

*

The overcast had gone when the first nail-paring of sun showed above the eastern horizon sending its light flooding swiftly across the smooth water. It flowed over *Trigger*'s periscope an instant before it illuminated the ships. There were still four of them, but their formation had changed. Harding had watched them change it in the first lessening of darkness before the day had come.

The two freighters were still in line ahead but, with the danger of a surface attack from astern gone, both destroyers were leading them, one to port and one to starboard. The convoy was zig-zagging too, but doing it regularly, unimaginatively, predictably and, apart from necessitating an occasional burst of speed from the submarine, the manoeuvres had caused Harding little trouble. At a range of three thousand yards he fired his last four bow torpedoes at the merchantmen, then ordered his ship taken deep.

At precisely the correct calculated running time for the first torpedo the characteristic sharp crack of an exploding warhead broke the expectant hush in the control room. Two more followed it at the proper intervals. There was no fourth.

The single miss made no difference, the freighters sagging lower and lower as though tired, finally to sink almost together. But until Petty Officer McIntyre was able to confirm that all reciprocating engine hydrophone effect had ceased, Harding knew nothing of that.

*

Lieutenant-Colonel David Furness knew nothing of it either. His B-17s, spaced four miles apart in line abreast, were extended over a large area of sea to obtain enough visual coverage to cancel out any errors in navigation. It had been the obvious plan to follow, but there had been no errors.

Lieutenant Winnick was a very good navigator and at the centre of the line 'Hedy Lamarr', which was the name Furness had given his bomber, passed at ten thousand feet directly above a destroyer steaming north at high speed towards another two several miles directly ahead of it.

Furness was not interested in destroyers. It was two freighters carrying some top secret equipment the British wanted sunk and if that was what the British wanted then that was the way it would be. He agreed a search pattern with Winnick and ordered it carried out.

*

It didn't surprise Harding when McIntyre told him that both destroyers were in sonar contact, as he had found it strange that they had failed to achieve that during his torpedo attack on the convoy. *Trigger* was moving fast at one hundred and eighty feet when the first pattern of depth-charges exploded.

The thunder-claps were vicious in their intensity and Harding stood, clutching the periscope hoist wire, feeling the deck rocking beneath his feet, listening to the surge of displaced water past the hull. Close. Too damned close. He ordered a radical alteration in course and a depth of three hundred feet, still using full speed because the noise of that would not be heard by the enemy until the turbulence created by the detonations had subsided. Glancing around the control room he saw the coxswain making careful chalk marks on the rim of the depth-gauge in front of him, adding to the total of depth-charges already recorded there. That made him smile and the smile carried affection. Although Ryland was the only coxswain he had ever served with in submarines, unaware that he was contributing to the creation of a mutual admiration society, Harding thought that the man's quiet competence, steadiness and cheerful acquiescence to anything that was asked of him must make him the best coxswain in the Service.

The second attack was less effective, the third more so and reports of minor damage reached him from various parts of the ship, but it was not until McIntyre reported that the two destroyers had been joined by a third that *Trigger* began slowly to die.

'I'm sorry, Commander,' Furness said into the telephone. 'We sectored half the goddam Tyrrhenian Sea and there was no sign of them anyplace. All we saw was three small warships. Destroyers I guess.'

'Did you say three, Colonel?' the earpiece asked him.

'Yeah. Two together, another some miles away heading to join them.'

There was a long pause, then 'Ginger' Donaldson's voice came from the receiver again.

'Colonel.'

'Yeah?'

'If you didn't see the freighters in that visibility after such a long search with so many planes they can't be there, can they?'

'Go on, Commander.'

'Well first, can you tell me what the destroyers were doing?'

'Sure, the one to the south was heading north like a bat out of hell. Had a wake a mile long. The other two were kinda circling. Slowly I'd say.'

'I see,' Donaldson said. 'Were they dropping depth-charges?'

'How the heck would I know? We were flying at ten thousand and – Wait a minute! There were what looked like circles on the water behind one of them. You suggesting there was a submarine down there?'

'I'd be prepared to bet on it, Colonel. *Trigger* had already sunk one ship in that convoy and was trailing the rest of them last night. I think she must have sunk those freighters before you got there.'

Furness barely heard Donaldson's last few words. His mind had jumped back over the weeks to the long-drawn-out misery he, Winnick and O'Halloran had endured in *Trigger*'s wardroom and he felt his stomach muscles tighten as they had done so often then in anticipation of the next series of appalling concussions.

He breathed in slowly, forcing his muscles to relax, then, 'You did say *Trigger*, didn't you?'

'Yes.'

'Forgive me if I hang up on you now, Commander,' Furness said. 'I've got some flying to do.'

*

It had been after the fourteenth attack that *Trigger* found the layer, the bathythermograph recording a sharp alteration in water temperature at a depth of three hundred and seventy feet, and Harding had ordered his battered ship taken below it. Immediately, the accuracy of the underwater assault had diminished, then ceased altogether with the layer deflecting, distorting the enemy's sonar transmissions, but he was afraid that the reprieve was only temporary. The destroyers knew he was still there, knew what he had done, knew too that with the repeated bursts of speed he had employed during his evasive manoeuvres his batteries must be low. They only had to wait in the knowledge that lack of power would prevent him distancing himself very far from them under the protective layer and that sooner or later he must come up and then…

Harding was very tired after more than thirty hours without sleep and the strain those hours had imposed on him, his crew less so because some had watched while others rested, his ship tiredest of all. As much for the purpose of keeping his brain active as in the hope of producing constructive thought Harding mentally listed the damage.

An unknown number of the 336 almost man-sized battery cells on board had been cracked by the onslaught. That was certain because hydrochloric acid had drained into the sumps of all three battery tanks. There was nothing he could do about that until the ship surfaced, if it surfaced. Numerous small leaks had been sprung in the hull, although most of those had sealed themselves under the colossal external pressure of the four hundred feet of water above them. There was nothing he could do about that either, except hope that the sea still finding its way in through the remainder did not make contact with the battery acid. If it did, chlorine gas and death would come hand in hand to all of them.

The electrical switchboards had suffered too, metal bolts shearing to let the equipment they supported inch out of position, producing arcing and earths where no earths should be. That *had* been dealt with, as had the fracturing of the base of the telemotor pump which, for an eternity, had deprived the ship of hydraulic power. During those endless minutes it had taken Lieutenant Menzies and his engine room artificers to realign and secure the pump, the physical effort required of the men operating the hydroplanes and steering by hand had reduced the residual oxygen in the air dramatically. So had the electrical arcing. So had the increased pulse rates of frightened men, his own included. The bitter tang of fright-sweat seemed to be lodged permanently in Harding's nostrils. He tried to clear it by blowing his nose, but didn't succeed, so used his handkerchief to wipe the sweat from his face feeling no shame at its presence because everyone was sweating. And that wasn't surprising, he told himself, when one considered that the repeated heavy discharges he had called on the batteries to make had raised the temperature of the deck covering them to 140 degrees Fahrenheit.

There were other odds and ends which weren't exactly right, he knew, but his exhausted brain refused to pin-point them for him. It didn't really matter. It was clear enough to him that *Trigger* was dying much faster now.

'What we going to do next, sir?' Able Seaman Norris had asked him when he had walked through the ship half an hour earlier. 'Attack them with the three stern torpedoes if they don't bugger off soon, but I'd rather keep the fish for a bigger target,' he had replied. Farcical of course, but the idea had brought pleased grins to the faces of those in earshot which was why he had voiced it. 'Surface and abandon ship' would have been the correct answer, but Harding wasn't ready to give that order yet.

*

As accurately as before, Lieutenant Winnick's navigation carried 'Hedy Lamarr' precisely along the invisible line connecting the airfield near Menzel-Temime with the circling destroyers. Nine other B-17s kept station on her, five to starboard, four to port. Because he was least affected by the reflected glare of the afternoon sun off the flat sea, the bomb-aimer of the plane furthest to the west sighted the targets first.

Alerted by the excited voice in his earphones Lieutenant-Colonel David Furness said, 'Nice going, Chuck. Now, if any other of you good ole boys are still awake, there are three Wop tin-cans up ahead kicking the shit out of a friend of mine. Let's take them. Follow daddy. Go!'

*

Harding had decided that if the battery and the air lasted that long, and if the temperature layer continued to provide *Trigger* with its protective umbrella, he would wait until darkness came before surfacing. That would give the crew a slightly better chance of getting away from the ship before he scuttled her, or the excitable Italians opened fire on them. The decision taken, there was nothing left for him to do and his thoughts turned towards Lee Lawrence, pretty Lee of the golden hair and the smile which uplifted the soul.

It had been a gently contrite letter which had reached him from the Pacific where she was reporting that war for the American public. She had had a short passionate love affair with a United States Army major, wished she had not, but could not promise that it would not happen again with somebody else. 'I get frightened, Peter,' the letter had said, 'and it helps. Do you remember that shelter in London where you held me during the big air raid and the days and nights that followed? Well, of course you do. That was love, I promise you, but fear was the seed from which it grew and with so much fear around I can't be certain that I'll come out of all this the sort of girl you would want to be engaged to if, indeed, you still do.'

The letter had ended with the words, 'Please, please tell me what you decide' and that made Harding very sad, not about what she had done, but because *Trigger* had sailed on the day that it had arrived and it looked now very much as though he would never be able to tell her that he didn't mind, that he loved her still.

Gascoigne was thinking about a girl too. She was beautiful, well brought up, sensual but nice, and existed only in his imagination. He wished very much that that was not the case, that he could have known somebody like that, got married perhaps and somehow miraculously avoided the sordid situations into which he fell so readily. 'Too late on all counts,' he told himself.

Not holding with women Chief Petty Officer Ryland was not thinking about them. He was thinking of the next beer-drinking session he would have with Chief Yeoman Yarrow. Well aware that their situation was precarious, he still had little doubt that he and Yarrow would go ashore again together. The skipper would think of something. He always did.

Unaffected by the temperature layer, Petty Officer McIntyre's passive sonar watch continued to record the slow circling of the destroyers four hundred feet above. His head had drooped forward until his chin touched his chest and most of his sleepy mind was centred on his mother's little house at Callander in Scotland. He was feeling glad that he had rewired it for her, even if the work had been unnecessary, when his ears jerked him back aboard *Trigger*.

'Cap'n sir!'

'Yes, McIntyre?'

'The destroyers have speeded up, sir. Going like blazes!'

'Attacking?'

'Don't think so, sir. I don't know what they're doing. Hang on a minute.'

That was when the thunder started. Not the stunning detonation of depth-charges with their surging aftermath of tons of displaced water, but the staccato roar of huge hailstones striking a tin roof, dozens, scores of hailstones. The tattoo ceased abruptly, then came again before repeating itself eight more times. Two long rumbling explosions accompanied the last of them and then there was silence. Harding found that he had been staring up at the deckhead as though he could see through it and establish the source of the uproar. That made him feel silly until he glanced around the control room and saw that everybody there was doing the same thing.

'All hydrophone effect has ceased, sir,' McIntyre said.

Harding looked at him and doubt must have been written on his face because the chief sonar operator added, 'It's a fact, sir.'

Very slowly Harding turned to face Gascoigne.

'Bombs, Number One?'

'I think so, sir.'

'Then bring us back to periscope depth.'

'Aye aye, sir.'

Trigger glided slowly upwards, periodically flooding water into her internal ballast tanks to compensate for a hull expanding fractionally at the decrease in the pressure it had been subjected to for so long. Harding was staring into the binocular viewer of the periscope when its upper lens rose above the surface.

Debris moving listlessly on the nearly flat sea. Patches of oil, some burning, some not. Corpses given a spurious appearance of life, rolling over as the moving periscope brushed them aside. An upturned boat. Life rafts, some with men in them, some empty. The last remaining destroyer three hundred yards away, listing heavily and on fire almost from bow to stern. Desolation. For the first time in months Harding thought about God, then stopped doing it because all that was much too complicated.

The onset of trembling fingered his muscles and nerve-ends, but his voice was steady and untypically formal when he said quietly, 'Very well, gentlemen. Let's go home.'

www.ingramcontent.com/pod-product-compliance
Ingram Content Group UK Ltd.
Pitfield, Milton Keynes, MK11 3LW, UK
UKHW040658140525
5908UKWH00009B/68

9 781839 013324